# The Girl,
# the Gold Tooth
## *& everything*

*A novel*

BY FRANCINE LaSALA

Diversion Books
A Division of Diversion Publishing Corp.
80 Fifth Avenue, Suite 1101
New York, New York 10011

www.DiversionBooks.com

First Diversion Books edition September 2012.

ISBN: 978-1-938120-64-0

1 3 5 7 9 10 8 6 4 2

*For Christopher. For always.*
*For ever. (In Blue Jeans.)*

"You were my compass star
You were my measure
You were a pirate's map
A buried treasure."
—from "Ghost Story" by Sting


"'Twas brillig and the slithy toves
Did gyre and gimble in the wabe;
All mimsy were the borogroves,
And the mome raths outgrabe."
—from "Jabberwocky" by Lewis Carroll

# PROLOGUE

Whenever Zander Randalls took the stage, you could be sure something magical was going to happen. An electric presence with shining silver hair, with a face that gleamed with wisdom and understanding, with an aura of passion and purpose ever-emanating, Zander Randalls spoke words so powerful, so powerfully spoken, he made a considerable impact every time he made an appearance. He was majestic, like an eagle. He was massive in stature and presence and form. He was very much a god to those who followed him, his message the very scripture that guided millions of lives.

On this night, he paced the stage at the Nassau Coliseum in Uniondale, New York, pontificating to a fully packed house of 17,686 (and then some, if you counted the awestruck stage hands, Coliseum staff, and members of the press who took in the show from the sidelines and backstage). But it wouldn't be accurate to say the seats were filled; the devout, frenzied and frenetic, generally took in the Word on their feet so they could proclaim their praises that much more powerfully. Indeed, the followers hung on every word that sprang from the silver tongue of the modern messiah. His message was so simple, so accessible. So very much theirs.

"If you can hear it, you can believe it!" Zander proclaimed. And the followers parroted back at astounding volumes. (Even the deaf emphatically signed their replies after taking in his message, signed by the many translators who circled the stage.)

"If you can feel it, you can believe it!" he cried out. And droves of audience members, tears in their eyes, began beating their chests with great passion and fury as they echoed back this sentiment to him.

"If you can *believe* it . . . " he began, and he paused.

"We believe it! We believe it!" came the cries from the audience. "We BELIEVE IT!!!"

"If you can believe it," he started again, and then more loudly, "if you can believe it, then you can know it to be true!" he screamed out, and they praised and screamed and fawned and shook their fists in a frenzied dance of ardent air-punches and frantic fist-bumps. The crowd lapped up his message like doctored fruit drink, slurping up every last word.

Somewhere in the tenth row a woman fainted, but that was okay. Someone always fainted. Somewhere in the balcony, a woman removed her blouse and threw it into the crowd, but that was okay, too. Not unexpected by any measure. Both women and men, in fact, were known to get so caught up in the religiosity of the Zander experience their passion could not be constrained by their clothing.

But that doesn't mean that all was right in this earthly paradise of self-affirmation. For somewhere in the sidelines, someone was plotting something foul, something that would soon bring down the House of Zander.

Because everything has a price.

# 1

It was the kind of day that made Mina Clark feel every breath of her forty-two years—and then some.

It was bad enough that the hot water heater was now broken and that neither she nor her three-year-old daughter, Emma, would be able to wash up properly. A problem for Mina, who hadn't taken a shower since Tuesday . . . or Monday? And it was already Thursday. Or Wednesday? No, Thursday.

But a bigger problem for Mina's tastefully decorated home had come when, during a regrettable moment's distraction on Mina's part, Emma, with her improbably nimble fingers, had managed to trip the lock on her father's cabinet of ancient art supplies. Delicious and dear, dark and demonic, Emma had not only managed to open the long-locked cabinet, but had also been able to unscrew all the tops of Jack's acrylic paint tubes, and was now awash in color from head to toe. And, alas, so were myriad walls and carpets, fixtures and furnishings. It was as if a Jackson Pollack painting had come to fiery life and burned through the bedroom, the hallway, and the living room of the Clark home leaving a trail of destruction that, like the water heater, there was no budget to correct.

What could she do? Could she wrap the child in plastic garbage bags, drive them down to their complex's community gym, and sneak Emma into the showers where she could rinse them both off? She considered this for a minute until she remembered that her car was in the shop. Again. Hit and run. Again. And she had no means to collect it from the shop until the insurance adjuster cut her a check.

This time, the accident had happened in the parking lot of Emma's elite nursery school, Acela Academy. Mina had taken Emma to her classroom, and when she finally emerged after a twenty-minute struggle with separation, someone had crashed in the passenger-side door of her car, without leaving a note. Scum apparently knew no social station.

The last time, Mina's car had gotten rear-ended as she sat waiting for a red light to change. The blood-curdling screams that came from the backseat, from a child seemingly unharmed but frightened beyond words, could have woken the dead. Mina considered that perhaps they had, and that maybe all the bad luck she'd been having lately was the work of one such spirit-formerly-at-rest who was hot with revenge at having been disturbed. And she also knew that was ridiculous.

Terrified, Mina had bolted right to the pediatrician—without calling the police or trying to chase after the driver who hit her. It seemed like Emma would never stop crying, and Mina was convinced that something was terribly wrong.

Dr. Swenson, a kindly gentleman in his late fifties, had carefully examined the screaming child and concluded, "She's just scared."

"Scared?" Mina nearly shouted as she tried to pull a wriggling, writhing Emma into her arms to console her. A raging octopus with chainsaws for tentacles. "Just scared?"

"Just scared," he said, sweet and soft-spoken, surprisingly audible over the cacophony.

"Well, how do I make her less scared?" Mina asked, and they both sized up the still-screaming tot, the mother with a face frantic with worry, the doctor with a cool, matter-of-fact gaze.

There was a long pause before he spoke. "Benadryl," he said.

"Medication?" Mina gasped. "But if you say she's okay, why am I medicating her?"

And just at that moment, Emma had stopped screaming. She gave a little shudder and a big sniff, and she let out a sigh. The drama was over.

"Well, she isn't crying anymore, is she," Dr. Swenson said, and gave Mina a warm, friendly tap on the back. "The Benadryl would have calmed her down. Even knocked her out," he whispered, with a wink and a warm smile.

"Oh."

Later that day, she had sat with her neighbor Esther, and told her what had happened. Esther gave her the same warm look Dr. Swenson had worn and assured her, "There's no way I could have raised my five kids without Benadryl."

Suddenly, what the doctor had said made sense. Mina had no idea what she would do without Esther, an octogenarian who lived next door. Esther had been so kind to Mina and Jack, Mina's husband. And Emma loved Esther so much. Her fashion sense arrested in the 1960s. Her curiously black beehive hairdo. Her amazing costume jewelry collection—each day a new piece!

And now Mina knew just who she should call to help straighten out the mess. Esther Erasmus. The only person who made living where she did bearable.

But as Mina approached the phone—that thing that had ruined her day every day, every week, every month for what seemed like decades—it rang. She checked the caller ID and, just as she had suspected, it showed an unidentifiable 888 number. Her heart stopped. Her breath got trapped in her throat as she watched the phone, praying for the ringing to stop. The machine would have picked up if it hadn't already been filled with messages she couldn't bear to listen to. Messages from people angrily making demands she couldn't honor.

Every ring reminded her why she couldn't replace the water heater. Why the dryer leaked condensation through the kitchen ceiling. Why her car was still in the shop.

On top of it all, her lower left molar was throbbing in pain, and had been for weeks. She hated that she was going to have to make an appointment to see her dentist because she deeply dreaded going to the dentist. But more than that was the dread she felt at how much it would cost, the same sense of dread she had felt at the ringing phone. Whoever it was on the other end of that phone wanted money. And Mina had none.

If you looked around Mina Clark's suburban home, you'd have been shocked to learn she had no money at all; the expansive, well-appointed space pretty much screamed that wealth resided here.

For one, the house was located in the very exclusive enclave of Easton Estates, a gated community of soulless McMansions that all looked much the same—and God help you if you didn't like it that way.

Stepping through the carved mahogany double door, you encountered a foyer the full height of the house, complete with a dramatic skylight that allowed sunlight to splash onto the terrazzo floor and sparkle off the speckled silver bowl with the cobalt blue dragonfly pattern resting on the foyer table. Mina knew she'd had that bowl for years, long before she lived at Easton Estates, but she had no idea when she had gotten it—or from whom or why.

Downstairs was a basement where Mina never ventured. It was always kept locked, and she didn't have the key. She wasn't exactly sure why she wasn't supposed to go down there, though she knew it had to do with her condition. Her strange condition. Yet another puzzle she was taxed to solve as she wandered daily around this strange house where she lived, desperate to piece together the life that had existed, the one she couldn't remember, the one from several years past.

To the left of the foyer sat a richly decorated dining room, and behind it a fully outfitted modern kitchen, sleek and cool with cobalt cabinetry and stainless steel appliances. It reminded Mina somehow of being in a submarine; she didn't like it at all.

Behind the kitchen was a small alcove Mina had gated off and made into a playroom. The room was a crazy jungle of colors and soft things, a wild juxtaposition to the submarine kitchen. Already awash in Day-Glo, the room took on a whole new level of color thanks to Emma's "artwork."

To the other side of the foyer was a formal living room, then a family room, and then behind that, another alcove that was purportedly Mina's "office"—though she rarely did anything in that room. She could have paid bills if she had money to pay them. She could have gotten some work done, if she knew what her work was.

Mina entered the small room and headed for the cassette player on the fairly antiquated stereo system, which was improbably hooked up to a state-of-the-art speaker system wired throughout the house. All things considered, she could only guess that there had been money in their lives at one point, and that the source of the money had unexpectedly dried up. She didn't need her memory to understand that this source of money had somehow had to do with her, that she could feel. Like most things in her life, she just couldn't understand why.

Mina pressed "play" and moved back through the house, heading to the kitchen to try to call Esther again.

*"What do you believe?"* the man's voice implored emphatically throughout the house.

"I have no idea," Mina absently answered.

*"What do you want to believe about you? What do you want to believe you are?"*

Mina wanted to believe something about herself. That she was something—was someone. That she had once done more with her life than sit around her house trying to remember who she was—that and chase around a maniacal tot. But there was also the fear . . . The warning that if she found out or remembered anything too fast, things could get much worse for her.

*"Who do you believe you are?"*

"I don't know," she said softly. "I don't remember."

The no memory thing was tough and seemed only to get worse by the day. As hard as she tried, Mina simply could not remember anything that had happened in her life before Emma was born. Even Emma's earliest days were a fog. She has no recollection of her pregnancy—whether it was "easy" or not, whether she was sick or not. The birth. The other mothers always wanted these answers. They were obsessed with natural or epidural, vaginal or caesarean, breast or bottle—and they were also obsessed with bonding with the mothers who had done things just as they had, and equally obsessed with belittling, tormenting, and alienating any mother who had done it differently. Mina hated mothers.

*"You can be WHO you think you are. If you think it, you can believe it!"* the voice encouraged.

Then there was Jack. Her husband, the phantom presence that shared this house and this life with her when he wasn't working late and weekends, or traveling for business. She didn't quite understand how they had no money if he worked as hard as he did; she didn't want to think about what else he might be doing.

Mina could not remember meeting Jack or falling in love with him. She could not remember their wedding day or any of the planning or preparation involved. It was hard to get a sense of him even now. She couldn't remember if she loved him, if she ever really loved him. Though she felt she had—and that she still did. Even in the small pockets of time they spent together these days, she could feel a warmth, a crackling flame, a shared affection and a desire, even if it was seldom acted upon by either of them anymore.

She barely got to speak to Jack these days—not even when he was at work. She'd called him earlier that day and had been verbally accosted by the receptionist.

"Balabaster Design Fittings," a young woman's voice had answered.

"Hi, may I speak with Jack Clark, please."

"Who is this?" the receptionist asked, her voice soaked in boredom and contempt.

"This is his wife."

There was silence at the other end.

"Hello? Is anyone there?" Mina had asked.

"Yeah. Jack's not permitted more than two calls a day."

Mina thought that was odd, but she replied, "This is only the first time I'm calling him."

"I recognize the number. You called earlier. You hung up."

Mina tried to remember if she'd called Jack earlier and then realized that she had indeed dialed his line . . . . just before Emma got into the paint. She relaxed and let out a small laugh. "Oh, right. My daughter. Our daughter. She's three and she—"

"Two calls. That's what you get. Buh-bye." And the girl hung up the phone.

So much for her husband sharing in any part of her life or Emma's.

*"If you feel it, you can know it to be true!"* said the voice on the tape, and Mina took a deep breath as she repeated the words under her breath.

Perhaps the saddest thing of all was that she had no idea where she came from. No recollection of childhood, of family. She had been able to piece together that there was no one left. But who was her mother? Her father? Did she have any brothers or sisters? These questions and a million more like them distracted Mina daily—and opened the door for Emma to do crazy things like paint the walls and the furniture.

"Out! Out! Out! Monny, I want out!" Emma shrieked from her playroom "prison," and the phone started ringing again. Mina hoped it was Jack, but when she saw it was a different 888 number, she angrily picked up the receiver and slammed it down again. Anyone who wanted to speak to her could call her cell phone, she rationalized. At least the vultures didn't know that number. At least not yet.

*"If you could, just think for a moment if you could . . . "* The voice paused and started up again with great passion and fury. *"If you believe you could be what you want to believe, would you finally . . . Would you FINALLY . . . Would you finally believe in yourself?"*

"Not likely," Mina surmised and dashed to the playroom to collect Emma. Except she had forgotten to mop up a large puddle of water that had formed under the ceiling from where the dryer had been mysteriously leaking and she slipped, old-film-wipe-out-on-a-banana-peel-style on the Italian ceramic floor.

"Monny! MONNY!"

"I'm coming!" Her whole body hurt as she tried to get up. And then the doorbell rang.

*"What do you believe?"* the man's voice demanded of her.
*"What do YOU believe?"*

"You bad monny. Bad, bad monny. I gonna hit-choo, bad monny!"

Mina picked herself off the floor and headed for the door.

"I gonna hit-choo in the head!"

*"What do you believe the Universe owes you?"*

Emma just kept screaming. The phone started ringing and the doorbell sounded again. "Oh fuck, alright, I'm coming!" she said.

*"If you know what you believe you need, the Universe will bring it to you! But first you must know what you believe you need!"*

"MONNNNNNNNY!!!!"

"I'm coming, baby. Hang on!"

"I want-choo now, monny! Now! Now! Now!"

Bedraggled, limping, covered in dried paint, Mina pulled open the door. And there, on the other side, stood her opposite. Serenity, manifest in a small-framed, advanced-aged "savior" known as Esther Erasmus, who was clutching a covered plate of something sweet and today wearing a bright, bejeweled pin that reminded Mina of a Tiffany stained-glass lampshade. Esther had arrived, as if beckoned by the Universe itself, and now Mina could finally breathe.

*"If you want it, you can bring it to you."*

"You shouldn't just open the door like that," Esther chided, though with a gentleness Mina had come to depend upon. The soothing calm in the chaos of her life. "You have to be careful."

"Esther, my goodness," Mina laughed as they stood in the doorway. "Here?" She shook her head. "I think the worst-case scenario would be that creep that runs the landscaping committee. And I think I could probably take him." Mina made a pathetic attempt at a laugh, as she and Esther both looked to the planting beds outside her front door—or rather, what had been planting beds.

"Those bastards," Esther said, with a succession of tsks. "I mean, I knew they would do this. But those bastards, all the same."

"That they would do this? To a neighbor?"

"That Charlie Witmore is a pain in the ass and everyone knows it. But the head of a homeowners' association holds a lot of power," she said. "Besides, widowers can be assholes in general. Trust me. I've known plenty of them."

*"If you want it, it can be yours."*

Starting off the seemingly never-ending list of things that had been making this the proverbial day from hell was the discovery this morning that the flowers in the planting beds surrounding Mina's front porch had all been brutally murdered. The night before, the entire landscaping committee had come and unearthed all of Mina's plants. As it turned out, bellflowers were expressly prohibited, as stated in the bylaws of the community.

Bellflowers had been the favorite flower of Charlie Witmore's now-deceased wife. At her funeral, there had been an ocean of bellflowers. And now, any time anyone at Easton Estates saw bellflowers, all they could see in their mind's eye was Kitty Witmore, made up like a pasty showgirl, in her pink-satin-lined coffin.

Shame rose in Mina's face and she looked away. "It was insensitive of me," she said. "I should have gone with marigolds. No one ever uses marigolds at a funeral."

"No one uses bellflowers either," said Esther, and Mina half-nodded in agreement. Esther placed a hand on Mina's elbow. "You don't think it was insensitive of them to come here in the middle of the night and massacre your garden?"

*"What you welcome will be YOURS!"*

"You have company?" Esther asked, a perplexed look on her face.

Mina didn't answer either question.

Esther craned her neck to look inside the house to find the source of the curious voice as she spoke. "I can't tell you what I'd have done had they messed with my yard," she shook her head and gave Mina a soft, powdery kiss on the cheek. "Honey, you're going to have to stop letting people push you around like this." She handed Mina the plate.

*"If you want it, it will come to you."*

"What *is* that? Is someone here?" asked Esther, gently pushing her way inside. "Who's that man talking? And where's the little one? Isn't it Tuesday?"

Tuesday! Of course. In the time that had elapsed since Mina chose door over daughter, Emma had gone silent. Almost too silent. Now Mina panicked.

"Here," she tossed the plate back to Esther and ran to the playroom. "Emma? Mama's coming! Emma! Are you okay?"

*"If you want it, make it yours! Goodnight!"*

"Goodnight?" said Esther, befuddled. "But it's eleven thirty in the morning."

Mina raced to the playroom and found Emma crunched up in a little ball, holding her knees, rocking and scowling. When she saw her mother had finally come for her, she regarded the woman with a sour grin and went on sulking. "I'm sorry, baby," Mina said, and bent down in front of the gate. "You know Mama loves you?"

Without warning, Emma's scowl switched to a smile, the sweetest and brightest smile Mina had ever seen the little girl wear. Instantly, Mina's heart filled with joy, with an intense and incredible sense of love from seeing her daughter like that, smiling at her so warmly, so beautifully. She wanted to scoop up the child, cradle her in her arms, and plant kisses all over her little painted body. She wanted to snuggle with her so much, it made her heart hurt. She took a breath and reached out her arms.

"Esda!" cried Emma, and ran to the section of gate that "Esda" now occupied.

"My goodness, baby, what have you gotten into now?" asked Esther, bemused, looking at Mina, not Emma.

"I paint!" a gleeful Emma boasted, and waved around the playroom to show Esther the extent of her masterpiece.

Esther looked at Mina, and Mina smirked, mimicked her daughter's hand movement, and showed Esther the "masterpiece" spread throughout the house.

"Oh dear," said Esther, another tsk in her voice. "Why didn't you drop this child in the bathtub right away? Is it because of that man in the house?" she asked, craning her neck into the next room. "Who's that man in the house?"

"Esther, what are you talking about? No one's here except Emma and me."

"Forget it," she said. "But dear, what happened here?"

"Kind of a funny story," said Mina, blowing a strand of her paint-encrusted bangs out of her eyes, and lifting Emma into her arms. When Emma nuzzled her small, warm head into the crook of Mina's neck, and she breathed in the fresh sweetness of the small one underneath the paint fumes, she knew in her heart that the look of love that Emma had shown had indeed been for her.

As soon as Esther learned the situation with the water heater, she immediately offered to help out—first by suggesting Mina and Emma shower at her house and then by giving Mina the name and number of a friend who could give her a good deal.

"Except I can't pay anything until the middle of the month," said Mina. "And even then—"

"Don't give it another thought. Bob will help you out, no questions asked. Just pay him what you can whenever you can."

"I don't know how to thank you, Esther. For this. For everything you do for us."

"Not to worry, dear. I was your age once. Small children, limited funds. Budget stretched to the hilt. I understand. I'm glad to help."

Mina really didn't know what she'd do without Esther.

"Why don't you walk through the backyard. Lord only knows what kind of fine or punishment that busybody Witmore's going to dream up over the two of you looking the way you do," she said, folding her arms in front of her. "The back door's unlocked. Why don't you grab some fresh clothes and walk on ahead. I'll straighten up a little here."

"Thank you, Esther," said Mina, warmly. "Downstairs shower then?" Mina and Esther had the same exact home configuration; she had been in Esther's house thousands of times, but even if she'd never been there before, she'd know exactly where the downstairs shower was.

"Of course, dear," said Esther.

Mina ran upstairs and grabbed clothes for Emma and for herself. In her bedroom she saw Jack's laundry still folded on his side of the bed from the day before, a reminder that he hadn't made it home last night, again. He'd taken the red-eye and headed right into the office. A stab of longing pierced her heart as she wondered if he'd be home early enough tonight for them to see each other. Or even have a conversation. She never knew these days. Jack was working all the time. One day running into the next. She headed out of the bedroom and down the stairs.

"I'm back," said Mina and she scooped up Emma into her arms.

"I'll be right behind you," said Esther. "I'll grab the cookies."

Mina slid open the expansive glass doors that led to the backyard and cut across the yard to Esther's. With every step, Emma writhed and squirmed to break free.

"I want to walk!" screamed Emma. "I walk!" After taking a couple of punches to the face, which were considerably painful for such small fists, Mina gave up and set Emma down.

Just as Emma's feet touched down, both Emma and Mina were knocked over by a powerful force, which Mina only identified as water once they hit the ground. She swung her head around to find Esther wielding a garden hose like a crazed naturalist who'd just captured a raging python by the midsection on some wild animal program. The spray must have been on full-force and Mina wondered for a moment how the hell Esther could be so incredibly strong. Could control such force with her small and aged frame, before wondering why Esther was trying to drown them with a hose.

Esther laughed out loud. "You didn't think I was going to let the two of you into my house looking like that!" she said.

Mina opened her mouth to speak and got pelted in the mouth with a hard stream of water. She looked at Emma, who she imagined must be terrified, and Emma looked back at her. Then Emma began to laugh maniacally, and she splashed her tiny hands in the water and now mud puddles that had formed in the grass. Mina watched Emma, face and hair and clothes and hands streaked in rinsed paint and brown mud and random loose blades of grass, who was now looking back at Esther continuing to spray away with mad delight. "Again!" screamed Emma. "Again!"

As the sun rose in the sky signaling high noon and Emma and Esther screamed and laughed with the hose spraying away, Mina gave in to the moment and joined in the fun, splashing and laughing and spinning around in the grass with Emma as Esther rinsed them clean. And she was feeling, at least for the moment, that maybe this late September day wasn't the worst day after all.

About an hour later, Mina and Emma, now both fresh and clean, sat at the kitchen table with Esther, sipping homemade hot chocolate and nibbling at the chocolate chip cookies Esther had baked for them.

Emma jumped down from the table. "I draw?"

Esther brought out for Emma a carousel of crayons and a giant-sized coloring book.

"I didn't know you had that," Mina said. "You let her play with crayons in your house?"

Esther laughed. "I keep these here for Emma, for when you drop her here. She really loves her art," Esther said. "I guess that explains the attraction to the paints. You're a painter, Mina?"

"Not me, no. Jack."

"Ah. I never took him for the artsy type. Well, you learn something new every day, I suppose."

Mina had a hard time thinking of Jack as an artsy type as well. She tried to remember a time before he wore suits to work. She was aware that there had to have been a time like this, because she did know that the paints were Jack's. It was another one of those things—a thing she could feel but could not intellectualize. She wanted so badly to remember one instance of Jack painting, to have a memory of him creating, a moment of something deeper. She wanted to remember just one example of the joy it gave him. It seemed there was no joy in Jack's life these days. Not his, not hers.

As Emma scratched colors onto the printed forms in the book, Mina could feel in her heart that this passion in Emma had come from Jack, and it made her smile.

Unfortunately, Mina had forgotten about the havoc being wreaked in the back of her mouth by her derelict molar for a split second—just long enough for a gooey chocolate morsel to land there and make her wince in excruciating pain.

"Are you okay?" said Esther.

"Sure," said Mina, desperately trying to clear the chocolate away with her tongue. "Just a little toothache. It'll go away."

"You probably ought to get that checked out," Esther said. "I've read stories about dental problems leading to death."

Mina rolled her eyes. "Stories?"

"True stories," said Esther, nodding emphatically. "There was this one woman with an abscess in Tennessee. Never looked after it, and it killed her. Left her four kids all alone in the world."

"Where did you read that?"

"The Internet."

Mina cringed again, for another reason this time. How long had it been since she'd been able to search for anything on the Internet? Since they had been able to pay for service? She giggled nervously. "Esther, I don't think you can believe everything you read on the Internet. Anyone can write anything they want on the Internet. I can write and post a news story about a crazy old bat who drowned her neighbors with a garden hose!" Mina snorted.

Mina was joking but Esther's silence made it clear she had gone too far. "I noticed Jack didn't come home again last night, dear," said Esther, taking a sip from a chunky white mug. This was the side of Esther that Mina, and Jack especially, could do without.

Mina played with a cookie on her plate and paused before answering. "You know how it is," she said casually, trying to brush off her own frustrations at the situation.

"It's a strange time in a marriage," Esther said, "when the children are young. The mother's life changes completely. The father's free to live the life he wants. Long work hours. Business travel," she took a long sip from her mug. "Sometimes they're fooling around. Sometimes they're just looking for a reason to be away. They're never trapped by children the way the mother gets trapped, you know." Esther zoned out for a moment after speaking these words, seeming to go to some faraway place in her mind and her memories.

After some time she looked up. "Are you thinking about going back to work? That helps sometimes, you know. With the loneliness. The resentment."

Mina felt the familiar surge of panic she generally experienced when anyone asked her about work, or anything else she couldn't remember for that matter. Panic and fear. She lost control of her mug and the contents spilled out over her blouse and the table. "Oh no!"

"Oh no," said Esther, and she jumped up to retrieve the paper towel roll sitting on the countertop. "I'm sorry, dear. I sometimes forget about the . . . you know . . . your situation. You don't remember yet what you used to do."

"I don't," said Mina, taking some of the towels and wiping up the spill. She looked up at Esther, hopeful. "Do you?" she asked.

Esther looked away. "Even if I knew the answer to that dear, you know I'm not allowed to tell you. It's for your own—"

"I know, for my own good," Mina snapped. "But I feel like even the smallest clue about the past, just someone giving me some kind of hint . . . I feel like it would help with everything."

"Don't worry, dear," said Esther, with a reassuring tap on Mina's hand. "Eventually, it will come to you. All of the answers will come."

"So they say," Mina said absently. "But when."

"Are you trying, Mina? Are you doing the exercises Dr. Barsheed recommended? The notebook?"

Mina was guilty. She barely ever did any of them. "How did you know about that?"

Esther looked embarrassed and paused a while. She smiled. "Jack told me," she said. And Mina thought that was strange, as Jack avoided talking to Esther whenever he could. Esther must have read her mind. "It was some time ago," she said. "When Jack was, well, around more."

Mina let it go. "You think I should do them."

"Could it hurt just to try?"

"I have. A little, I guess. I use the notebook, but . . ."

"But?"

Mina sighed and shook her head. "It's been years already, you know." Tears began to well in her eyes. "I just want to feel normal again."

"You will," said Esther, the grandmotherly warmth finally returning. "Dear, what was that man's voice in your house today?"

Mina felt warmth rising in her cheeks. The tapes. She had no idea why she had them, but she always played them. They spoke to her somehow. They made her feel connected. But she was embarrassed to admit that, so she just told Esther: "I just found those, tucked away in the hall closet. He's some new age guru or something, I don't know. All I know is that when I listen to them, I feel better."

"But he doesn't really *say* anything," said Esther, a twinge of concern in her voice. "I mean, he says words, but from what I heard, that's all they are. Common sense words. There isn't anything he says that anyone wouldn't already know."

"Maybe," said Mina. "But there's something about the way he speaks. It feels like he's speaking right to me."

"Well," said Esther. "You know that's how all those woo-hoo guys make their money. A bunch of common sense Jesuses spouting common sense, *insights*"—and she curved the word insights in air quotes. "I don't jump for Jesus in general, so I'm not going to get into what I think about those kinds of people." She looked at Mina, whose face was now scrunched by doubt, insecurity, and worry. Esther smiled warmly at her. "But if it makes you happy, I suppose I can't see the harm," she said, and then looked away.

Esther rose from the table and collected the mugs, which she brought to the sink. Emma crawled into Mina's lap. "See my picture, Monny? I make you!"

Welling with pride, Mina looked down to see a black-outlined portrait of pouty Disney Princess Ariel completely scratched over in diarrhea green crayon. She and Esther shared a glance before Mina squeezed Emma tight. "It's beautiful, sweetie. I love it," she said, and kissed her daughter on the top of her sweet and precious head.

Back home, Mina waited for the water heater guy Esther had called for her. Emma was building structures with oversized Lego-like blocks, then knocking them down, shrieking with joy, as Mina wandered around the "submarine" in search of something to make for dinner. But how many would be eating tonight? She hadn't heard from Jack all day.

Mina saw the light flashing on the answering machine, nothing new, but wondered if maybe among the messages was word from Jack, who had forgotten again to dial her cell phone instead. She garnered the strength to hit "play" and took a deep breath as the robotic voice relayed just how many messages were available (sixty-two) and how many were new (fourteen). She kept her finger on the "delete" button as she endured the sometimes terse, sometimes disarming, sometimes unnervingly creepy voices of creditors chanting on between the beeps.

"Mrs. Clark, this is Bob. Mrs. E called me. Looks like I'm not going to be able to get there until about five or so today. Figured I'd give you a shout so you weren't sitting around waiting for me. I'll try you back in a bit." Mina wasn't used to being treated with such courtesy and kindness, and relaxed somewhat before advancing to the next message.

"Hi it's me." She let out a sigh. Jack.

Emma darted into the room. "Daddy!"

"Doesn't look like I'll be making it home for dinner tonight, guys. Sorry."

"Daddy! Daddy! DADDY!"

"Shhh, sweetie. I need to hear what Daddy's saying."

"That new regional manager I told you about, Amber Fox—"

"DADDY! DADDY!"

*Amber Fox? New regional manager? Who?*

"We're all stuck here—"

"DA-DA! I want Da-da!" Emma screamed, garbling anything Jack had to say about Amber.

"Anyway, I'll try not to be too late. Hopefully you'll still be up." When his message stopped, Emma darted back out of the room and Mina went to replay it to try to make out what she thought she had heard, just as the phone rang again. Forgetting herself, she picked it up.

"Jack?"

"Mina," said a man's voice. Not Jack. Not familiar, but friendly. "How's it going, Mina?"

"Who is this?" she asked, sadly knowing that just because she didn't recognize the voice didn't mean she didn't know the person on the other end. The voice was so inviting. So disarming. She couldn't help but feel a small glimmer of hope that this was a friend.

"You don't know who this is, Mina?" the man's voice asked, sweetly. Warmly.

She was now starting to feel a little guilty about not recognizing him. "I'm sorry," said Mina. "I'm very sorry but I don't."

"It's me," he said, reassuringly. "It's Anthony." Mina squinted her eyes and mouthed the name, trying to retrieve at least some vague picture of who this man was to her and why he seemed to be on such familiar terms with her. "You gonna leave me hanging forever, baby?" his tone now changed from sweet to something that seemed more salacious. And then he sang, "When you gonna pay?"

Mina froze. "I'm sorry?"

"Come on, baby. Let's not play these games. Give Anthony what he needs. Give Bankcorp what we need." Mina felt paralyzed. Immobilized. "You're over a hundred days behind already," he said, his voice now growing colder. "How long you gonna make Anthony wait?"

Mina slammed down the phone. She was shaking. Finally she breathed, and the phone rang again. When the machine picked up, the caller hung up. She looked down at her watch. There were still a couple of hours before Bob would be coming, and she wasn't going to spend them here.

"Emma!" she called. "Playground. Come on." She grabbed her oversized purse, swung it over her shoulder, and flipped open the stroller. Emma bounced into the seat, Mina strapped her in, and off they went.

# 2

Easton Estates, "A Haven For Harmonious Living" (as the sign in front helpfully explained to anyone wondering), was envisioned in 1995 by billionaire real estate tycoon Edward W. Easton III as a well-to-do community for empty nesters over the age of sixty-five seeking a new "nest." Not necessarily a less expansive or spectacular nest than the one in which they'd raised their kids, but one they could call their own—one where they could continue to live a comfortable life, one not muddied by memories of the way their children had destroyed their original homes during the "growing years." Which is not to say that offspring and their offspring weren't welcome. The homes were designed with plenty of guest rooms.

For all his business vision, however, Mr. Easton hadn't anticipated the socioeconomic shifts that were to come in the ensuing decades. He had not imagined in his wildest dreams that offspring might fly back to the nest in droves to live, or that families with young children might see the benefits, mainly financial, of living in a gated condominium community versus a private home. Also unforeseen by Easton was something of a civil war that would eventually begin to brew between these groups—the Nesters and the Empty Nesters. The older people resented the chaos of the younger families; the younger families fumed at the crankiness of the curmudgeons. Harmonious living indeed.

The older people worked to keep "the kids" (anyone under the age of fifty-five) in line by making sure they occupied every seat of power available in the community; over the course of the past decade, however, younger families were starting to equal, if not outnumber, the old folks. And the oldest residents were losing their numbers as their numbers came up, so to speak. Which is one of the reasons that Easton Estates also boasted one of the prettiest playgrounds in the town.

While technically it was only for the residents, there were always dozens of nonresident kids climbing the jungle gym, riding the slides. And this day was no different. As the children swung and chased and played, the mothers clustered in cliques on various benches, sipping fancy coffees from tall paper cups as a gaggle of nannies of all nationalities looped through the playground equipment and guarded the precious ones.

In this neighborhood, the early autumn uniform of motherhood generally consisted of stylish boots, snug-fitting designer jeans, down or fur vests draped over thin cashmere sweaters, and oversized, overpriced designer sunglasses. One of the mothers, though, was always inexplicably dressed in a dark designer suit, wearing pantyhose and pumps, her straight blonde hair chopped into a no-bullshit bob.

Mina's less stylish clothes, dotted with various patches of encrusted mystery, were only part of what made her feel left out among the other mothers here. She wheeled the stroller to an empty bench in the shade that was nearly covered in dried bird shit. Knowing she couldn't possibly ruin her clothes sitting here made her feel better, even a little smug, about what she wore.

On the other side of the playground, also on the outskirts of the mothers' group, was a woman Mina knew definitely lived in her complex. Harriet Saunders. Harriet had a daughter Emma's age, Brittany, who was in Emma's nursery school class. She also had two sons and a daughter who were older. And a son who was younger. Harriet, too, was out of uniform, wearing a peasant blouse and boho skirt. She kept to herself, her arms folded over a fairly ample bosom, as her children swarmed around the playground like savages, with the exception of the littlest boy, who clung to her like lint.

Harriet waved Mina over; Mina waved back and pretended not to notice the invitation. Instead, she bent over Emma to release the stroller harness and Emma sprang out. She ran toward a group of other kids. No panic. No fear. No insecurities. Mina was proud. She watched Emma with the other children for a few minutes and, sensing Emma felt safe and fine and happy, she opened her purse and pulled out her ancient Sony Walkman, the only portable device she had that could play her prized tapes. She put on her headphones. She pressed "play."

"What's your purpose here? What's your purpose in this life?" the man's voice asked, and she took out her notebook and pen.

As Esther had earlier shamed her into remembering, one of the recommendations from Dr. Barsheed, her shrink, was that she carry a notebook and pen with her. Anytime she found herself with a free minute to think, she was supposed to take out the notebook and simply scratch into it with a pen. He believed, as he explained to her, that if she just took pen to paper, at the very least marking the paper in lines or squiggles or doodles, eventually the random lines would start to become words, and the words would help Mina unlock the secrets she'd been repressing along with her memory. Frustrated and bored by it, Mina had dropped the exercise for a while, but had decided to give it another shot.

In the first several weeks, Mina had sat with her notebook, her pen in hand but never touching the paper—just hovering. When she finally got over the hurdle of actually writing something, all she could manage was straight lines. As a result, the first several pages of the notebook looked like something Emma had done. Eventually, she had been able to expand the scratchings into shapes and squiggles, and had now, by the middle of the book, advanced to doodles.

"What are you trying to accomplish here? What is the meaning of your purpose here?" the voice on the tape asked of her.

With the sun on her face making her calm and relaxed, Mina began to scribble into her book. Loops and lines appeared on the page, and then an object began to emerge from the etchings. A long pen-like shape, two fingers or long leaves on each side of it. As she sketched, the image began to take form. It was an image she recognized, an image that with every stroke of her pen made her feel closer to grasping something, knowing something—something just beyond her reach. But what was it? What was she grasping for?

This had never happened to her before, and she was starting to get excited. She really felt she was on the verge of something now and her heart raced as she drew. What did this image, now with legs and antennae formed, clearly a dragonfly, evoke in her?

*"What does it all mean?"* the man's voice asked.

She could feel it. She knew it. She was right on the cusp of getting it and then . . .

And then someone began tapping her on the shoulder.

"Is dat your child?!" Mina looked up, the sun in her eyes. A silhouette of a woman, clearly one of the nannies, shadowed her. "Hey, lady? I'm talking to you. Is dat one yours?" Mina pulled off her headphones.

"I'm sorry?"

"I said, is dat your child?" And the woman pointed to the sandbox, where a commotion had broken out.

A little girl, not Emma, was crying, "Stop that! Give it back!" as another child repeatedly tore off and replaced the head of a doll, laughing manically all the while. The sun may have created a heavenly aura around the aggressor, beaming down on her shiny platinum locks, but Mina knew this child was no angel.

"I break this!" Emma squeaked in delight, her bright blue eyes shining. "I break this!" a slight glint of innocence sparkling through the ever-prevalent state of mischief.

"Emma!" she screamed and jumped up. She raced over to the sandbox, grabbed the doll away from Emma, and handed it back to the crying girl.

"I'm so sorry," Mina said, and the girl squeezed her doll and buried her face in her nanny's stretch pants. The mothers, sniffing drama, began gliding over.

"Let's go Emma. Now," she said, panicking, not wanting to face them and their judgments.

"No! I don't want to go, Monny! I don't want to go!" Emma fought with the strength of an army against Mina, who desperately tried to pack the simultaneously squirming and stiff child into the stroller. With a swift, gentle karate chop to Emma's mid-section, Mina finally bent the child into the seat, got the safety straps fastened, and raced away from the fray.

"Hey, I think you forgot something," Harriet called after her.

Mina whipped around to her bench. There she saw a man, probably somewhere in his mid-sixties, with a salt-and-pepper beard and a black wool hat. He was standing over her things.

*Didn't they pay a premium for security around here?* she wondered. *Why was just anyone off the street permitted?*

She watched him pick up her notebook and purse as she quickly pushed the stroller toward him.

*And then to just rob her in bright daylight!*

She raced over to him and he smiled at her, a smile so warm and kind it nearly disarmed her. "This is yours, yes?" He spoke with a thick Russian accent.

"Excuse me!" she snapped, and she snatched her things away from him.

He nodded at Emma. "I saw the child. This one, she's . . . how would you say . . . feisty." He laughed. "I know this type. My niece, she is like this."

Emma began to scream and cry. Mina stuffed her notebook and her tape player into her bag in a huff.

"What you listen to on there? I did not know they even made those anymore," he chuckled.

"I don't see how that's any of your business. Who do you think you are, touching my things like that!"

"Ah, Alex meant no harm, I promise," he said, shrugging his shoulders. "It looked like you needed to, ah . . . make yourself quick exit. I get this. I am just trying to help."

"Well, thanks but no thanks," she said, spinning on her heel and wheeling the stroller away.

"That child is out of control!" she heard from the group as she passed the mothers again.

"I think she was a C-section," said the business-mom.

"Definitely C-section," quipped another.

"Well, I'd say that certainly explains things," yet another agreed.

"Hey, see you later?" Harriet shouted after her. "Parents' Night?" And Mina felt a stab in her chest at having forgotten something that should have been so easy to remember.

Mina finally escaped, with Emma still crying her head off. She tried to ignore the child as she wheeled out of the playground and down the road to their house. There seemed to be more people out walking than usual, and they all stared at Mina, regarding her with disapproving faces as she and screaming Emma passed.

Within two minutes, Emma passed out and Mina could breathe again. She was now even starting to enjoy the walk, even though it was all uphill in this direction and made her shoulders and the backs of her legs tired and sore as she pushed the stroller. She was thin as a rail but took this as a definite hint that she was out of shape. Or maybe just getting old.

Now that Mina and Emma presented the picture of domestic tranquility, pretty mother pushing sleeping child, the neighbors all smiled at Mina while they watered their lawns, gathered and gossiped, walked their dogs. One guy, holding the leash for a pooch that reminded Mina of Lady from *Lady and the Tramp*, was speaking with a woman who had a small toy poodle at the end of her leash. He smiled, big and bright, at Mina, and he and his companion both waved to her with their other hands, in which they were holding plastic shopping bags with small lumps in them. Mina wondered if they even realized they were waving bags of dog shit at her.

Ten minutes later Mina was at last home, pushing a still-sleeping Emma up the driveway. Parked there was a white van with bright blue lettering that read, "Bob's: We're the Best In the Business!" A man, Bob, she surmised, was standing at her front door. As she approached, she noticed the garden beds were now brimming with bright red and orange mums. She hated mums, vehemently. But she had no idea why.

"Mrs. Clark?" the man called, and started walking down the driveway to meet her. "I'm—"

"Bob," she smiled, pointing a thumb at his truck. "Please call me Mina."

"Will do, Mina," he grinned. There was a gold flash in his otherwise pearly white smile. It caught the sun and the glare caught her attention. A gold tooth. So unusual. "A pleasure," he said. He knelt down. "Now, who's this?"

"That's Emma," she whispered. "Please don't wake her . . . "

"I wouldn't dream of it. I got three of them myself, you know. I know how it goes. So you want to show me the problem?" he asked, and they headed inside.

Bob went right to work and replaced the water heater within the hour. Emma had woken up during that time and was playing peacefully with blocks in the kitchen. Esther had agreed, happily, to come sit with Emma so Mina could attend Parents' Night. On her own again. She tried to ignore the pang of resentment that stirred in her, but these resentments were building, and were getting harder and harder to ignore.

"That should do it," Bob said. "Let me know if it gives you any trouble. I'm not that far from here." He scribbled onto a clipboard and tore off the sheet. He handed it to her. "So here's what you owe us, just parts. Pay whenever you can. Labor's on me," he said. When Mina started to object, he waved his hand, dismissing her concerns, "I don't want to hear otherwise. I *told* you, I got three of those." Smiling at Emma, he said, "Folks helped us. Glad to help when I can."

"Thanks, Bob," Mina said, and she walked him to the door.

"By the way," he said, "took care of that dryer for you too. You don't want to let that kind of thing go, you know. Leak's because the vent needs to be cleaned from time to time. That's all condensation pooling up, causing the leak. But it could be worse. Ignore a blocked dryer vent and you might find yourself with a fire."

"Good to know," said Mina. "Thanks again."

It was close to dinnertime now and Mina realized she'd never taken anything out of the freezer to prepare. Not that it mattered—not to Emma or her. She really only cooked for Jack. She opened a can of tuna and a sleeve of crackers, and, voila!, dinner was served.

After they ate, Mina gave Emma a bubble bath and dressed her in her pajamas, and by 7:00 Esther had arrived. Esther had changed her outfit. She now wore a brown track suit with sandals. Instead of her Tiffany-inspired pin, she had on a large three-toned necklace that resembled three snakes coiled around each other.

"Nice necklace," said Mina.

"Really? I never much liked this piece. I was thinking Emma might want it to play with."

"I think it may be a little too nice for Emma, but thank you," Mina giggled.

"I think I can be the judge of that," said Esther, with a hint more smugness than seemed necessary. Then she changed her tone. "Have a nice time, dear," she said, tentatively scanning the room with her eyes.

Mina was embarrassed. "Uh, sorry for the mess. I didn't have time to straighten up and—"

"Don't worry, dear. I know you expect old Esther to clean up for you."

Mina was horrified. "Oh God, no. Of course not!"

"Oh come on," Esther chuckled and shook her head. "I'm just teasing you, Mina. Really, you have no sense of humor sometimes," she gave Mina a gentle nudge out the front door. "Try and have a good time. I know there were few things I looked forward to like Parents' Night." Esther cackled, and closed the door behind her.

3

Mina had to take a cab to the Acela Academy, which swallowed almost her entire grocery budget for the week. Jack wouldn't get paid until the following Wednesday, and she mentally calculated how many diapers she would need for the next several days, hoping she'd have enough. She definitely did not have the mental stamina this week to try potty training again.

Mina looked pretty tonight, in a clean pair of dark, crisp blue jeans and a powder pink cashmere sweater that went well with her pale coloring and light blonde hair. Even though it looked nice, Mina felt it didn't particularly suit her. In fact, it was a top she wore rarely, really only on occasions like these. She had no idea why she even had it, as wearing it made her feel like an impostor. Though, in fairness, almost everything about her life made her feel that way.

Entering the school, she soon spotted Harriet, who had also come sans husband, but with Clingy McLinster in tow. Harriet, Mina noticed, was still wearing the same, now considerably dirty, clothing she had been wearing at the playground earlier. Harriet was the only woman who ever made Mina feel like a better mother, and Mina had to admit to herself that she was kind of happy to see her.

"Over here," Harriet shouted, waving wildly from the other side of the room, bouncing her small one on her knee. "Hey! Mina!"

While Mina made her way over, braless Harriet pulled her shirt completely off over her head and smushed babe to bosom, scandalizing a Ralph Lauren-clad group of parents congregating nearby. "What's your problem!" she challenged. "It's natural! It's perfectly natural!"

Mina knew that no one in the room had any issue with mothers breastfeeding in public. Not Mina. Not any of the other members of the Acela community. But Harriet had a way of taking things maybe just slightly too far. Sitting fully topless in the hallowed halls of the Acela Academy was one of those times, but there were hundreds of others Mina could recall since she had been able to recall anything at all, like the time Harriet had shown up drunk at a community meeting, her entire brood swarming around her, all with red, sticky, highly contagious conjunctivitis. When someone on the board suggested maybe she and her children would be more comfortable at home, she had told them all to go fuck themselves.

Mina rationalized it was too late to pretend she didn't see Harriet now, and she wandered over to her.

"I'm so glad you're here," Harriet said, pulling Mina into a tight one-armed hug and then pressing her lips against her cheek and lowering her voice to say, "Because I just want to fucking kill everyone else here."

Mina couldn't help but laugh.

Harriet pulled away and darted her head around like a bird. "Where's the squirt?"

"Home," said Mina. "With Esther."

Harriet gasped. "Are you kidding me? You left her with that old bat? Shit, I would never trust any of those old fuckers with my kids. You want your kid to be safe, leave her with me."

"Esther's my friend," said Mina. "She loves Emma."

Harriet shook her head and pursed her lips. "Nuh-uh," she said. "No fucking way. None of those old coots love any of us and you know it. How can you be sure that old witch isn't boiling up your kid in a cauldron somewhere?"

"I don't have a cauldron in my house."

For some reason, this satisfied Harriet, and Mina had figured out why. Mina could smell booze on Harriet's breath and she wished for a second she too had thought to have a drink before coming to Parents' Night.

As if reading Mina's mind, Harriet reached into her oversized purse and pulled out a travel coffee mug. She offered it to Mina. "Oh, no thank you. It's a little bit late in the day for me to be drinking coffee. I'll be up all night," Mina said, politely waving it off.

"It's a gin and tonic, dummy," Harriet laughed. "Go ahead. I have a few," and she opened her purse to prove it—four additional mugs lined up like soldiers.

Mina felt a twinge of discomfort. "But aren't you, you know, nursing? Isn't that supposed to be, well, bad? Drinking?"

Harriet seemed to consider this for a moment. "Better for both of us," she said, snuggling the babe. "Makes us both more . . . uh. . . calm?"

"Oh," said Mina, and thought to herself, who was she to judge. Wasn't the perceived "judginess" what she hated most about other mothers. She decided to be gracious. Open-minded. The child was calm. Of course this made sense. Somehow?

"Thanks," said Mina. She clutched the mug and took a healthy gulp.

Within twenty minutes, the dog-and-pony show that was Acela Academy Parents' Night had started to become tolerable, even fun, especially after Harriet's young one had a meltdown during the phys. ed. presentation and finally passed out in his stroller.

Mina and Harriet moved from room to room together, half-listening to fundraising pitches and making fun of the speakers by scribbling notes back and forth to each other in Mina's notebook.

At the presentation given by the director of admissions, Portuguese-born Ernesto Garcia, the night took an uncomfortable turn for Mina, who seemed to have all of a sudden developed a weakness for Portuguese men.

There was nothing particularly attractive about Mr. Garcia. His face was creased, his hair was greased, and he was even a little bit ugly. But as he encouraged the parents to bring in friends, relatives, and general acquaintances, he spoke with the slightest lilt of an accent, which swirled around his words like hot fudge swimming in ice cream. She couldn't look away from him, except when he made eye contact with her.

"You look like you're going to pass out," Harriet whispered. "Your face is all red!"

"It's the gin," Mina lied, putting a hand to her face to try and cool herself down. But with every word he spoke, she could feel heat rising in her.

"No more gin for you!" Harriet snorted. "You look like a goddamned tomato!"

An angry "Shhhh!" sounded from the front of the room.

"Sorry," Mina mouthed. Harriet blew a giant saucy raspberry and Mina burst out laughing.

By the final event of the night, a parents' reception in the dining hall, Mina was so buzzed she was having trouble feeling her lips. And now that the other parents were drinking too, which made them considerably less smug, the night was getting bearable.

Then Harriet acted up again, tugging wildly at Mina's sleeve. "What?"

"Who's that?" Harriet asked.

Mina squinted in the distance. "Don't know."

"Look. They're coming right for us," said Harriet, pointing. "Look! They look like they know us. They're smiling at us." Sure enough, a well-heeled couple was making a beeline for their table. "What the hell do we do? Do you know them? Dammit. What the hell are their names?"

"I can't help you," said Mina. "I can't remember."

"Oh, gosh. Sorry."

"No, no. It's not because of that."

"Well, how are you doing with that?"

"Good days and bad, I guess." She managed a weak smile. "Like anything else. It's just been going on so long."

"How long now?"

"I don't really remember."

"Sorry," said Harriet, seeming uncomfortable.

"Oh, I'm sorry. I didn't mean . . . I guess sometime after I had Emma, but the details are still a little fuzzy. I don't remember being pregnant with Emma. I don't specifically remember anything about her being a young baby. I don't know. It's all either totally black or gray."

"Hey, I used to teach a memory class," said Harriet. "I'm surprised I never told you this, you know, all things considered."

"Well, we really never talked that much before tonight."

Harriet pursed her lips. "Good point. Well, I can't bring it back, I'm not a magician. But I can help train you going forward to remember things—like people's names. Like these guys."

"Uh, okay. But how exactly does this help us now?"

"Huh?"

"I mean, we're probably already expected to know who they are and—"

"Don't worry about it. Let's just move forward, shall we." Harriet now wore a serious expression. "I promise you. It never fails."

"Except . . . "

"Except what?"

Mina hedged before speaking. "Except . . . if it works so well . . . Uh, then why don't you remember their names?"

"That's because I'm shitfaced!"

As luck would have it, the couple was intercepted by one of the administrators on the way to the table, and at least for the next several seconds, Mina and Harriet were in the clear. They each took a deep breath.

"Here's our chance," said Mina. "Tell me the technique."

"Okay, so here's how it works," Harriet said, and she leaned in, conspiratorially. "You *associate*."

"Okay?"

"Yeah, you know. Make an association. Like, say her name is Barbara."

"Her name is Barbara?"

"No. I mean maybe. I don't know. Just say it is."

"Okay," said Mina, nodding.

"Now, check her out. Barbara. What about her can we associate with 'Barbara'?"

Mina nodded. "Her blue suit? That starts with 'B.'"

"Yes, because she'll always be wearing that suit," Harriet smirked.

"Oh."

"Boobs!" Harriet exclaimed, loudly enough to silence the room for a second or so. "Boobs," she then whispered, as if that would make it right. "Barbara has big boobs. Boobs, Barbara. Barbara, boobs. Get it?"

"But what if her name isn't Barbara? Now I can only think of her as being Barbara."

"But what if it *is*!"

"Well, what if her name is Annie. Or Giselle?"

Harriet shook her head. "Her name is not Giselle."

"What makes you so sure?"

Harriet rolled her eyes. "You're really not getting this at all, are you?" she said. "Because if her name was Giselle, she'd be lithe and graceful. Like a gazelle. See? Giselle. Gazelle." Harriet nodded in "Barbara's" direction. "And look at her, all stocky and top-heavy."

Mina realized that Harriet was definitely shitfaced and so was she. She tried to save face. "I don't think it works that way," she offered.

"Well, I'm going with Barbara. She looks like a Barbara to me," Harriet said, and slurped the last drop of cocktail from the last travel mug. "A Babs!" she shouted, a glint in her eye.

Mina sighed heavily. "I think I'll just call her Harriet."

"Barbara" and her husband never made it over to their table and the night finally came to a close. Harriet and Mina stepped outside.

"You want a ride home?" Harriet asked.

"Thanks, but I already called a cab," said Mina.

"Great idea! I'll come with. Just give me a sec." Harriet darted back inside and then out again. "It's on me!" As Mina didn't know if she was going to be able to afford the additional fare, she was relieved. Now she might even have enough money left over to buy some fresh fruit and vegetables. She wondered if there would ever again be a time in her life that buying groceries would not be such a struggle. Feeling a chill, Mina wrapped her arms around herself.

"Not too cold to wait out here?" the question was lightly seasoned in a familiar Portuguese accent. Mina turned her head to see Mr. Garcia leaning against the outside of the building. He was smoking a cigarette, which he stubbed out before walking toward her.

Mina's heart began to race in her chest as he approached, and a thousand tiny tingles crackled to life under her skin. "I noticed you in my lecture today. You and your friend. Your lovely blonde hair. I have a weakness for blondes," he said, lighting a new cigarette. He stood only a foot away from her now, and she could smell his cologne. And cigarette smoke, at once inviting and repulsive. The essence of him, manly and foreign and ugly as hell. So confusing. All so confusing.

In her mind she kept repeating Jack's name, but it had been so long since Mina had been intimate with Jack—she couldn't even remember the last time. And while it may not yet have gotten to the point where the very breeze could arouse her, a man like this wasn't the breeze.

"I could lend you my coat," he said, and he began to undress.

"Oh, that's okay," Mina partly whispered, her voice disappearing with the loss of her breath. It felt like he was making a pass at her, but between the alcohol and the essence of the man, she couldn't trust herself. "My ride should be here any minute."

"Why don't I drive you."

"That's okay," she said, just as Harriet pushed her way outside again, the baby still asleep in the stroller. The cab pulled up to the entrance.

"Goodnight," Mina gasped, and she dove into the cab. Harriet tossed the baby into the car after Mina, collapsed the stroller with one hand and tossed it to the floor, and then sat down beside her.

The cab pulled away and Mina watched from the back window as Ernesto slid his coat back on and pulled another cigarette from the inside pocket. What if she had taken him up on his offer for a ride? Would she have been able to resist him?

"We should have a play date after school tomorrow," said Harriet as they drove away. "We'll come to your house. You can make us all lunch!"

"Uh, sure," said Mina.

Harriet shook her head. "We'll bring a pizza, dummy," she said, and punched Mina in the arm. "Wow, you really don't have a sense of humor at all, do you?"

"I do."

"Sure you do," said Harriet. "Driver, what's the fare going to be," she shouted to the front seat.

"Oh, that's okay . . ."

"Don't be ridiculous. You probably saved our lives by reminding me not to drive us all into a tree. I got it covered."

"Thanks," Mina said, as a new wave of relief washed over her. No one spoke again until the driver dropped Mina at the top of her driveway.

"Don't forget about tomorrow," Harriet said, and Mina nodded. The driver peeled out of the driveway and into the night.

When Mina entered the house, she noticed the downstairs had been straightened up, and some of the paint had even been scrubbed off the walls and the floors, a faint trace of it remaining as a permanent reminder to Mina not to lose track of Emma again.

"The little one's asleep," said Esther, pulling on a sweater as she greeted Mina in the foyer.

"Esther, you truly are a saint," Mina said, and pulled her into a hug. "Can you stay for a glass of wine?"

Esther eyed her suspiciously and Mina hoped she hadn't slurred the words she'd just spoken, or that her face wasn't still flushed from the unexpected flirtation she'd been a party to.

"How was your night, dear?" Esther asked, seeming not to notice any of it.

Mina relaxed. "Crazily enough, I actually had a pretty good time with Harriet Saunders."

Esther regarded Mina coolly and took a long pause before she spoke. "That woman's trash. You should not be associating with her."

"Oh, she's alright," Mina sang. "She's just a little kooky."

"She's a loose cannon and she makes it difficult to live here." She folded her arms in front of her. "Her and all those kids."

"But don't you also have five kids?"

Esther's eyes went dark. "I had my kids under control," she said. "The way that woman carries on. The way those kids behave. And that husband of hers. A child himself! Just disgraceful."

Mina did not want to get into it with Esther. She wanted to make nice, and she asked Esther again if she'd like a glass of wine.

"Thank you, dear, but I'm afraid I can't," Esther said, now warm again. "I'm a little tired from chasing that Emma around. Not so easy for a woman my age, I'm afraid. Especially with this knee acting up again. And then there's my wrist. Oh Mina, don't even get me started," she said. "I'll make you terrified of getting old." Mina walked Esther to the door and gave her a soft kiss goodnight on the cheek.

Mina looked around the house and decided that if Esther at her age could get so much accomplished, surely she could try her hand at taking off some of the paint, or at least getting it to fade, as Esther had. She opened a bottle of wine, grabbed some cleaners from under the sink, and began scrubbing. The scrubbing apparently made her thirsty; by 9:45, she was surprised to find herself halfway through the bottle. By 10:00, there was still no sign of Jack.

Slightly tired, slightly more tipsy, and feeling lonely, Mina picked up the phone. She dialed Jack's line but there was no answer. She hung up the receiver, poured the rest of the wine from the bottle into her glass, and dialed another number. The phone rang three times before an automated voice answered.

"Thank you for calling First Federal. Please be advised that if you have been instructed to call this number that this communication is with a debt collector attempting to collect a debt, and any information obtained will be used for those purposes. If you know your party's extension, please dial it now. If not, please hang on and—"

Mina dialed four-one-five-six, and a woman answered the line. "Kim Harris."

"Hi Kim. It's Mina."

"Case number, please."

"Oh come on, Kim. Aren't we past this by now?"

"Case number, please?"

At least this one Mina knew by heart. "Four three nine, two seven zero, zero zero, B as in boy, nine three nine."

"One moment please," the woman said, and Mina could hear fingertips darting across a keyboard. Next came a litany of security questions about her name and Jack's, their social security numbers, their address, their dates of birth, their mothers' dates of birth. Mina didn't know her mother, yet she knew when she was born. She didn't have a single memory of her mother, but she knew this random fact because it seemed not one of these collectors would take a penny from her without it.

"Are we done?"

"You know I have to stick with the script."

"Sorry."

"Please be advised that this is a call from a debt collector attempting to collect a debt—"

"Yeah, I called you—"

The woman spoke over Mina, "—and all information obtained will be used for that purpose."

"Okay, now?"

"Sorry, girl. But you know I have to do that. I'm probably in enough trouble for all the hours I've spent on the phone with you. This is why they don't like us to speak to the same people more than twice."

"Thanks for making an exception."

"Look, you know I like you. But if it's ever my ass or yours, you know who's going down, right?"

Both women laughed.

"So how's your day?" Kim asked. "Anything special?"

"Not really, no."

"What about with Jack? Things improving there?" Mina didn't answer. "Uh oh. Tell Kim. What's going on?"

Mina hesitated. "It's . . . It's nothing, really."

"It's never nothing, sweetie. If you're feeling something's off, something's probably off."

"He has a new boss, just out of nowhere. Never mentioned anything about it till today. And it's a woman. Amber Fox." The words jumped out of her mouth, surprising her, as she hadn't given Amber much thought until this second.

"Amber Fox? Sounds like a stripper's name!"

That's exactly how it had struck her as well. Some buxom hot babe as the daily dominatrix of her husband's time . . . Maybe it was the booze talking, but she couldn't seem to stop herself. "Do you think he could be having an affair?"

Now Kim hesitated. "He's not having an affair."

"How do you know?"

Kim let out a sigh. "I can't believe I'm having this conversation. Okay, it's like this, baby. You owe us money. A lot of money. And you're not too quick to pay. So we keep a lot of tabs on you. On Jack."

"Oh," said Mina.

"Honey, we know all kinds of things about you I'm sure you wish we didn't."

"I wish you hadn't told me that."

"Sorry. Hey, let me change the subject on you for a minute."

"Oh Kim, I can't now. Jack doesn't get paid until next week and I don't . . . But of course you know that already."

"Don't be so sensitive, Mina. You know what this shit is about—you and me. Just because I like you doesn't mean I can't do my job."

"I know, I know. I'm sorry," said Mina, sincerely.

"But that's not even what I was gonna say."

"What do you need to ask me then."

"Not *ask* you. Man, are you ever self-centered. I got something to *tell* you. Something about *me*."

"What? What is it?"

Kim was quiet. "Nah, I ain't gonna tell you."

"Oh, come on. Tell me!"

"I'm gettin' married!"

# 4

Emma bounded into Mina's bedroom at what seemed the break of dawn the next morning. Jack's side of the bed had been slept in, but Jack was gone.

"I see Daddy! I see Daddy!" Emma shouted, bouncing up and down, and right into the bed. She was dragging the bunny-thing with her. Emma inexplicably called the bunny "PP," and Jack wanted to throw it away. "It's going to give us all the plague!" he'd said on numerous occasions. "It's going to be the death of us."

Mina didn't think Emma was ready to get rid of it yet, but she insisted Emma keep it in her bedroom so she couldn't lose it. Emma didn't always listen so well.

"I see Daddy!" Emma shouted.

"Oh, sorry, sweetie," said Mina, pained at how much Emma wanted to see Jack. "I think he left for work already."

Emma's face scrunched into a scowl. "No! I see Daddy! I *see* Daddy!"

"I know how much you miss him," she said, pulling the child into a hug, and getting a whiff of PP, which, ironically, kind of smelled like old urine. It was disgusting, though Emma believed the aroma was pure heaven, and could often be found shoving the mangy ears into her nostrils and breathing in ecstatically. The stench made Mina aware of a slight hangover, and a wave of nausea rose with the aroma. She made a mental note to throw it into the wash that day. "Perhaps tonight, angel."

Emma's face was now bright red. "No! I see Daddy. I see Daddy!" she insisted. "And he give me this!" Seemingly out of the air, Emma produced a wooden dolphin that was the size of a banana. As she whipped it out from behind her tiny frame, she somehow managed to stab Mina in the side of the face with the dolphin's tail, right in the very spot where her tooth would apparently now resume its daily throbbing. "Ouch!" Mina shouted so loudly she even startled herself. Emma jumped off the bed and ran out of the room.

Poking the pain in her mouth with the tip of her tongue, Mina was sure she tasted blood as she checked the clock. How was it already after eight?

And then the phone rang, and Mina ducked into the shower to avoid it.

The Acela Academy had been established in 1947 when a surge of post–World War II "welcome home celebration" babies had come of near-school age, and James P. Rhinequist, the founder and original headmaster, smelled opportunity in all the baby powder. On top of that, the economy was experiencing a postwar lift, and Rhinequist was the kind of man who was only comfortable when other people's disposable income landed with him. So instead of creating a school that would start educating children from first grade, the norm at the time, he thought, why not start children at four, three, or even two! The trend to send babies to school didn't really pick up until the mid 1960s or so, but by that time, Acela's graduates were already applying to, gaining acceptance to, and attending the ivy leagues.

More than sixty years after the structure was erected and the first students enriched their young minds within its stately brick walls, Rhinequist's heirs were still raking it in from wealthy parents who dreamed of investing their own heirs with the means to sustain their own wealth in adulthood. The children who attended Acela had never seen TV, had no idea who Elmo was, had never consumed a Happy Meal. No sugar had ever passed their lips. No food that wasn't 100 percent organic had ever been absorbed by their delicate systems.

In this newest "class," through which Emma and Harriet's Brittany were being indoctrinated daily in the culture of the elite, Emma could pass if she never mentioned her fixation with Elmo and chicken nuggets, but Brittany definitely stood out, like her siblings before her. Like the parents who were raising her. For while Harriet had some wholesome ideas in line with the ideals of typical Acela parents, she was still a kook, and most of the mores that guided her were her own, based on whatever she felt they should be at any given moment.

Jack had gotten a ride to work that morning—Mina could only guess from whom—and left Mina a note to use his car. They were really late now, so she raced to the school, pained all the while by Emma's sliding back and forth with every sharp turn in the car seat Mina had haphazardly installed.

Mina scooped up Emma and hauled ass to the front door just as it was about to be locked by none other than Mr. Garcia. "You made it," he trilled as Mina raced through.

Because she was late already, and because "school" would last less than two hours at this point, Mina decided to stick around after she dropped Emma off. But, terrified she'd have another encounter with Mr. Garcia, she opted not to sit in the lobby. Instead, she headed back to Jack's car to wait.

The first thing she did was to reinstall the carseat. Then, back behind the wheel, Mina reached into her purse and pulled out her notebook, along with her Walkman and headphones. The machine had been running since the last use, unfortunately, and the batteries were dead. Mina then noticed that Jack's car had a cassette player (her car did not), and she felt a surge of relief as she turned on the car, slipped the tape out of the Walkman and into Jack's tape deck, and pressed "play."

*"You are the light of the world. Did you hear me? That's right. It's YOU. You are the light of the world. Now repeat after me: 'I am the light of the world.'"*

Mina shrugged her shoulders and whispered the words as she flipped through her notebook. She opened to the page with the sketch she'd scribbled the other day, the dragonfly that seemed to have appeared out of nowhere.

*You are the salt of the earth. That's right. That's what I said. It's YOU my friend. It's you. The salt of the earth. Now repeat after me: 'I am the salt of the earth.'*

Mina again repeated the message absently as she traced the dragonfly with her finger. What did it mean?

A rap on the window knocked her out of her thoughts. She spied Harriet on the other side of the glass, Linty clutched to her side like a purse. She immediately shut off the tape and opened the window.

"We still on for today?" asked Harriet.

"Today?"

"Playdate. Your house. Pizza on me."

"Oh, right," Mina said.

"Here's what we'll do. We'll pick up the kids and then the pizza, and then I'll follow you home. I think I'm going to sign all mine out for the day. It's a drag sometimes coming back and forth and back and forth for them. And I kind of have a little headache today," she said with a wink, "even though you pretty much drank all my hooch."

Mina opened her mouth to defend herself and Harriet shrieked and pulled back. "Whoa! What are you, a vampire or something?"

"What are you talking about?"

"Your mouth. You're bleeding."

"Oh, shit," Mina said, and she pulled the rearview mirror to a position where she could see into it. "Shit. Shit. Shit."

Linty started to fuss and to paw at Harriet's chest. Harriet knocked his hand away. "You're going to have to get that looked at."

"It's nothing, really," said Mina, dabbing at the inside of her mouth and at the trail of blood that had trickled down the side of her chin with an old tissue she extracted from her purse.

"Yeah, that's pretty much an emergency," Harriet said. "You can't let dental things like that go, you know. People can die—"

"No one has ever died from a dental problem," said Mina, shaking her head. "What is it with you and Esther."

"Do not compare me to that old bag of mothballs."

"Then don't say the same things she says," Mina replied, feeling smug and triumphant.

"Okay, well, if it isn't lethal, it's at least gross," said Harriet, as Linty pulled up her shirt and she knocked his hand away again. "Call your dentist."

"There's no way they would see me on such short notice."

"Tell them you have stigmata of the fucking mouth and they'll see you. I'll call them."

"I'd have to call Esther. I don't know if she could watch Emma on such short notice."

"For reals?"

"Well, I don't trust babysitters."

"What about *me*?"

"What about you?"

"Duh. You know, I do have a few kids of my own. They're all alive and well, Mina. I could watch Emma for a couple of hours while you go get your mouth fixed."

Mina had a flash of Emma grasping on to the blades of the ceiling fan, spinning around and around while Harriet's kids took swings at her with a broom, piñata-style, as Harriet, oblivious, drank from a giant jug of booze in the kitchen and blabbed away on the phone.

"Oh, thanks," she said, "but I don't think . . . "

"Consider it done," said Harriet. "I'll even watch them all at your house, where I'm sure everything is locked up and childproof," she continued, as Linty found a way under her shirt and to her breast. "Fuck, I hate when he does that!" she said, looking to Mina for support. "Just like his father. Won't take no for an answer. I keep saying to myself, 'Today's the day I'm gonna wean,'" she shook her head. "And then the day passes."

"Right," said Mina, unsure how to reply. "Well, I guess I'll call, but I don't think . . ."

"Time's up," Harriet shouted and plucked Linty from her breast. "Come on. Let's get the brats."

Half an hour later Mina drove up her driveway, with Harriet in her minivan behind her. Before Mina could turn off Jack's car, the doors to Harriet's minivan flew open and all the kids sprang out, like those springy snakes that come in the trick cans. The kids chased each other around the yard and right into the freshly planted patch of mums. "Don't trample the flowers!" Harriet called, and they ran back to the grass. Mina couldn't help but feel a stab of disappointment—her wish that Harriet's kids destroy the flowers would now go unfulfilled.

Mina extracted Emma from her car seat and everyone headed inside. The second they passed through the door, chaos erupted, with kids running everywhere, jumping all over the furniture, screaming wildly. "The basement?" Harriet shouted.

"Oh, no. I . . . We don't go down there."

"Why the hell not?" said Harriet, panic evident in her voice. "Where do you store them?"

"The playroom. Right off the kitchen."

Harriet shook her head. "Well, I suppose that will have to do for now. But for how long?" said Harriet dramatically. "For how long?"

Harriet began herding the children through the house and into the playroom just as the phone started to ring. Now it was Mina's turn to panic; she hadn't unplugged it.

One ring became two, then three, then four. "Are you going to get that?" Harriet shouted from the other room.

Mina thought quickly. "Uh, no. I think it's rude to answer the phone when you have company, don't you?" Mina was proud of herself for coming up with what she thought was a pretty good reason.

"Well, if the phone stops ringing after a handful of rings, sure," said Harriet, who had now entered the foyer with Mina and paused to listen. "But that's like six or seven already. Don't you have a machine?"

At that, the ringing stopped, and Mina could breathe, until Harriet started heading out the front door. "Where are you going?" Mina panicked again.

"Pizza's in the car," she said.

Mina went back to the kitchen and set out paper plates. The children, strangely, were all playing together quietly as Harriet retuned. "Food!" she screamed, and the pandemonium returned. Once seated with their pizza, however, the savages calmed again.

"So tell me why you don't trust babysitters again?"

Mina, starved, had just taken a rather large bite of food and frantically chewed before trying to answer.

Harriet laughed. "Oh, I know why! It's because you only have the one kid."

Mina shook her head and swallowed. "No, I don't think that's it. I just don't like people I don't know that well being alone with my child. The world is crazy, you know. You don't know who you can trust. It's not safe."

"Well, that may be true. But I'll tell you—if you had five like I do, you'd relax on that a little. You'd realize there isn't anything more crazy out there than exists in your own house."

Mina was horrified. Did this woman not know about kidnapping and pedophiles and murderers? "You can't be serious!"

"Well, no, I'm not being serious. Not really. What I meant to say is that when you have more of them, they lose some of their 'preciousness,' you know? I mean, you'd still rip the head off of anyone who ever tried to harm them, but you tend to beatify them a little less."

"I guess," said Mina.

"So when are you having another one anyway?" Harriet said, taking a bite without bothering to chew before she continued. "Emma would be much nicer with a sibling. She'd have to be."

The question hit like a stab in the heart. Mina was sure she wanted more children. But how could she? In her current mess of a mental state? In their financial condition? She took a deep breath and tried to relax. "Emma's perfectly nice. She simply requires more attention, more attention from me. It's her personality type. I read somewhere that difficult children act out the way they do because they didn't get enough attention in the womb. Not enough stroking or talking to or music being played to them . . ." Though Mina could remember none of her pregnancy and had no idea if anything she was saying was true in any way. But she couldn't help herself from motoring on.

"And then breastfeeding—and you understand this. Children who aren't nursed, or nursed long enough, these kinds of children also tend to act out."

At this, all the kids jumped out of their seats, chased each other around the kitchen, and then, getting a look that could kill from their mother, dove over the gate, back into the playroom.

Harriet raised an eyebrow at Mina. "That's all just bullshit. You must know that. Don't you know that?"

"Bullshit? But studies have been done. These are facts. Experts have said—"

"Yeah, they tell you all that because they want your money. Just like the baby products industry does everything they can to make you feel incompetent and keep your kids from growing up. Haven't you noticed how the patterns on diapers get cuter the larger the sizes? By the time I had Brittany I didn't use diapers after the first six months. Just held her over the toilet when it was time."

"Wow. I've heard about people doing that. So how long did it take you to train her?"

"About eighteen months, but that's not the point."

Just then the phone started to ring again, and Mina ignored it again.

"For Christ's sake, who the hell keeps calling you?"

Mina felt the usual heat rising in her cheeks. "It doesn't matter. If it was important, they'd call me on my cell. And they'll call back later, I'm sure."

"Okay, because it won't bother me at all if you just pick up the phone and—"

"It's okay," Mina snapped, and the phone mercifully stopped ringing. They sat together in silence for a moment.

"So how's your memory thing coming along? Anything working yet?"

"Not really."

"Are you doing the notebook? I've heard people have made a lot of headway with the notebook."

"Somewhat. But I just can't seem to get anywhere significant, you know?"

Just then they were interrupted by a shrill scream. "Monny! The boy taking my doll! He bad!"

Harriet spoke right over her. "That's because you have no brain-space," she said. "Send that kid to daycare one full day a week and your brain will start to free up. I think that's going to be your key to remembering. Just try it. You'll see."

"Monny, he bad! MONNY!"

Mina shook her head. "She has Esther. They play nicely together."

Harriet's eyeballs nearly popped out of her head. "Are you fucking serious? Come on now. You know it isn't natural for her to be hanging out with a hundred-year-old bat all the time," she said, and took a bite of pizza. Then, without swallowing, "Ever wonder what would happen if Esther just dropped dead?"

Mina had never considered that and now started to panic. "I . . . I . . ."

Mina's face started going white and Harriet changed her tune. "That's not going to happen, I'm sure," she said, unconvincingly. "But I still don't see why you let her spend so much time over there."

"What do you have against Esther?"

"I don't know," Harriet said. "There's just something about her."

"You hate everyone in this neighborhood over sixty-five."

"Sixty, but who's counting," said Harriet, and both women laughed.

"You are a very bad boy," said Emma, almost too calm, and a giant thwack was heard from the play area.

Linty began to scream and cry. Just at that moment, Harriet sprang a leak in her shirt and, of course, the phone started ringing again. Both women said, "Shit!" then, "Ooops!" then "Shoot." Harriet ripped off her top and grabbed Linty. Mina said, "I guess I better get that."

"Oh good, it's you," she said. Lucky for Mina, this time it was Jack. "Did you get my message?"

"Message?"

"Yes. I called before. Spoke to some snotty girl. She didn't tell you?"

"Who? Amanda?"

"I didn't ask her name. I asked to speak with you and she was rude. She hung up on me. Are you really only allowed two phone calls a day? I mean, aren't you in sales?"

"I never heard of that before. Are you sure that's what she said? Sounds a little ridiculous."

"Are you telling me you think I'm making this up?"

"No, no. Not at all. Uh . . ."

"You must have some idea of who answers the phone. It wasn't the usual person."

"Oh, right. Amanda, I guess. Amber's new recruit." Just hearing him say the name "Amber" irritated her to her core. They spoke only a few moments after that, exchanging small talk like a couple of acquaintances. When she couldn't bear it anymore, she asked him for information about their dentist.

"You actually like him a lot," Jack said.

"Why do I find that hard to believe?" she said.

"Seriously," he laughed. "You do. You'll see."

Mina was literally shaking as she sat in the examination room waiting for Dr. Samuels to arrive. There was nothing about this space that inspired calm or confidence. The walls were stark white. All the surfaces were porcelain, cold and sterile. A profusion of lethal-looking torture implements in gleaming stainless steel were laid out threateningly in plain sight on the table next to her. She could only imagine which of these would be used on her this day.

Adding to this, Mina was feeling incredibly anxious, as she had not been able to get a hold of Esther and so had left Emma with Harriet and her kids. At least she had remembered to unplug the phone before she left.

But that small sense of relief soon gave way to a new fear. What if something happened, something bad, and Harriet couldn't find her cell phone because one of her kids took it and she tried to use the house phone to call for an ambulance. Would she let Emma bleed to death before seeking help from Esther?

Panic lodged like a tennis ball in her throat, and that's exactly where it stuck until there was a knock at the door. Before Mina could respond, a kind-looking man in his late sixties entered.

"Mina Clark! As I live and breathe," the man beamed and he bounded over to her. He clasped both of her hands in his. "How long has it been!"

"I'm not exactly sure," she said, squinting at his face, trying to remember him, or the flash of gold in the front of his smile. A dentist with a gold tooth? This was a person she was supposed to trust with the state of her mouth?

Dr. Samuels' expression went to serious now. "I'll tell you how long it's been, Mina. Three years. Three long years! I mean, last time I saw you, that baby of yours wasn't even a glint in Jack's eye," he said, smirking and shaking his head. "You got pictures?"

"Sure," she said, and she pulled out her cell phone, clicked through to her photo screen, and handed the phone to him.

"That's a beautiful child," he said, and now smiled again, the bright fluorescent light bouncing off the gold in his mouth and right into her eyes. "She looks just like you, when you were that age."

Mina was taken aback. "You knew me when I was three?"

He now wore a look of patient concern. "Mina, I've known you your entire life."

"Sorry," she said, and looked away.

"No, I'm sorry. I guess I didn't really believe it was true. I thought you were avoiding me, like you always do." He shook his head, pained. "So it's really true then? You don't remember anything?"

"Not really. I mean, I remember some things. But my past, it's pretty much gone."

"Well, I can't say I'm surprised. You know. Considering what happened to you."

Mina felt a surge of fear and panic, but along with it, a nagging curiosity. "What happened to me," said Mina, hoping she could play it cool and extract even a small nugget of information from the dentist.

But he caught himself in time. "Oh, wait. I'm not supposed to tell you anything. I'm supposed to wait for you. Oh gad-darn it. I hope I didn't mess things up. I hope I didn't make you worse."

"But you didn't tell me anything."

"I didn't, I guess. But I did say it was terrible."

"So what happened to me was pretty terrible then?"

"Oh, it was bad alright," he said. Then he smiled. "Oh, you're a tricky one, aren't you!" he smirked. "All right now, let's take a look in that mouth of yours and see what's going on."

Mina was disappointed. She opened her mouth and tilted her head back, and Dr. Samuels poked around in her mouth with a pick and a mirror. He let out a gasp.

"What is it?" asked Mina.

Dr. Samuels closed his eyes and turned away, as if he'd just witnessed someone strangle a kitten. "It's amazing we have the relationship we do, Mina. I've known you forty years and seen you maybe fifteen times. I don't think it's giving anything away telling you that you don't like me very much."

"No, that's not true. Jack says I do like you. I really do. And you seem nice and kind to me. Of course I like you."

He dismissed her with a wave. "If you liked me, if you really liked me, you'd come see me every six months, or twelve at the very least. You don't do that. You never did that."

"I'm sorry, I think I'm just afraid of—"

"I know, you fear commitment. You don't want to have a proper, steady relationship with me. You just want to use me when things get bad. Like now."

"But that's not a personal thing. You're a very nice man and—"

"It's just that I like you so much, it's heartbreaking. This, this thing with you and me, it's just not going anywhere."

"Where are you going with this?"

Tears began to well in his kindly eyes. "I mean, you come in here, always on a whim. Always when it's a disaster for you, Mina. And yet, if you came in more, you would see that I could take care of you. These things, they wouldn't happen to you. If only you took better care of your teeth. If only you let me help you take better care of your teeth . . ." he trailed off.

Mina opened her mouth to speak and he spoke over her. "I know, I know. It's not really your thing," he said, and motioned for her to lean back and open her mouth again. "And now we have to see . . ." He screamed.

"What? What is it?"

He sat down in the chair next to her. "Mina, I gotta level with you. I've never seen a bigger disaster of a mouth in my life. I don't think I can help you anymore. I don't think I have the skills, for one. But I just don't have the heart for it anymore."

Mina put her hand over her mouth.

"Here's the thing, kid. I just like you too much to keep torturing you like this. Every time I see you, it's something new. And never just a cavity. It's always a disaster. It's always epic."

"I could try and take better care of my teeth. I could try and come in more often."

"People don't change, Mina. You may say you will, but you're not going to change. I'm sorry. I just can't know you anymore. Not like this."

"Are you . . . Are you breaking up with me?"

He looked at her now with a solemn face, a tear in his eye. "I'm afraid I am, kiddo. I'm sorry but I just don't think we should see each other anymore. At least not like this."

"I don't get it. There must be something else. It's my balance, isn't it? I owe you money, don't I?"

"Well, yes. You do. But that's not really my area. The ladies in the front take care of that. They'll tell you. But don't worry about that."

"I *do* worry about that," she said.

"Well, I'm serious when I say that I don't. I make all the money I need from reimbursements. I actually make a pretty kick-ass living on reimbursements. Anything I collect from patients, well, that's really just bonus money. If you never paid your balance, no one would ever care. But I never told you that."

"Of course not."

"But that's not actually the point, is it? Rinse."

Mina complied. "I guess not."

"Look, because I like you, I have a suggestion for you. A place I just discovered." He opened his mouth and tapped his gold tooth with his finger. "They did me and they were great," he said, "Highly recommended." He rolled in his chair over to the table across the room, picked up a card, rolled back, and handed it to her.

"Pearls of Wisdom?"

"Yeah, I know, it's a terrible name, but I promise you Mina, this place will blow your mind. Seriously."

"But it's all the way in Queens. Why would I—"

"Just give them a call."

Mina looked away. "Sure."

"You're not going to call, are you?"

"No."

"Well, then I will call them for you." He picked up the phone. "Hi, this is Dr. Samuels from . . . oh, you remember me. How nice. Well, I'm just fine thank you. Perfect, actually. Could not have done a better job myself," he said and he winked at Mina. "Anyway, I have that woman here that I told you about. Yeah, that one," he smiled and nodded at Mina. "Can you guys fit her in tomorrow? Two thirty? Great. You're the best!"

Dr. Samuels hung up the phone and came back over to Mina. "You know they even offered me a kick-back?" he beamed.

"Oh, good. So they're ethical too."

"Don't be such a stick in the mud," he said. "Honestly, I don't know how Jack kisses that mouth of yours—literally. But don't worry. They're going to clean you up and good. And you might even enjoy yourself!"

"I find that hard to believe."

"Lean your head back once more and let me see if I can do something temporarily to help you out here. Consider it a parting gift."

Mina returned home to the sound of a vacuum running. "Harriet?" She couldn't imagine Harriet was cleaning her house. Unless one of her kids broke something and she was just hiding the evidence. "Emma?"

A woman she'd never seen before rounded the corner with the vacuum, turned it off, and began winding up the cord. "Oh, hello," she said, as if there was nothing unusual about her being there. "That was some job with the paint. I understand it was even worse. I tried to get it, most of it, but I think you'll never be done with it."

"I don't mean to sound rude or ungrateful, but who are you?"

"Me? I'm Kathleen."

"Hi Kathleen. What are you doing in my house? And where is my kid? And my friend?"

"Had to kick them out. There was no way I could to do what I needed to do with them around. Those kids are animals. Especially that little blonde one. Looks like an angel, but that child's the devil, bless her."

"Where are they now?"

"They're at the playground. I hope you don't have one of those sandy playgrounds," she said, scanning the room and her hard work.

"So, not be rude again, but why are you here? I didn't hire you."

"No. You didn't. A friend of yours called me. A guardian angel I believe is what they said."

"I'm sorry, but I can't pay you—"

"Ha! I've already been paid, missy-pie. No way I would have done a job this big without getting paid first. And handsomely, I might add. You have nice friends."

"But who?"

"Not allowed to say."

"Of course. So you're done here?"

"Enjoy it while it lasts."

"Thanks, Kathleen."

"Of course."

Mina showed Kathleen to the door and took her card, though she knew she'd never be able to call her. She couldn't help wondering what the charge was for cleaning her house. And then wondered if she couldn't make some cash cleaning houses. She had an image of herself, hair wrapped in a kerchief, peacefully humming and scrubbing a floor, like Cinderella in the Disney movie. And then Emma, her head on fat cat Lucifer's body, streaking sooty footprints across the floor.

The playground was in full swing as Mina approached, and, amazingly, all the kids seemed to be playing nicely. Even Emma was sitting quietly, digging with Brittany in the sandbox with a set of plastic beach toys. In fact, everyone seemed to be getting along. It was weird. It was almost eerie. Some older people were perched on benches watching the children play. Harriet was even chatting with a handful of the mothers, and they all smiled and waved her over.

Mina tread carefully, feeling like she'd walked into an alternate universe. Either that, or a very big other shoe was soon to drop.

"Do you guys know Mina?" Harriet asked.

"Hi Mina," said a woman in her late thirties with long reddish hair, sounding very much like she was drugged up on Valium or Seconal. "I'm Starla's mommy. Starla's my star, she just is. Have we seen each other before? Mommy And Me maybe? I just love Mommy And Me. Don't you? I love being a mommy."

Next, the business-mom extended a hand. "Her name is Claire. Claire, you have a name. Your name is Claire and you were Claire before you gave birth and you'll be Claire when your little star stomps all over your soul when she's a teenager and then leaves you for college without taking a glance back."

She turned to Mina. "I have a name. My name is Ellen. I live here. You don't see me here a lot because I work. I have a job. I have a kid but I have an *identity*. And I live right here, right here in Easton Estates. And that's my kid, right over there. His name is Hunter. He lives here with me. But not my ex, that son-of-a-bitch. No way. Hunter's usually here with his nanny. She had to take the day off, and then so did I. So I'm here at the playground while my goddamned assistant is heading a meeting for me and trying to steal my job." She finally released the vise grip she had on Mina's hand.

"I'm Marie," said the brunette to Ellen's left, lightly pushing Ellen to the side. "You live by Mrs. Erasmus, don't you?" she asked sweetly.

"I do," said Mina.

"Sorry!" said Marie, and all three women busted out laughing.

Harriet looped her arm around Mina, in a creepily territorial way. "I hope you don't mind us coming here," Harriet said. "My kids wrecked your house. Well, you know. Beyond how it was already a mess."

"You didn't call someone to clean my house, did you?" Mina asked. "Because you really shouldn't have—"

"Clean? No. That's funny, though. You should see how we live. 'Squalor is the new black,' as they say!" said Harriet, beaming at her own perceived cleverness.

"Who says that?" said Ellen.

Harriet's smile fell. "I just tried to get them out of there before they broke anything else."

"Sorry?"

"Uh, I mean before they broke anything. I meant to say *anything*. Anything at all. No one broke anything. Why? Did it look like something was broken?"

Just then came a loud plopping noise, like a melon dropping to the ground. Mina whipped her head around; Harriet kept talking as if nothing happened.

"Harriet!" Ellen called. "Harriet!"

Harriet rolled her eyes and held up her hand. "Busy here."

"Dude, he fell out of the stroller. Again," said Marie.

"Oh shit," said Harriet. She jogged back to the fray, where the mothers and nannies surrounded the fallen, screaming child. "What are we going to do with you." She picked up the child and hugged him to her breast. At which point he immediately went to undress her. "Mina, gotta split. Call you later. I mean, if you'll answer."

Harriet collected her kids and took off. Emma didn't seem to notice her playmate was gone as she went about her business in the sand, and Mina headed over to her favorite bench. She sat quietly for a moment before pulling out her notebook and pen; the pen dropped to the ground. At that moment, she heard one of the nannies sounding off again. "Whose child is this? Whose child is this?!"

Mina could now hear the sound of another child crying, and Emma's maniacal laughter. She dove behind the bench to find her pen. And then, "You are hiding or you are teaching life lesson?" The words were spoken in a thick Russian accent.

Mina looked up as the man continued to speak. "You know that the small one needs to work it out for herself. Not like rest of these American women. Think they have to be on top of everything," he shook his head. "Kids never learn anything. But not you."

She was embarrassed. "Actually, I just dropped my—"

"You can't hide there forever, you know." He knelt down next to her. "In fact, I think you can't hide there at all. Everyone can see you."

He was holding her pen. "I think you dropped this?"

"How did you get that so quickly?"

"Ah, that's my secret," he said, and he smiled. On some level Mina knew she should fear this man, this strange grisly man with his strange accent and black wool hat. He looked like a longshoreman, or at least a cartoon depiction of one. Maybe it was the cartoonishness of the man that made him less threatening?

"You don't remember me?" he said. "From yesterday?"

She held out her hand and he handed the pen to her. "Of course. Thank you," she said.

"Please, allow me to introduce myself properly. I am Alex. I am from Moscow," he said.

"You do know this playground is only for residents. For people who *live* in this complex."

He regarded her quietly. "You are right. I am guilty. I do not live here. But my niece does. I think I told you, I look after her."

Mina looked over at the group of children, which had now quieted down. "Which one is she again?"

She couldn't see Emma but was relieved when the child raced over and hugged her mother's legs. "Stranger danger! Stranger danger!"

"That's okay, Emma," said Mina. "This isn't a stranger. This is Alex."

"Don't talk strangers! Don't talk strangers! Esda say no talk strangers!"

"No, Emma. This is Mommy's, uh," Mina hedged as Emma was entirely right that this was a stranger, that the black wool hat on a mild September day almost surely meant that he was dangerous, or at the very least up to no good. Yet she didn't fear him. "Mommy knows him."

"Hello Emma. I am Alex." He kneeled to her level, and offered a hand to her. She pierced him with her icy blue eyes. She tentatively offered hers in return, and he gave it a gentle shake. "It's nice to meet you, miss."

"I don't like you."

"Emma!"

"That's okay. She is smart one not to like Alex. You like magic, Emma?"

Emma eyed him suspiciously. He turned to Mina. "Tell me, you have one of these things—that you wrap in your hair to hold it up?"

"A barrette?"

"No. That makes...how you say," he held his hands up to either side of his head. "Pigtails?"

"Oh, a ponytail holder. Sure." She reached down her sleeve and produced one for him.

"That was like magic trick."

"I have hundreds of them."

He turned to the child and held the elastic over his pinky and ring finger. "Okay, Emma. You see this band, that I just took from Mama?"

She nodded.

"You want to see it jump?"

She nodded.

"Okay, I need your help." He leaned in closer to her. "Blow on my hand, please." And she did just that without hesitation. "Now tap the fingers the rubber band is on." And she did. "Now repeat after me: 'Applesauce and gravy!'"

"That's ewwwwww!"

"I don't chose the words, but I promise they work. Let's give it try. Repeat after me again, 'Applesauce and gravy!'" And she did, and the rubber band danced to the other side of his hand.

"Amazing," said Mina absently, feeling somehow that this wasn't the first time she'd seen this trick. And then a strange sensation came over her.

"Again!" squealed Emma. And the man did the trick again. Emma lost interest and ran off, but the man did the magic trick again, now for Mina.

Mina watched as his hands moved and it was crazy. It made no sense, but there was something about this moment, this trick, this man. She had a flash of feeling. A good feeling. Hands like these on a younger man. A summer day. A sensation that made her feel like she'd been here, in this situation, somehow, before.

He asked, "You like magic, Mina?"

"I think I do," she said, overwhelmed now that this simple trick was starting to open a door for her, a realization that might be a memory? She felt a little woozy and unstable about this happening to her, over this, and now. It must have showed.

"Are you okay, Mina?"

"Can I ask you something, something that might seem a little strange?"

"Of course."

"Do I know you?"

He smiled warmly. "What do you think?"

"I think I've never been to Russia. But, I don't know. There's something familiar about you. I guess this all seems weird to you," she said. "I'm sorry. A couple of years ago or so, I had an accident or something. I really don't remember anything about my life before that. Anything or anyone. But every now and then, I don't know, I just *feel* something. You know?"

He was quiet. He cocked his head. "Tell me."

"This must seem so crazy to you. I mean, you just met me and here I just told you my whole life story—"

"No, Mina. Not crazy at all."

She smiled, feeling safe and secure until a realization shook her within. "Wait, you keep calling me Mina. But I never told you my name!"

"You didn't?"

"I'm sure I didn't."

He was quiet for a moment. "You didn't have to," he said, and she held her breath, feeling that finally she was going to get some answers about something. "It's on your pen," he said.

She checked the pen and, sure enough, there it was. "So it is," she said, shaking her head. "So I don't know you. Wow, sorry. There was just something about that magic trick you did. Something that made me start to remember, or I thought made me start to remember."

Now Emma raced back and Mina lifted her in her arms.

"It is okay," he said, sweetly, sympathetically.

She looked up at him. "I know, this probably sounds crazy to you. But you're the first person in a really long time I felt I may have known. Before. But of course we don't know each other. Silly . . . " She readjusted Emma's weight on her hip.

"Oh, I didn't say we didn't know each other," he said. "But it's not for me to tell you, is it? Isn't it for you to figure out?"

"Yes."

"Ты мой ангел," he said.

"Ты моя сила," she shocked herself by saying. She gasped and threw her hand over her apparently foreign mouth, which had apparently been deceiving her by speaking English all this time. "What the fuck?" Mina felt like her head was going go explode. She spoke Russian? She spoke and fucking understood Russian?

"What da fack! What da fack!"

"Shhh. No, Emma. Bad, bad words." Emma nodded.

Alex cocked an eyebrow at her. "So not everything is buried?" he said.

Now feelings began to consume her, feelings that were growing in intensity by the minute. Not only had she understood what he said to her, "*You are my angel,*" she had replied, and in Russian, "*You are my strength.*"

These were not the words of passing strangers. These were the words of people who knew each other. People who knew each other . . . intimately? What was going on here? Electric currents of emotion began connecting in her, emotions not just connecting but exploding. She felt safe and secure and connected, at peace and terrified all at once.

She then began putting it all together. The accent. Her apparent "thing" for accents. Of course! This was why! She gasped. Had she been some Russian spy who was masquerading as an American housewife? That might explain some of her boredom with her life, sure. Was this her partner in the KGB? Did KGB operatives even have partners? Was he her . . . *lover*? She jumped back.

"What wrong, Monny?"

Alex regarded her coolly for a while, eyebrow again cocked. "What is it, Mina? What are you thinking?"

"We weren't . . . you know . . .intimate?"

Alex exploded into laughter.

"What?" Mina snapped defensively.

"You are so, how you say, adorable. Such a little простак sometimes," he said, tears streaming down his face, he was laughing so hard.

"I don't see how that's warranted——"

"Good-bye for now, little one," he said to Emma, tapping her on the tip of her nose with a fingertip. "See you again, Mina," he said. He was still laughing as he walked off.

And now, instead of learning something more about herself and where she'd come from, Mina had another mystery on her hands. Why did she speak Russian? And why did this man Alex think she was a simpleton?

As the sun began to set over Easton Estates, Mina sat with Esther on Esther's front patio, still somewhat shaken from the events of the day and the fact that she apparently understood Russian and spoke it fluently. Should she tell Esther about what had happened with Alex at the playground? Perhaps not everything, but that she had met someone she might know? Would Esther be able to tell her something about it, about herself? Or would it make Mina seem unstable? More unstable than usual.

"Monny talk to stranger," said Emma, who was apparently going to take matters into her own tot-sized hands. "Monny talk to stranger in park."

"Emma, sweetie, it's not nice to tell on Mommy," said Esther, taking a sip of tea. "But she's right, dear. You should probably not be talking to strange men in the park."

"I know, I would never do that. But this was different. I can't explain it, Esther," said Mina, noticing that Esther was wearing two iridescent beetle earrings. She made a mental note to ask her about them later, a note she would of course forget. "There was just something about him. Something familiar," she continued. "Safe, even. You know? Which is kind of weird," she said, stopping to take a sip from her mug, "because he's Russian. From Moscow, even. I could barely understand him," she lied with a forced chuckle.

Esther stared at her a moment, and shook her head. "Mina, I'm eighty years old. I'm from a generation that believes the only good things to come from Russia are vodka and vodka. If I ever see some strange Ruski prowling around the playground, you can bet I'll be the first to call security."

"Alek doos magic!" Emma gushed.

"You let Emma talk to him too?" she shook her head. "Dear, you need to have a little more fear in you. Especially when it comes to the safety of your child."

"Are you kidding? I think I probably live in constant fear, thank you very much," said Mina defensively. "I mean, especially since Jack's never around. What would happen if I fell down the stairs and snapped my neck in half? Then what?"

Esther gave her a gentle pat on the leg. "Just never have more than three drinks and you'll be fine, dear. After that, it starts to affect the legs. Before that, avoid the stairs."

"Seriously, Esther. I've thought about this. What if something happens to me?"

"Nothing's going to happen to you," Esther soothed. "As long as you avoid Russians." The sun caught one of the beetles hanging from her ears and it seemed to come to life. Mina blinked her eyes several times and the beetle stopped moving.

"How do you know that? What would Emma do? She's so little. Would she even know what to do?"

"You worry too much."

"But what if—"

"Emma, come here, sweetie." Emma ran over to Esther and Esther pulled the child into her lap. "If anything happens to Mommy, what should you do?"

"Gramma Esda!"

"That's right, sweetie. Come find Gramma. And where does Gramma Esther live?"

"Numba six!"

"And where is number six?"

Emma pointed to the front of Esther's house. Esther looked at Mina. "Told you."

"Okay, I feel better now," she said, relieved.

"As long as Esther's alive, you can count on Esther," said the kindly old woman.

"I'm glad you said that," Mina said. "Reminds me that I need you to look after Emma a couple of hours tomorrow. I mean, if you can? I have to go back to the dentist. A different one, actually. Some place in Queens."

"Harriet's not available?" Esther asked, somewhat coldly. Mina looked away, guilty. "I understand she trashed your house?"

Mina was embarrassed and then realized she'd figured out who'd sent Kathleen. "Hey, you didn't . . . "

"What, dear? Didn't what?"

"Forget it," Mina smiled. What would she ever have done without Esther.

# 5

Jack came home long after she was asleep and left before she awoke the following morning. The only indication that he had been home at all was that he had taken his car. Mina called the body shop to see if hers was ready yet.

"Hi, can I speak to Phil? Please tell him Mina Clark's on the phone, checking to see if the insurance adjuster made it there yet to evaluate the damage."

There was no response.

"Hello? Is anyone there?"

"Did you say . . . Mina Clark?"

"Yes."

"The VW?"

"Yes. The black wagon."

"Oh."

"Is there a problem?"

"Hang on a second, I gotta put you on hold." He must not have pushed down the hold button all the way because Mina could hear everything that came next.

"Phil. It's the broad with the VW."

"Oh, shit. You're kidding."

"Well, what are we going to tell her?"

"Dunno. This never happened to me before."

"Well, technically it happened to her."

"Yeah, but we're kind of involved in a way now, don't you think?"

Mina started panicking.

"She's such a nice lady. I hate to tell her about this."

"Well she can't be that nice if she doesn't pay her bills."

"I can hear you!" Mina shouted into the phone. "What happened to my car?"

A silence and then, "Uh oh."

"Hi, Mrs. Clark. This is Phil."

"Phil, what happened to my car?"

"Uh . . . well . . . It kind of got . . . uh . . ."

"Phil. What. Happened. To. My. Car."

"Uh, it kinda got repossessed."

"What?"

"The guy just came. Said you were a couple of months behind. Just drove it off. A shame too, because it came out real nice and—"

"You couldn't have called me first? Told him the car didn't run? Maybe stall for a tow?"

"What a great idea! I'll have to remember that. If it ever comes up again. I mean, not like it ever would. Twenty-three years in business and I swear this never happened once."

"Always a first time," said Mina, and she hung up the phone. She reached into her bag to grab a train schedule and mysteriously pulled out a wad of twenty-dollar bills. "What the...?" she said, confused about how this stack of money got there, though relieved to have the extra cash. She reached in deeper and pulled out even more cash. "So odd." She took two of the twenties and slipped them in her wallet; she stashed the rest of the cash in a drawer in the kitchen.

Mina dropped Emma off with Esther and took a cab to the train station. She made the 1:15 with enough time to buy herself a ticket and a Snapple. Such a strange feeling it was for her to buy these things without stressing or straining over it. How long had it been since she could just buy something extra? Anything at all?

She found a seat next to the window and pulled out her Walkman. She forgot she hadn't replaced the batteries, though, and she stuffed it back into her purse. She considered bringing out her notebook again, but she then thought better of it. When did she get a chance to just stare out the window and daydream? Without a child gone wild to stalk?

The train departed the station and Mina sat back and watched the scenery roll by. Large expanses of green yards, many with large in-ground swimming pools. A sprawling golf course. A cemetery as pretty as a park. As the train wove through its westbound route, the manses and green expanses began to give way to industry and squalor, with houses stacked close together, then attached houses, and then no houses at all. Just a sea of concrete and brick and fire escapes and slums.

Mina exited the train at her stop and climbed the stairs to the street. She walked a few blocks west and finally arrived at the address given to her by Dr. Samuels. While the state of the neighborhood had unsettled her at first, all dilapidated and depressed, by the time she arrived at the address she felt relaxed, though she couldn't imagine why.

The building that housed her destination was certainly right at home in the neighborhood. Something like moss or mold grew up the front, while paint peeled from the door. A lighting fixture hung by the side of the door, its glass frame smashed and broken and its light bulb exposed. Mina wasn't sure if this was a dental practice or a crack house; she pressed the buzzer anyway. When the door responded with a humming noise, she pushed it in.

No traits of the building's outside were present within, however. The foyer was absolutely pristine, a shiny metal and glass vestibule nestled in a natural stone. Sleek and modern, it seemed to glow.

The Pearls of Wisdom lobby was painted in rich, earthy hues, and tasteful art covered the walls. The reception desk, sitting prominently between butter-soft black leather couches, seemed carved out of marble. If there was anything about this space that remotely resembled the neighborhood, it was that the reception desk was encased in bulletproof glass. Mina wondered just how bad this neighborhood was if even the dental practices got robbed.

As Mina approached the desk, the receptionist beamed a perfect smile. Mina, feeling self-conscious, held her hand over her mouth as she spoke. "Hi, I'm Mina Clark. I have a two-thirty with—"

"Of course, Mina," the receptionist said, punctuating Mina's name with a flip of her improbably shiny black hair. "I'm Midori. May I call you Mina?"

"Sure."

"Great! We've been expecting you, Mina." Midori looked down at her clipboard. "Now, let's see. Looks like we'll be starting you off with a facial by Shayla and then a massage with . . . Ooooh, lucky you!" she gushed.

"I think there's been a mistake—"

"My God, you're right," said Midori. "Massage before facial. Of course. Let's go with Alain for mani-pedi."

"Oh no . . . "

"I know. Weird having a man do your nails, right? But I swear you'll never go back."

"No, I don't think you understand. I'm here to see the dentist. I have this molar—"

"Ah. No one explained this to you?" Midori asked. Mina shook her head. "At Pearls of Wisdom, we like to take the 'nasty' out of dentistry. We see no reason why a dental treatment can't be handled like a spa treatment, and we like to make sure our customers are as relaxed as possible and have the most enjoyable experiences possible."

"I've seen ads for dental spas before but I always thought they were a ploy," said Mina.

Midori chuckled. "Well, yes. Those places are. Just a massage chair in the examination room. So silly. But not here. We know it takes more than a label and an ambience to create an experience. When's the last time you enjoyed going to the dentist, Mina?"

"I don't think I ever enjoyed going to the dentist."

"Well, that all changes today," Midori said. "Why don't you have a seat? It will just be a minute."

"Aren't there any forms . . . "

Midori chuckled. "Oh, no. We don't do forms here. Too stressful, don't you think?"

"Sure," Mina said, and she sat down on one of the couches. She noticed a series of controls on the arms. Heat and massage, with various levels.

"Dat's some shit, ain't it?" Mina looked up and saw she wasn't alone. She hadn't realized another woman had even come in. "Get you all loosey-goosey out in here before they reach in and yank all your teeth out up in there!"

The woman was roughly Mina's age and African American. Physically, she couldn't have been more Mina's opposite. While Mina was fair, porcelain skinned with nearly platinum blonde hair, and thin and lithe, this woman was pure ebony, and she seemed to gleam and shine. On her head she wore a black skull cap, embedded with sequins, and from her earlobes hung gold hoop earrings so large a full-grown adult could've worn them as bracelets. Mina tugged absently at her small white gold hoop earrings, which were embedded with blue diamonds; the other woman's earrings blazed with shimmering rhinestones. While Mina wore light khaki cargo pants and a simple powder blue top, this woman was wrapped head to toe in a black jumpsuit, a scarf of bright swirling reds and oranges with a fringe of brightly colored pom-poms pulled around her shoulders.

The scarf was fastened right in the crevice of the woman's bosom with an oversized dragonfly pin, and this was the element of her outfit that Mina most noticed. Now she was seeing dragonflies everywhere and she couldn't seem to look away.

"Wat-choo staring at, Lily?"

"I'm sorry," Mina said, embarrassed that the woman had caught her staring like that. "I was just noticing . . . "

The woman looked Mina in the eye and fondled her dragonfly pin between her thumb and forefinger. "Lily, you do not need to strain your eyes to get a look at these babies," the woman said, and shifted her hands to her breasts, now cupping them in her hands. "And yes, they are one-hundred percent real. And they are fantastic. I know."

"No, it wasn't that. It was . . . I'm sorry."

"Don't worry about it," said the woman behind the desk.

"Yeah, don't you sweat it none, Lily."

"Excuse me, but my name is Mina. Why do you keep calling me Lily? Do I know you?" When you had no idea who you were or where you came from, of course anything was possible. After all, who could have guessed before yesterday that Mina spoke Russian?

"Mina, we're ready for you," Midori called.

"Be sure you go for the happy ending, Lily. It's worth it!" the woman said, and slapped her legs, laughing.

A tall young man emerged from behind the reception desk. He could not have been more than twenty-six, with a taut, muscular build obvious even underneath his T-shirt and yoga pants. "This is Paolo," said Midori. "He's from Portugal."

"Paolo? Shiiiiitttt!" called the other woman waiting. "You lucky fucking bee-atch! Go for the happy ending for sure!"

"Hello Mina," Paolo said, with an accent, naturally, and he gently clasped her hand. "Come with me. Let's begin."

It was the kind of attraction you could feel in your ears. In your fingertips and toes. Your lips. In places you can't even imagine there are nerve endings, like the ends of your hair. It was the kind of attraction that washes over you and consumes you fully. The kind of attraction you can only feel for a stranger in a situation that will never be consummated—probably more of a deification than an attraction, but that didn't make it any less real.

"Why don't you make yourself comfortable," Paolo told her, handing her a steaming mug of tea and motioning to a chair in the corner. "Please take off your clothes—all your clothes is best," he said, exuding raw, hot sex. "There's a silk robe for you to wear, hanging on a hook behind that screen. Please put it on and make yourself comfortable. But you will need to take it off before we begin, yes?" he said and he licked his lips.

Mina gulped as the young man left the room. It's just a massage, she told herself. This wasn't cheating. People had massages every day. Married people. Athletes. Newlyweds. Honeymooners. Just a massage. A medical procedure, really! She peeled down her clothes and slipped into the robe. Her skin tingled when it made contact with the soft, cool silk.

She took a seat in the chair and placed her feet in the aromatic foot bath prepared for her and quickly relaxed into the setting. The room was almost dark, but a lighting fixture that resembled a Japanese paper lantern gave the room a warm glow. The walls were painted a soothing moss green, and in the dim light she could barely make out the images that hung around the walls in wooden frames. Every surface in this room exuded softness and warmth; there were no metals or porcelain or hard materials of any kind.

There was a light tapping on the door. "Are you ready, miss?" Paolo asked from the other side.

"Just a minute, please," said Mina, and she placed her tea mug down on a wooden bureau. She slipped off her robe and climbed onto the massage table, which was softer and more inviting than her own bed.

As Mina lay on the table, Paolo came in.

"Are you ready, Mina?" he asked, igniting a new wave of tingles in her as she waited for him to begin. She tried to think of every possible vision that could knock the tingles out of her. Esther in her underwear; Harriet nursing all her children at once; Charlie Witmore nude.

"Your accent," she said, her voice nearly cracking. "I'm trying to place it. Where did you say you're from again?"

"Iowa," he deadpanned.

"Oh," said Mina, now embarrassed that she was hallucinating accents.

He laughed lightly. "No, I am kidding. I am from Cascais. In Portugal."

"Oh," she said.

As soon as Paolo's warm, oiled hands touched her skin, it was all she could do to not become completely aroused. He rubbed her back and shoulders, then he moved down her back, grazing the area right above her buttocks, kneading and rubbing her lower legs, her inner thighs. Mina could feel all the knots being worked out of her, but there was the other part of it too. The part of her that was on the brink of release with every touch. And then . . .

"Okay, Mina. We're done here," trilled Paolo. "Unless . . . "

"Unless?" she gasped.

He leaned over her and whispered into her ear. "Unless there's something more I can do for you today?"

"Uh, no. We're good."

"Are you sure?" he said, and seemed shocked. "Because Paolo—"

"No, really," she replied abruptly. "But thank you."

Before Paolo left, he brushed the side of her face with the back of his hand and she almost exploded from this last touch. "Enjoy the rest of your visit then," he said, and he left.

Mina was flushed. Her skin was on fire. She desperately wanted a shower—a very cold one—but she heard another knock at the door. She was both panicked and intrigued that maybe Paolo did not take no for an answer. "It's Midori. Can I come in?"

"Oh. Yes," said Mina, and Midori bounded in. "Great news! It looks like your insurance company's going to spring for the cucumber wrap. Any interest?"

"I'm not sure. How long will it take?"

"Half hour, give or take," said Midori. "Do you need to make a call?"

"I should probably check in with the babysitter."

"Great, please feel free to use the phone on the bureau," said Midori, surprising Mina, who hadn't noticed a phone in the room. Why would there be a phone in this room? Just as Mina was about to ask, Midori turned to leave. She stopped at the door. "You know, most everyone opts for the cucumber wrap after a session with Paolo. I have no idea why when they can just have Paolo," she said with a wicked glint in her eye, and she left.

Mina would have used the room phone had she actually known anyone's phone number, but instead she dug into her purse, found her phone, and speed-dialed Esther. "Good timing," said Esther. "Jack just came to pick Emma up."

"Jack's home?" she asked, and now she felt a pang of longing. Jack was home, at a normal hour, and all she wanted to do was go home. But she hadn't even had her tooth looked at yet.

"Let me put him on the phone," Esther said.

Mina explained to Jack what was going on, though not about the orgasm she'd nearly had at the hands of Paolo. "Sounds hilarious," he said. "Look, don't rush home on my account. I got things covered. And you deserve a treat."

"Jack, I have to tell you something. My car . . ."

"I know, sweetie. They called me at work."

"I'm so sorry."

"Hey, don't worry. We'll get it back. Just try and relax, okay?"

"Okay."

"I'll see you later," he said, and hung up the phone.

Following the soothing cucumber wrap, Mina had a manicure and pedicure, followed by a facial. Two hours later, Mina Clark, polished, primped, and more relaxed than she had been in years, was escorted to the dental office to finally have the procedure she'd come in for. "Dr. Putter will be with you in just a few moments," said Midori. "Here, drink this," she handed Mina another steaming mug.

"No, thank you. I really shouldn't . . ."

"Just drink it," Midori said. "It's tea."

Mina sat back and sipped her tea. The massaging examination chair was warm and inviting, made of the same soft leather as the couches in the lobby.

She looked around the room, amazed that the examination room looked almost identical to the massage room. Nearly twenty-four hours earlier she had been in a room that served exactly the same purpose as the one this was meant to serve, but it could not have been more different from her usual dentist's office. The cistern was a green, cool marble, with a marble basin. The implements of unspeakable torture were tucked away, out of sight.

Mina wondered why all dental offices couldn't look like this. She felt none of the usual fear or dread. None of the panic of anticipated pain and torture. Just a deep, cool serenity. She sat back in the chair and soon drifted off to sleep. When she opened her eyes, a handsome man in his mid-forties was standing over her, smiling.

"I'm sorry," she said. "I was so relaxed. I guess I just dozed off."

"Happens all the time," he said.

"Okay, well, I'm ready," she said, and opened her mouth.

"Ready?" he said. "We're done!"

"Done?"

"Sure. I just took care of everything while you slept. You didn't feel anything?"

"No," she said, and she tapped the side of her mouth. "I'm not even numb from the Novocain."

"No Novocain here. Not necessary. I'm going to let you in on a little secret," he said, and leaned in conspiratorially. "The only reason it ever hurts when a dentist works in your mouth is that people have a tendency to tense up. That's the problem, you see. When people are relaxed and receptive, they don't need it."

"Huh," said Mina, but she wasn't really buying that. "So what did you do to me?"

"Hmmm," he said, rubbing his razor stubble with his hand, "I think I'll spare you all the gory details. It's never really a pleasant scene to describe, when you've just shattered someone's tooth out of their mouth with a hammer and chisel."

Mina winced.

"But suffice to say, you won't be feeling any discomfort back there anymore." He whipped put a hand mirror. "Check it out."

Mina took the mirror and angled it to see the back of her mouth. She was shocked to find a patch of gold where her tooth had been.

"Oh my God!" she said.

"Pretty, isn't it?" he asked. "You like it?!"

"I don't know what to say."

"Well, it's not really a million-dollar smile, but beauty like that usually runs about three grand," he offered.

"Three thousand? I'm sorry. I can't afford that," she said. She tapped the crown with her finger. "Can you pop it out?"

"Relax, Mina. It's fully covered."

"How can that be?"

"A mouth as bad as yours is actually a bigger risk for the insurance company. Fixing it is way cheaper. Bad dental hygiene can kill you, you know."

"So I've been told."

"Did you know your life insurance and health insurance were covered by the same provider?"

"Um, no, I didn't, actually. And why do you?"

"I just know. The point is, the company rationalizes that if they pay out now, even a coupla grand or more, that's a lot better than a coupla mil. when your bad teeth actually kill you."

"Oh."

"Have a great day, Mina!"

Fifteen minutes later, Mina was back outside and heading to the train station. The sun was falling in the afternoon sky and as it shone off the buildings, each unique and with its own character, despite most of them looking like they could crumble to the ground with one good wind, Mina thought that this area actually seemed to have more soul than where she lived. Except things were looking less familiar than when she came. She feared she was going the wrong way now, but she kept walking, hoping things would start looking right again.

As she walked, Mina tapped the side of her mouth repeatedly, amazed that there was not even a trace of pain. She ran the tip of her tongue over her new tooth, and it was smooth and strangely cool, considering that it had been sitting in her mouth for a while now. As she walked, she kept digging at it, waiting for it to warm, but it never did.

"Diggin' for something good?" It was the woman who had been in the waiting room with her.

"Oh hi," said Mina.

"Oooo-weee, do they hook you up in there!" said the woman, rolling her tongue across her teeth. "I feel like a new woman. Um, and that Paolo . . ."

"Oh, so you had the massage then?"

"Best ever."

"And the cucumber wrap?"

"What? Fuck no. Do I look like a damned salad to you? Nuh-uh. I had me some Paolo!"

"Oh my."

"Don't know why anyone chooses that damned wrap," she said, shaking her head. She pursed her lips together and shook her head. "Name's Char-a'tee, by the way, Lily. In case you're wondering. Char-a'tee Pryce. My friends call me Char."

"It's very nice to meet you," Mina lied, "but I really have to be going."

"But you really don't know where you're going, do you?"

"Of course I do. I just . . . uh . . . well . . ."

"Oh, come now, Lily. You don't know where da fuck you are, do you? Come on. Tell ol' Char."

"I don't. I don't know where I'm going."

"Well then, it's a good thing God's gone and sent you some charity. Char-a'tee Pryce, at your service."

"Your name is really Char-a'tee Pryce?"

"Your name is really Lily?"

"Actually, it isn't. It's Mina. Mina Clark."

The woman eyed her up and down and laughed. She held out her hand, her fingernails painted in green and orange stripes. Mina's newly manicured pastel-pink fingertips looked anemic in comparison as she went to shake Char-a'tee's hand.

Char-a'tee shook Mina's hand aggressively as she pursed her lips. "Nah. Your name is definitely Lily," she insisted.

Mina started to feel confused. Maybe this woman was someone she knew? It couldn't be weirder than the Russian in the park. Maybe her name really was Lily? "You know me," Mina said, more than asked.

The woman burst into a giant cackle. "Uh, no," she said, gasping between bellows. "I just call you Lily 'cuz you the whitest creature I ever seen." And she began to laugh manically again.

Mina felt stupid. She wanted to cry. Char-a'tee took pity on her. "So where you ending up tonight, Lily? And what are you driving there?"

"Funny you should ask," said Mina, choking back her tears.

"Come on. I'll walk with you. Now tell me what you're driving . . . No! Wait! Let me guess. This is you, right? Silver BMW?"

"No. Actually."

"Aw, yeah, I know. Bet-choo drive a white car."

"No. My car's black."

"Well, look at you. I bet it is. Now, let's see," she said, looping her arm through Mina's as they walked. "Wait!" Char-a'tee screamed and stopped dead in her tracks.

"What?"

"Look over there. See that?"

Mina squinted across the street where she saw two people sitting in a car arguing. "Ain't nothing funnier than folks fighting in cars. I don't know why it's so funny, but damn! Look at those two!"

Mina had no idea what it was about the scene that was funny, but she couldn't help laughing. "That is sort of funny," she said.

"Bitch, that's some funny fucking shit!" Char-a'tee said. "Okay, let's see what else we got on the street here looks like it got some class," she said.

"Look, I appreciate your help, but—"

"How about this? This SUV?"

"No."

"So that ain't your car either, huh? Well, I don't know . . ."

"I'm sorry. I tried to tell you, but I actually took the train."

"What? You mean to here? From Long Island?"

"Yes."

"Whatever for?"

"Well, it's kind of a funny story," she said.

"I like funny stories."

Mina didn't know why, but she somehow told Char-a'tee the entire story, from her car being hit in the nursery school parking lot to it being repossessed at the body shop.

Char-a'tee shook her head and clicked her tongue while Mina spoke. "Well, you can't be taking no shit like that," she said. "No sir."

"But I was late with my payments. It's what you agree to and—"

"How long you have that car?"

"I don't know, a few years?" she replied, which was the truth because it was at least as far back as she could remember.

"Um-hmmm," said Char. "So you telling me you made about, say fifteen thousand dollars' worth of payments, at least, on that car?"

"Sure. I guess that's about right."

"So what you saying is the damned bank stoled that car from you."

"Well . . ."

"Damned car's overpriced. You already paid what it's worth," she said. She looked Mina dead in the eyes. "They stole that damned car from you, you know that."

"I guess."

"Well, now we gonna get it back."

"I don't think that's such a good idea," Mina said.

"You cannot let these muther-fuckers walk all over you like that," Char-a'tee said. "You gotta take 'em by the balls. Show 'em who's in charge. So come on. Let's go get your mutha-fuckin' car back."

Mina's feeling of panic abated when she saw she'd arrived where she needed to be.

"Oh look, the train station," she said. "Thanks a lot. It was really nice meeting you, Char-a'tee."

"Char."

"Right. Really, *Char*. Thanks again!" she called over her shoulder as she darted away.

# 6

Thanks to being distracted by Char-a'tee Pryce, Mina missed her train. By the time she got back to the burbs, it was dark and chilly. She called Jack from the train station for a ride home but he didn't answer. Neither did the machine. Had she plugged the phone back in? She tried his cell, but there was no answer there either. She tried calling Esther, and again, no answer.

Mina spied a cab, but doing the math quickly in her head, she surmised she didn't have enough left in her wallet for the fare. She almost kicked herself for not taking more of the cash she'd found. She thought for a second that perhaps she could take a cab part of the way home, then realized that the only places around her own community were other gated communities, and there was no way they were going to let her in, even to get dropped off. She decided to take a chance on Jack again, trying him on his cell phone. Still not getting an answer, she wrapped her arms around herself and decided to walk.

Forty-five minutes later, the security guard in front of Easton Estates waved her in, albeit reluctantly, and she walked the last half mile from the gate to her house.

Mina was frustrated when she walked up her front lawn and saw all the lights on in the house. He was home after all. At least Jack had thought to flip the outside light on for her. That small, almost thoughtless favor warmed her heart, but only a little.

And then, when her eye caught sight of the mums in her planting bed, the warmth turned into hot rage. She hated mums but she knew it wasn't the mums themselves that made her so angry. It was that they were planted in her yard, around her home, without her consent. That what people would see when they came to her house, that what people would associate with her, were the flowers she detested most. Mina uncharacteristically stepped off the paved path that led to her front door, and, with just the tip of one shoe, she smashed one of the grotesque, offensive, prickly-looking flowers into the ground. And she had to admit, it felt pretty good.

"Mina," Jack's voice called from the door. "There you are." He was standing there in the doorway, an actual, living, breathing Jack, not the phantom holographic illusion that sometimes lingered in Mina's consciousness like a severed limb. It was really Jack. Her Jack. Wearing jeans and a T-shirt that read: "The Truth Is Out There." *The X-Files* suddenly popped into her head.

"What are you doing to that poor little flower?"

Something that may have been a memory was now knocked away by guilt. Mina looked down at her foot. "I don't know why I did that. I'm sure I don't like mums but . . ."

He laughed. "Oh no. You hate mums. I mean, not like I'm supposed to tell you that or anything." He stepped off the porch and took her in his arms. "But it's not like I'm telling you anything you don't already know." She relaxed into his embrace. He smelled of musk and sandalwood. And paint. And all the rage in her just melted away.

"You look pretty." He leaned in and whispered into her hair, his hot breath on her ear setting her skin on fire. "Why didn't you call? I would have come for you."

She pulled away, now starting to feel annoyed again. "I did. I called your cell phone." The moment was gone.

"Oh, but I never answer that—"

"The landline is unplugged again."

Shame and stress filled his beautiful brown eyes as he absorbed her words. "Disconnected?"

"No, they didn't do it." He sighed in relief. "I did it. Too many calls."

"Well, we need to make it stop somehow. They called me at the office, you know."

"Which they? I mean, aside from the car." He couldn't answer. For both Jack and Mina, all the "theys" seemed to swim together like a cloud of algae ready to bond and become something other, something that could crawl right out of the water and change life as they knew it. An insidious life form, forming to destroy them.

"Well, what does it matter," he tried. "Come on in. Emma's got a whole 'Pandora' scrawled out in finger paint."

"Pandora?"

"From that movie? *Avatar*?"

"Oh . . . right . . ." She had no idea what he was talking about and she was annoyed briefly that he seemed to find time on his numerous business trips to watch movies—and that he'd be so out of touch as to think this kind of movie would be appropriate for a three-year-old to have any knowledge of, let alone try to recapture in fingerpaint.

He looked at Mina, an innocent sincerity now emanating from him, an almost boyish sweetness that she knew was part of the reason she loved him like she did. His thick mane of black curly hair. His soft, warm eyes. His smile, which when sincere, like now, just lit up his whole face. "She may have something going there."

Mina entered the dining room to find the table covered in oversized sheets of paper and Emma standing on the table covered head to toe in paint.

"She really likes art, you know," said Jack, smiling warmly, even a little sadly, watching his daughter play with her paints. Mina felt a twinge of guilt, knowing without asking how much he envied the little girl her ability to paint so freely. To just do what felt natural and what felt good.

"Wait, oh frack!" Jack yelled, darting over to the stove where a pot over-boiled. Mina smirked; this reference she knew. *Battlestar Galactica*. Taking in his handsomeness, his sexiness, even as he was, in his natural state, kind of a sci-fi nerd who loved cheesy sci-fi TV, she knew with everything in her that she loved this man, even if she could not remember all the hows and whys. He pulled up the lid and tried to tame the steam monster. "Dammit!" he cried, dropping the lid that had burned his fingers.

"What are you doing over there?" Mina asked. "You hurt?"

Jack sucked on his fingertips. "I'll live."

Mina moved toward the stove. "What are you making?"

"Nothing. Just tossing together some stuff I found around the kitchen. Figured I'd toss it over some rice," he said. Which sounded like it had to be dreadful, but Jack had a knack for whipping up something wildly and deliciously gourmet from the decay of whatever was left over in the fridge. The "creative" in him. The artist.

"Smells great," she said.

"Yeah, that's just the garlic," he said. "Toss that and a little olive oil into a Staten Island landfill and you'll up the real estate value tenfold."

Mina had to admit it all smelled pretty great.

"MONNY!"

She turned her attention to the table where Emma, and yards of once-white paper, were now slathered in a rainbow of paint. "Oh no," she gasped.

Jack laughed. "It's okay," he said, wiping his hands on a kitchen towel. "All washable. I checked the label before I bought them."

"You *bought* her new paints?"

"Well, I think we're probably better off with washable in the long run," he said, pointing his thumb at the faded shadows of color that still lingered on the kitchen and dining room walls.

"Huh," said Mina, knowing the term "washable" on children's art products was more a suggestion than a guarantee. Mina now accepted that Emma's art experiment was going to be part of the decor as long as they lived in the house. Or until they could afford to repaint and refurnish everything. So forever.

"So you have cash," she asked, embarrassed at how desperate and hungry the question had sounded.

"It was three bucks," Jack said, and shrugged his shoulders.

"Jesus." Mina felt resentful. With another three dollars, she probably could have afforded the cab ride home. She started to feel rage and resentment rise in her. Why was it okay for him to throw money around like he did? And she was equally annoyed at herself for feeling this way over three ridiculous dollars.

Then the oddness of Jack's presence at home struck her. "Why are you here?" she asked, in a tone considerably less matter-of-fact than she felt.

Jack jumped to the stove and dipped a wooden spoon into one of the pots. He brought it to his lips and tasted with a satisfied "Mmmmm." He offered the spoon to Mina and she pressed it to her lips. She could definitely taste chicken, mushrooms, lemon, white wine, butter. She had no idea what else he had put in there, but it was delicious.

At the taste of the food, and the thought of him making it, Mina's anger ebbed, and she collected dishes for setting the table. But she was still curious. "You never answered my question," she pressed. "It's not even six o'clock. How are you here?"

"Amber was out today," he said. "Out of town, actually. I figured I was caught up with all my work, why not come home and see my girls?"

Just then, Emma swooshed into the kitchen, her hands a rainbow of potential home disaster-making, wet Day-Glo paint.

"Back! Back! Back to the table, young lady!" Jack shouted, and Emma scurried to her seat.

"How did you do that?" Mina asked.

"Do what?"

"Get her to listen to you?"

"I gave her a good beating before you got home."

"Jack, be serious."

"I was just firm with her. Try it sometime."

"I'm firm with her."

"Okay."

Mina felt dismissed and it annoyed her. "Well, how would you know that? It's not like you're ever around—"

Jack stroked her face with his hand. "Hey, come on. I'm here now, aren't I? Can't we just try and get along? Enjoy the time while we have it?"

"Sure," said Mina, as she cleared away Emma's paints to set the table.

"And we're ready," Jack gushed, pouring the food into a giant serving bowl. "Let's eat!"

They sat down, and Jack spooned heaping portions onto each of their plates before serving himself.

"Tell me about the dentist. I know it's your favorite!" Jack said with a wink to Emma.

Mina tapped the back of her mouth with the tip of her tongue again. The feeling of cold metal in her warm mouth. "It was really weird," Mina said. "Can you imagine? A spa in a dentist's office?"

"Sounds genius to me," he said, as he shoveled food into his mouth. "So what did they do to you?"

Mina thought about the nearly orgasmic massage, and tried to refocus. "I got a new crown," she said. "It's . . . uh . . . well, it's kind of gold . . ."

"You got a gold tooth!" Jack shouted with glee.

"Well, no. Not a tooth. A crown. A thing they put over your tooth when you don't really have a tooth left."

"Gowd tooft! I wanna see gowd tooft."

"It's not a big deal," said Mina, and Jack and Emma looked at each other and shook their heads.

"Not a big deal?" said Jack. "My wife's gone ghetto-fabulous and that's not a big deal. Come on, open up and show it!" he said.

"Gowd tooft! Gowd tooft!"

"Well, if you insist," said Mina. She put her finger to the side of her lips and pulled open her mouth. "See?"

Jack and Emma burst out laughing. "Ghetto fabulous indeed!" Jack said.

"Can we drop it now?" said Mina, and the family respected her wishes and turned their attention to their plates. By some miracle, Emma behaved through the entire meal, and she finished every bite.

"Look at you, little lady," Jack beamed. "You cleaned your plate."

As someone who had meals with Emma regularly, Mina cried out, "Oh no!"

"I clean my plate!" said Emma, grabbing the napkin next to her plate, scrunching it into a ball, and rubbing it all over her still-saucy dish. "I clean my plate!"

"The cup!" Mina called. "Grab the cup!" Thankfully, Jack was able to grab Emma's open cup before she poured her drink out so she could finish the job.

After dinner, Jack and Mina finished their wine as they gave Emma a bath and wrapped her soft little body in warm pajamas, but not before Emma made seven or eight further requests to see the tooth. Each time, she squealed with delight. They tucked her into bed together, and she was asleep before Jack finished reading *Pinkalicious* to her.

Jack grabbed Mina by the hand. "I have something for you. Dessert," he said, and he shot her an impish grin. She nearly lost her breath as he led her out of Emma's bedroom, but felt a terrible pang of disappointment and frustration as he turned away from their own bedroom and down the stairs.

"Sit down," he said, and headed into the kitchen. "And close your eyes."

She sat for a moment by herself and soon she felt Jack's presence next to her. "Open your mouth," he whispered, and again she complied. The next thing she knew, a luscious sensation swirled in her mouth, a velvety surge of creamy chocolate.

"You like it?"

She opened her eyes. "I love it. It's heaven!"

"Open," he smiled, and he fed her another bite.

"This is the most wonderful thing I've ever tasted," Mina said, as she savored every luscious morsel. Then the flavor took on a whole new dimension . . . no longer a food but a place, and before she knew what was happening, the word "Paris" slipped from her lips.

Jack stopped cold. "What did you just say?"

"Paris," she said. "I know. It's silly, right?"

"No," he said. "Here, keep eating. Tell me what you're feeling now. What you're thinking."

"We've been to Paris," she said. "Me and you."

"Yes."

And memory began to trickle over her like a light drizzle of rain. "It was warm. Spring? It was . . . It was . . ."

"Come on, take another bite," he urged.

She squished the chocolate around in her mouth as more images started popping up for her. "We were sitting in a cafe. A cafe on the river. A man was . . . juggling?"

"Yes . . ."

"And then, another man, he drew our picture?"

Jack now had tears in his eyes. "Hang on, I'll be right back," he said, and he jumped up from the table and headed for the basement. He reached into his pocket and pulled out a key. "Keep eating!"

Mina took the spoon in her hand and stirred the smooth mousse around on her plate. The cafe. The river. The juggler. The painter. All as real for her as the mousse in her bowl. All a part of her, now coming back.

Jack raced back into the kitchen, a package under his arm. "What about the painting? Anything coming back to you about that?"

"It's not a painting, is it? A caricature. Yes, that's right."

"And . . ."

She closed her eyes. She smiled. "We're wearing formal wear, hanging from the Eiffel Tower like King Kong and Fay Wray . . . A tuxedo on you. A wedding gown on me. My hair pulled up in a bun. A beaded bodice . . ."

Jack produced the package, carefully wrapped in brown paper, and tore it open for her. "Is this what you see? Is this what you remember?"

The drawing was exactly as she had remembered it, in all its comic absurdity. "He made me King Kong," she pouted.

"You were a little curt with him. I think he was getting back at you."

"Ah," she said, and she stared at the drawing, the first stirrings of her memory finally returning. She noticed a necklace drawn around her throat and pulled the image toward her to take a closer look.

"What is it?" Jack asked, and Mina absently clutched at her throat.

"A pendant," she said. "A dragonfly?" Jack looked panicked and tried to snatch the drawing back, but she held on to it too tightly. "My necklace?" she asked, the fingers of her other hand at her throat as if the pendant was something she always wore and had suddenly lost without realizing until now. "What happened to my necklace?"

Jack was silent. He looked away.

"What?"

"Sweetie, I'm sorry. I can't tell you that."

"But the dragonfly. It means something. Something important, I'm sure. The other day, in the park. In my notebook. I started sketching a dragonfly. It means something to me."

"Dr. Barsheed . . ."

"Forget Dr. Barsheed. I need to know. Jack, please. I need to know why."

Jack took her face in his hands and kissed her gently. "You'll figure it out. I know you will. But not now," he said, and he kissed her again. "Try and stay focused on Paris, on what you remember."

Mina sighed. "Our honeymoon. The hotel. La Villa Maillot. The room key with the red tassel. The odd golden wallpaper in the room. The tiny bed . . ."

Jack pulled her close and kissed her more passionately now. "Yes, the bed. Let's hear more about the bed," he whispered, his hot breath on her neck seeming to melt her clothes away.

"We spent a lot of time in that bed, didn't we?" she said, and she pulled him in to a deep sensuous kiss. "We didn't see much of the city at all, did we?" she said, and then gasped as he ran his lips across her ear, the edge of her chin, the side of her neck.

"We're not going to make it to the bed," he said, and he lifted her off her chair and carried her into the living room, where he laid her gently on the floor. She looked up at him as he kneeled over her, unbuttoning his shirt, then helping her out of hers and her bra.

He lay down next to her, running his fingertips up and down her exposed torso, gliding across her breasts, gently grazing her nipples. "Oh Mina, you're so beautiful. Do you know that? Look at this body of yours. Look how amazing you are."

He rolled on top of her, kissing her with equal parts tenderness and passion. Hungrily, he peeled off the rest of her clothes and his and she nearly exploded when he entered her. The whole time he lay nearly flat on top of her, their faces, their mouths, never apart. When they finished, Jack brushed the tip of her nose with his soft lips and collapsed next to her.

"I miss you, Mina. I just love you so much."

They lay on the floor, fully entwined, for what could have been minutes or hours more, the warmth of their bodies and their deep affection negating the need for cover of any kind.

"Let's finish the wine," Jack said, and jumped up to retrieve the bottle and glasses.

"So are you going to tell me about the mums?" he asked when he returned, a playful lilt in his voice.

"I don't know why I did that," she said. "They just made me so angry, all smugly sitting there without my wanting them."

"Flowers make you angry."

"Apparently," she said, and sipped from her glass. "But I think it's just those. Just the mums. I hate mums, don't I?"

"You do."

"Why? Why do I hate them so much."

"I can't tell you," he said, and she rolled her eyes, "I can't tell you because I really don't know. Never have. Just one of those things."

"Huh," she said.

"So," Jack said, and drained his glass. "You want to finish the job?"

"What do you mean?"

"Come on, let's grab our jackets," he said, and they threw on their coats over their naked bodies.

The next thing Mina knew, they were outside, garden shovels in their hands.

"Mums, listen up! You have irritated my wife by your . . . smug . . .?" he looked to her for confirmation and she nodded. "Smug commandeering of our garden. Prepare to die!" He dove like a madman into the flower bed and began uprooting the offensive red and orange blooms with his shovel.

Mina began to laugh uncontrollably. "Are you going to make me have all this foul flower blood on my hands alone?" he said, and she kneeled down and joined him, as they dug wildly and laughed raucously.

Within five minutes' time, the deed had been done. The patch of flowers was restored to a patch of dirt, and Jack and Mina collapsed on the grass in a fit of giggles.

"Fuck you, Witmore," Jack yelped, holding up his shovel for emphasis. "Fuck you and your fucking mums!"

Mina glanced up and saw Esther's bedroom curtains rustle shut. For a moment she was embarrassed, but Jack broke that by leaning over and kissing her again. He started to run his hand up and down her body, stopping between her legs, but Mina, knowing Esther was watching, grabbed his hand and held it. "Inside," she said, nodding with her eyes to Esther's window.

Jack shook his head. "That nosy old bag spoils all the fun," he said.

Mina helped Jack clean up the kitchen and they headed up to their bedroom. They took a shower together to rinse off the guts of the mums and slid into bed.

They made love twice more before drifting off into a deep sleep.

A little girl, about six years old, stood facing a marsh on a cold, gray day. She wore a greenish-gray dress that seemed to match her surroundings. Her blonde hair hung over her shoulders, and even though her face was not visible, her posture made it evident that she was sad, so very deeply sad.

A man approached her, his face also obscured. He was dressed in a black suit that graced his tall, lithe, yet muscular build like it had been designed just for him. He didn't need to say anything for her to know he was there, and she didn't turn to face him when she spoke. "Will I ever see her again?"

"I'm sorry, peanut," he replied, his voice soft and kind. "I'm afraid not."

The girl's shoulders began to shake and it was evident she was crying, but she still never turned. "Why not?!" she cried. "Why not?! It's not fair! It's just not fair!"

"It's okay, peanut. It's okay," the man said, and rested his hands on her shoulders. "It isn't fair," he continued. "Life isn't fair. I'm sorry you have to learn this now, precious one, but life is what it is. It's fleeting and it's not fun."

"So what's the point?" the little girl said. "What's the point of it then?"

The man stroked the little girl's head, gently caressing her hair and pulling it into a loose ponytail that then unspilled at her back. "Just remember this, and remember it always," he said. "It won't seem like this while you're small and people, strange people, will be making decisions for you. But you are the one in control, sweet one. You are the one who will make your life what it will be."

At that, a dragonfly darted into the marsh, shiny blue and green and gold, like the colors of a peacock. It hovered between them as it sparkled, a beautiful and exotic and strangely armored creature.

"How will I live?" she said to the air, or to the man, or to the insect. "How can I get by when no one's looking after me any more? Now that Mama's gone." The dragonfly darted away.

"I will always be here for you," the man said. "I will always be looking out for you, even when I have to be away. You can count on me, I promise," he said. "Your mother's absence is a gaping hole for me too. No one will ever understand what you feel like I do," he said. "I miss her so much." His voice cracked.

The dragonfly flew back to join them and the man knelt down to face the girl, unfazed that his designer suit pants were now soaking in cold, wet mud. They faced each other, a sweet little girl with soft, pink, damp cheeks and glassy blue eyes, and a ruggedly handsome man with chiseled features and gleaming white teeth.

He took her small face in his hands, and as he wiped her tears away with his thumbs, he said, "Believe in yourself, peanut. If you need to be reminded that you are not alone, think of our friend over there," he nodded at the dragonfly. "He's not really like you, you know. All his protection is on the outside. His armor. Not you, peanut. Remember that there's nothing on the outside that gives you the armor you need to stay strong. It's all in here," he said, and he pointed to her small heaving chest. "It's all inside. It's all within *you*."

The dragonfly hovered between them once again. "He's more like me, I'm afraid . . ." his words trailed off. He shook his head. "That doesn't matter now. Not really. But when you need me, when you need to be reminded of the love and support you will always have from me, just think of him," the man said. Then the dragonfly began to expand and expand. Its wings shot out to crazy proportions and all its colors went to black. It took the form of a great, giant, black dragon as it cast a black shadow over the swamp and the man and the child, and Mina shook herself awake.

She sat up in bed, but Jack wasn't there. She looked at the clock. It was only five-thirty, but she heard muffled voices in the bathroom. She slid off the bed and padded quietly to the door, and heard more clearly that Jack was on the phone.

"Look, I'm sorry, but I have to be here sometimes too."

A silence was followed by Jack's heartbreaking words, "I understand, but this is my family. You know how it is with my wife. She isn't well . . . I have to make her think everything's normal sometimes so she doesn't totally crack but . . . But yes, okay. I'll be right there. Sure. Okay. Sure. Whatever you say." Mina heard Jack flip his phone closed and she raced back to the bed, hid under the blankets, and pretended to be asleep.

Jack emerged from the bathroom fully dressed in suit and tie, and, without so much as a glance at his wife, lifted a packed suitcase off his side of the bed and left the room and the house.

Mina took a deep breath as she thought about the little girl in her dream and the dragonfly. The man and the crazy dragon that the beautiful insect had morphed into. The shadow and the darkness it cast over marsh and everything.

And the fact that her husband had just now left her like a one-night-stand.

# 7

"What do you make of that? This dragonfly thing?" Mina asked, looking around Dr. Barsheed's office, which was decorated in a kind of red wallpaper that always made Mina think of formal dining rooms. He rested his chin on his thumbs, his hands creating a cage around his face, the tips of his index fingers tapping his nose while he listened. Mina had never known Dr. Barsheed to reply to any question, including "How are you?" without taking this long, nose-tapping pause. It was a little annoying.

"What do *you* think it means?" asked Dr. Barsheed. His index fingers down, he was now massaging the bottom of his black beard with his thumbs.

"Well, I don't know what it means," she said quickly. "That's what I'm trying to get from you. To tell me—"

A pause. A long, thoughtful pause. A pause drawn out longer than anything should ever be drawn out. "No, no, no. Not to tell you. No one can or must tell you. We've been through this. It can be very dangerous. You are here to figure it out for yourself." Dr. Barsheed spoke with a thick Middle Eastern accent and Mina was relieved that at least in this situation, the accent aroused nothing in her but confusion, as she couldn't always make out all the words he spoke.

"With all due respect, Dr. Barsheed, I feel like I could be coming to you another twenty years and I'm not sure even then anything, any of this, will make any more sense to me. When are things going to start to make sense? Are you sure what we're doing is actually working?"

Dr. Barsheed nodded. He paused, of course, then placed his fingers to his nose again. This time he slid the tips down below his nostrils and sniffed, grossing Mina out. "To be fair here, Mina," he said, and waited, and took another sniff, "no successful therapy is instant. It will take years more, indeed, to get to the heart of your memory loss. This time and the last time."

"Last time? What last time? What do you mean, last time?"

Dr. Barsheed's brown skin turned bright red. He answered quickly. "What? What other time?"

"That's what I was asking you," said Mina. "What did you just say? About the last time?"

He pulled his hands away from his face and shuffled through her file. "There was another time?" Dr. Barsheed played dumb as he thumbed through his notes.

"You just said there was another time. 'This and the last time' you said. Wow, I mean, you just said that!"

"I said that?" he challenged, pointing to his chest. "Me?"

"Well, didn't you?" said Mina, starting to doubt herself.

He looked down at her file and began shuffling through papers. "Ah well, one way or the other, you know I can't tell you anything about that," he said, not looking up. "But, uh, why? What do you remember?"

"Nothing. I remember nothing. Not then, not now. I only brought it up because you did."

"Oh yes. Of course, of course," he said, with a dismissive nod of his head. "Well, you know I can't tell you anything." He returned his hands to his face.

Mina was about to explode with frustration. "Okay, but I have to be honest here. That's what I don't understand. The *why*? I mean, *why* would giving me just a hint make me less stable? Make me more vulnerable? Wouldn't it help, I mean, in the long run, if I just had a clue? Just a little light to help find my way?"

"I told you before, and I'll tell you again. This kind of therapy, it's not meant to be instant. If you start to remember, when you start to remember, things could get out of hand very fast for you. You start to remember things, and one thing leads to another, and, well, in your case . . . Because of what happened in your case . . ." He shook his head. "Well, one thing might lead to another and when it all rolls back, and rolls back too fast . . ."

"What . . .?"

"It could take your mind for good."

Mina and Dr. Barsheed stared each other down, and she realized only now that they were opponents in a poker game of her mind. If she had ever trusted this man, that was all over now. There was no way she'd be telling him about remembering her honeymoon and chocolate mousse in Paris. Things were going to be different now. She could feel it.

"Looks like our time is up," said Dr. Barsheed, not looking away to reference a watch or clock.

"Looks that way," said Mina, and she got up and left.

"Monny!" shouted Emma as Mina passed into the waiting room.

"How did it go, dear?" asked Esther.

"Next Tuesday at three?" asked the receptionist.

Mina picked up Emma and gave her a big squeeze. She looked at Esther, whose jewel du jour was a butterfly barrette positioned right at the base of the beehive. "I'll tell you in the car," she said, and then she turned to the receptionist. "That won't be necessary, thanks," she said, and stormed out, leaving Esther to chase after her.

"What do you mean not necessary? Did you tell him about the dragonfly? About Paris?" said Esther, panting after her.

"Let's just say this session was revealing," Mina said. "Revealed very clearly that I'm wasting my time with this quack and his 'theories' about my mental state."

"Mina, Dr. Barsheed is a renowned psychiatrist. One of the best in the business."

Mina stopped and faced Esther. "He told me there was a 'last time.'"

"He *told* you that?"

"You mean it's true? This has happened to me before? I've lost my memory before?"

Esther looked away. "I don't know."

"Esther?"

"Honey, I truly don't know," she now said, looking Mina right in the eye. "You should ask Jack."

"At least tell me . . . Have I been seeing Dr. Barsheed since you knew me? Has there been anyone else?"

"Well, there isn't anyone else. Not of his caliber."

"I still don't understand how I ended up with him. I mean, all things considered, he's not exactly a match for me."

Esther looked punched in the stomach. "It was me," she said, pained. "I recommended him. His work with human memory, the studies he's done—"

"Oh. Well, then how did you find him?"

Esther was silent.

"Esther, where did you find this guy?" Mina asked, propping a slipping Emma onto her hip.

Esther looked away. "Uh, the Internet."

"Ah yes, the source of all information. The holy Bible of information. Esther, most people your age won't even go near a computer and here you devour everything you read on the Internet like it's scripture. Why is that?"

Esther puffed her beehive with her hand. "I'm progressive."

Mina shook her head and smiled. "I'm sorry, Esther. I didn't mean to snap at you like that. I know you're always looking out for me. You're like family," she pulled Esther into a hug, and Emma wrapped her small arms around Esther's neck. "I'm not myself today," she said. "Please forgive me."

"Of course, dear," Esther patted her softly on the back. "Should I take you two to the playground? I have to meet the ladies for mahjong."

"Sure, thanks."

Esther was unusually quiet as they rode back to Easton Estates, and Mina felt pretty guilty about it. She knew that even though Esther had accepted her apology, it would be a long time before she would really be forgiven for blowing up at her like that. She tried to think of something to say, then realized it would be best to leave it alone. Emma fell asleep the instant the car started rolling and therefore offered no help in breaking the uncomfortable silence.

"Here we are," said Esther. She looked back at Emma. "I guess you'll need the stroller. Let me pop the trunk."

Mina considered asking Esther to just drive them home, but she already felt like she was asking too much. She pulled the stroller from the trunk, extracted Emma from her car seat, and placed her in the stroller gently. As soon as she shut Emma's door, Esther sped away, and Mina realized her purse was still in the front seat of the car. She'd get it later.

Mina rolled Emma to the playground and noticed all the usual suspects mulling about. She didn't feel like chatting with anyone, and pointed to the stroller with sleeping Emma as she put her finger to her lips in a "shhh" gesture, then pointed to a bench on the other side of the playground. The mothers all gave her the "thumbs-up," and she relaxed into her bench.

"I was wondering if you would show today." The accent was undeniable.

"Oh, hello Alex," she said curtly.

"Ah, you are not happy with Alex. This I understand. I should not maybe have laughed at you like that. It was just . . . so . . . how you say . . ."

"смешный," she replied, more resigned than shocked that such a bizarre and foreign word would fall from her mouth like that.

"Ah, yes. *Ridiculous*," he said. "May I sit, while the little one sleeps? We can, how you say, chat?"

Mina was annoyed, but her curiosity about this man and what he could possibly tell her was far stronger. And now that she was left to figure out all her mysteries without the interference of Barsheed, she was going to do things her way. "Okay," she said, "but only if you're going to start talking."

"But Dr. Barsheed—"

"Dr. Barsheed is out of the picture now," said Mina. "And what do you know about me and Barsheed? Why do you know—"

"Are you sure that's a good idea? I mean—"

"I don't trust him any more. It's all me now."

Alex smiled. "This is good for you," he said, with a familiarity that should have made her uncomfortable but didn't. "You sound more and more like you every time I see you."

"You mean the Russian spy me?"

He laughed. "Mina, you're no spy."

"Oh, so the mail-order bride then?"

"No. Not bride. Not that either."

Mina took a deep breath. "Then what? Why do you know me? Why are you Russian—and am I Russian too? Why do I understand you better when you speak Russian to me than when you speak English with your accent? Look, I'm ready to lose my mind if I have to, but you have to help me piece this together. Please. If you know me, you have to let me know how."

He took a deep breath and he sat down next to her. He leaned over, placing his elbows on his knees. He flicked away a loose thread from his jeans. They sat in silence a few moments, watching the other mothers and nannies round up the children and take them away from the park. They were alone. There was something unsettling about them being all alone in the park right then, beyond the natural trepidation any woman might feel alone in the near-dark with a man she didn't really know. She couldn't place her finger on what she was feeling.

She put it back on him. "You're not talking."

"No. That is not it," he said. "I just don't know where to begin."

"Okay, well then how about you start from when we met?"

He sat back and scratched his beard. He looked at her with tenderness and affection, without even a trace of lust. She mentally crossed "lovers" off her list. But if not that, what was it?

As Alex finally opened his mouth to speak, Emma cried out, a shrill, blood-curdling wail. Mina bent down to see what was wrong, and as she leaned over, Emma projectile-vomited all over her. "Oh shit!" she said, wiping her face with the back of her hand.

Alex kneeled down next to Emma, touching her forehead. "She is burning up."

"Burning up? She was fine ten minutes ago!"

"This is how it goes with children. Surely you know this."

Mina imagined she did, but she now felt herself slipping into panic mode as Emma's crying became more intense and fierce. It was getting dark. Her phone and her purse were in Esther's car. Her own car was in some impound lot somewhere. All the other mothers had left the playground. She was alone with her ill child and this weird Russian stranger she had no idea why or how she knew. What were her options?

"We need to find doctor," said Alex. "There is doctor here? In complex?"

Mina had no idea. "Emma's doctor is a few miles from here. But, uh, I don't have a car."

He nodded. "Yes, I know. So we call—"

"My phone's in someone else's car. My purse . . ."

"Ah."

"Wait. How did you know about my car?"

"Not important."

And then the reason she had been so ill at ease being alone with him became apparent. "And where's your niece? You said there was a little girl you watch over—"

"Mina, listen to me," he stared pointedly at her, his hands now on her shoulders. "You need to trust me. Can you trust me?"

*Absolutely not, you crazy cryptic Russian lunatic,* Mina thought. Then Emma threw up again and nearly choked on her own vomit. "Okay."

"Come on."

The events of the next twenty minutes were a blur to Mina. Her child was burning with fever in her arms, and Mina was certain Emma was on the brink of death. All she could recall between the playground and the doctor's office was riding in the back seat of a speeding car, clutching Emma to her, crying into her baby's hair and praying softly that this strange Russian man she knew without knowing how hadn't poisoned Emma and wasn't leading them to their deaths.

But no, he apparently was not. Because they arrived at Dr. Swenson's office.

"You don't have an appointment!" the receptionist cried at them as they pushed their way into the examination area. Mina pleaded with her eyes and then the woman took a good look at Mina, caked in a now-crusty layer of kid puke. "Oh, gross! Come on, come in!"

The receptionist led them to an examination room and came back a minute later with a clump of wet paper towels and a clump of dry. "Here," she said, gagging. "Just try not to get any of it anywhere. Oh God, ew," she said, and left.

Mina tried to put Emma down while she wiped her face and hair but Emma wasn't having any of that. So she held Emma in one arm while she made a feeble attempt at getting herself clean with the other. Then Alex took the dirty paper towels from her and threw them away, not before giving her another quick swipe with the wet one. "You missed this," he said and she smiled at him. Maybe he wasn't so bad after all.

Dr. Swenson finally came and Alex stood quietly by as Mina held on to Emma and the doctor examined her. She threw up again, this time all over the doctor. "Happens all the time," the doc said cheerily as he pulled a bottle of Children's Advil out of his pocket, opened the bottle and measured a dose with one hand, and managed to get Emma to swallow it.

"Fever's high," he said, as if the child from *The Exorcist* wasn't about to erupt again in his office. "Once we get that under control, she's going to pop right back to normal. Well, you know. Relatively speaking."

Dr. Swenson deftly stuck a swab in the back of Emma's throat. "I bet it's strep," he said. "We'll know in a few minutes." He darted out of the room.

"Makes sense," Alex said. "You used to get very bad strep. Gave us a lot to worry about."

Mina started to shift the pieces together in her mind. A deep affection, not a romance. He knew things about her. He knew about her past. But she surprised even herself when she blurted out, "Are you my father?"

He answered quickly. "No. Not that."

Mina found it odd that this strange Russian man could know something so personal about her, but as Emma started to whimper and wail, she turned her attention back to her child. "Well, whoever you are, thanks for helping us."

"Of course."

Dr. Swenson darted back into the room with a small bottle of pink medicine. "You'll need this," he said, and placed it down on the counter. "Excuse me," he said, and he darted back out of the room.

When the examination room door opened next, it was not Dr. Swenson who entered. Instead, it was a familiar personage, large and in charge, and sparkling in her bright pink scrubs and trademark sequined cap.

"That's impossible," said Mina.

"Lily White," said Char. "Well, who'd'a thought we'd meet again like this? Shit! How you doin', girl?"

"Who is your friend?" Alex asked, clearly amused.

"Who da fuck is this?" Char asked.

"Alex, this is Char-a'tee. Char-a'tee Pryce. Char-a'tee, this is Alex. I'm sorry. I don't know your last name," she said, looking to Alex.

"Charmed," said Alex, offering a hand to Char.

"Are you shitting me?" said Char, looking Alex up and down.

"Char. Please," said Mina. "The child."

"Oh, sorry. But the shit coming out of me ain't the most damaging shit going on in this office, if you know what I'm talking about." Now she nodded to Alex.

"What's the problem with Alex?" she asked, even though it was a question she'd been asking herself since she'd met him.

"He's full of shit."

"What are you talking about?" said Mina.

"Yes. Please let us in on joke," Alex said.

Char only clicked her tongue repeatedly as she turned her attention back to Mina. "How's the . . .?" and she tapped her own tooth with a fingernail decorated in a pink and green harlequin pattern.

Mina self-consciously covered her mouth.

"They sure do some fine work at that Pearls of Wisdom," Char said. "The dental services ain't bad but the getting serviced—"

"Char-a'tee, please!"

Char laughed. "Char. Please. And Lily, I ain't gonna give your secret service with Paolo away!"

"I went for the cucumber wrap!" Mina snapped.

"Yeah, and like I already said, girlfriend, you missed out!"

"Pearls of Wisdom?" Alex interjected. "You mean that so-called dental spa on forty-third? In Bay—"

"The one and only!" Char confirmed.

"Mina, what did they do to you?"

"You mean besides rock her world?" Char asked.

"Gowd tooft!" Emma cried out, and sunk back into Mina's embrace.

"Gold tooth?" Alex parroted, seeming both confused and concerned.

"Poor love," Char said. "Ain't she a sweet one? She walked over to the counter and held up the bottle Swenson had left for them. "Yep," she said, "this is the miracle stuff. Five doses of this and she'll be done."

She handed the bottle to Mina.

"What do I do with this?"

"You gotta give it to the little one," Char shook her head at Alex, as if to say, "Can you believe this one?" Then she caught herself and looked back at Mina. "Look, baby's gonna be fine. Just bad strep," she said.

"I *knew* this!" said Alex.

"She just gotta take the meds and she be fine. Happens all the time."

Mina rested Emma in the crook of her arm as she unscrewed the bottle using both hands and pulled out a dropper filled with bright pink, milky liquid. Mina placed it in Emma's mouth but just as she was about to squeeze in the medicine, Emma whipped her head away with unimaginable force and the pink liquid landed everywhere but in Emma.

"You gonna have to try again," said Char. "Go on now."

Mina tried again, this time getting some of the liquid actually in Emma's mouth, which Emma then spritzed and sprayed all over Mina and, it seemed, the examination room.

"Girl you can*not* let that child walk all over you like that. Hold her down. Let Char show you how it's done."

Mina held on to Emma as the liquid skillfully poured from the dropper down Emma's tiny raw throat. "See that?" said Char. "She's gotta know who's boss. And you gotta show her."

"She makes good point," said Alex.

"Say what?" said Char.

"I said—"

"Yeah. Uh-huh. I know what you said. Shit," she said.

"I don't see how—"

"Lily, you ain't buying that shit are you? You blonde and pretty and all, but I didn't think you was dumb."

"Why does this woman keep calling you Lily?" Alex asked.

"Chuh. Listen to that? Most bullshit Russian accent I ever heard. Who'd you say you were again?"

"Is this some kind of joke?" asked Mina.

"That accent. That's the joke. Lily, baby, tell me you know that accent's a bunch of bullshit."

"What are you saying . . .?" She looked at Alex, who was watching Char-a'tee, a cool expression on his face.

"Well played, Miss Pryce," he said in perfect English. "Or is it Missus?"

"It ain't any shit you need to know," said Char. "Why don't you cut the bullshit and tell her who you really are."

"It's not for me to tell her," he said.

"Uh-huh. That's what I thought," she said.

"What is she talking about? Alex, what's going on?" Mina pulled Emma close to her, the both of them covered in dried vomit and wet, sticky amoxicillin, not really sure which of the characters here in this office confused her more.

"I'll leave you to it then," Char said, and she closed the door behind her.

Alex kneeled to face Mina, nothing but kindness in his eyes. He placed a hand on her shoulder. "I speak with an accent because I thought it would put you at ease," he said without a trace of an accent.

"Okay . . ."

"Accents relax you," he said. "They make you feel, well, at home."

Accents made her feel a lot of things, lately especially, but "at home" was not a label she would have used. "I don't understand."

"Look, while I'm on board for the most part with you giving Barsheed the boot, I do agree with him that realizing too much at once can be dangerous. So let's take this slow, okay?"

"Okay . . ."

"Let's see. Where can we begin here," he said. He stood and started pacing the room. "Has anything started coming back to you about before? Beyond the magic trick, which you used to love, by the way," he said, a faraway look on his face. "We all did. Well, until the day you figured it out and—"

"And?"

"Oh sorry. I shouldn't be leading you. But without thinking too much about it, had anything been coming back to you? Did the magic trick bring anything else back?"

"I don't think so . . ."

"Well, what about Lucy? Do you remember Lucy?"

*Who the hell was Lucy?* Mina wondered. She thought about telling him about Paris, but she still wasn't sure if she could trust him. And the dragonfly. That had to mean something. "I keep seeing dragonflies."

"Yes, I know. I saw the sketch in your notebook." A look of concern washed over his face.

"What about dragonflies? Tell me. What about the marsh?"

He shook his head. "I fear this is too much, too soon. Can you meet me tomorrow, Mina? Without Emma?"

Just then, Char burst back into the room. "Where we goin'?" she asked.

"I'm not going anywhere . . ." Mina started to say.

"Oh no, I think you gotta hear what this clown gotta say," she said. "But I don't think you should be meeting him alone. Don't think I trust him yet."

"But I don't even know *you*. How do I even know I can trust *you*?"

"Honey, you gonna have to trust and accept yourself some sweet Char-a'tee. My mama didn't name me this for nothin'."

"I think she's okay," said Alex. "Trust me?"

Mina rolled her eyes. "Yes, because . . ."

"I think she's okay to be part of this," Alex said. "I think she can help."

Mina looked to Alex and Char-a'tee. Both were smiling brightly. Emma stirred in Mina's arms. She looked up for a moment then nuzzled her tiny sweet vomit-encrusted hair back into Mina's neck. "I tired, Monny."

"I don't know. Emma's not going to be up for being with anyone else tomorrow. She's so sick."

"Child, one more dose of that magic potion and she's gonna be up terrorizing your house by dinner time."

"I should be getting her home now," said Mina.

"I really have to go. I have another appointment." Alex handed her two twenty-dollar bills. "This should cover a cab. Pay me back whenever—it doesn't matter."

"Thanks."

"Meet me tomorrow then? Both of you?"

"If Emma's better," she said, doubt in her voice, "I can meet you for an hour or so while she's in school."

"Great. How about the coffee shop on Ninth?"

"How about some place with a little more class," Char-a'tee sassed.

Alex smiled. "The Paramount. Breakfast. Nine-thirty."

"Deal," said Char.

"Sure," said Mina. Alex ducked out, with Char following behind. Mina called a cab from the phone at the receptionist's desk. While she waited for the car, she took herself and a considerably perkier Emma into the bathroom to clean up.

When they returned home, Mina saw that Esther had left her purse by the front door. She was relieved she didn't have to go over and retrieve it. She and Emma were both so tired.

Once inside, she tried to call Jack but the call went right to voicemail. She pulled Emma into the shower with her and afterwards changed them both into clean pajamas. Mina gave Emma her medication, which she took obediently. She tried to reach Jack again, but with no luck. She decided that Emma should sleep with her in her bed. So she got PP the bunny from Emma's bed, and the two of them snuggled up together and fell asleep to *Blue's Clues*.

The next thing she knew, Mina was in a playground. Not the playground at Easton Estates, but one she seemed to recognize all the same.

"Whatcha doin?"

Mina looked up to see a little girl standing over her. The girl was wearing brown plaid bell-bottom pants and an orange turtleneck. Mina thought this was a strange way to dress a child, but other things were stranger right now. What was she doing sitting on the ground? What was she doing wearing a gingham dress and matching knee socks? And why was she all of a sudden a child again?

Mina didn't know how to answer the little girl's question, because of course she had no idea what she was doing—in these clothes, in this body. She looked at the ground in front of where she sat.

"Jacks!" she said, perhaps a bit too excited.

"I like jacks," the little girl said. "Can I play with you?"

"Sure," Mina said.

"I'm Lucy," the girl said.

"I'm Alessandra." The name fell out of her mouth on its own, but she felt completely sure that she wasn't lying to the girl.

"Can I call you Ali?"

"Okay."

So the girl sat down with Mina-Ali and the children played happily for a while as the sun rose higher in the morning sky.

Suddenly, a shadow fell over them, the shadow of an adult. Lucy stopped playing and she stared point-blank at Mina. "Emma is in danger," she said. "You need to watch out for Emma."

Mina awoke with a start. She looked to Jack's side of the bed, and Emma and PP were nowhere to be found. "Emma?" Mina cried out, and she jumped out of bed. "Emma! Where are you? Emma!"

She raced around her bedroom. Into the bathroom. Into the hallway. She darted through the hallway calling out for her daughter, but there was no response. "Emma!" she cried, as she headed into Emma's room. There was no sign of her anywhere. She raced down the hall and was about to head down the stairs when she heard a small voice coming from the hall bathroom.

"Hi Monny," it said. Mina frantically flipped on the light and found Emma, her diaper off, sitting on the potty. Emma smiled big and beamed, "I do-ed it!"

Mina took a deep breath and then tried to exhale the "crazy." She knelt in front of her daughter and pulled her into a big hug. "I'm so proud of you, baby! Good for you!"

Mina and Emma went through the motions of getting ready for their day, and Mina called a cab to take them to Emma's school. But when they headed outside to the front of the house to wait for the cab, Mina's car had mysteriously returned, a typed note stuck under the windshield wiper blade. "*Thanx to Random Acts of Char-a'tee!*"

# 8

Mina was first to arrive at the restaurant, but Alex followed shortly.

"Table?" asked the hostess, and Alex nodded.

"No, booth, please," Mina replied, wanting privacy. Mina followed the hostess, with Alex trailing behind. He slid in across from her and they picked up their menus, as if this was a normal meeting of two people over a normal breakfast. Minutes later, Chara'tee appeared. Alex moved in to allow her to sit with him, and she shook her head at him dramatically and pressed up next to Mina, squishing her against the wall.

"Order me a Bloody Mary, baby," she said to Mina as she stared at Alex. "So what you gots to tell us, old man?" she said.

"Maybe we should all have a drink. Mina, make it three, please."

"What am I? The waiter here?" No one answered and when the waitress returned, Mina ordered three Bloody Marys.

"Three?" the waitress asked.

"Yes, three, please," said Mina, and the waitress left.

"Well?" Char challenged. "What you gotta say for yourself?"

As Alex opened his mouth to speak, Mina's cell phone sounded. "Sorry," she said, and checked the caller ID. An "888" number. They had found her cell number. It was only a matter of time. She silenced the call and turned her attention back to the meeting. Char and Alex shared a knowing glance, and it embarrassed Mina, this glance between two people who didn't even know her.

The waitress returned. "Three Bloody Marys," she said, and placed all the drinks in the middle of the table.

Mina's phone sounded again, this time another 888 number. "Dammit," said Mina, and she silenced it again.

"Girl, you give that phone to me!"

"I'm sorry?"

"I said, give the goddamned phone to me," Char tried to snatch the cell phone away from Mina. "Lily, baby. You can't let these motherfuckers walk all over your pretty blonde head like that!" she shook her head. "Shit."

"She has a point," Alex chimed in.

"It's not that simple," said Mina. "You wouldn't understand."

"Why is that, baby? Cuz you thinking old Char's skin tone means she don't got nothing they want?"

Mina was aghast. "That's not what I meant!"

"Lily, honey, that's racist!"

"No, I'm not racist," Mina pleaded. "I didn't mean to imply—"

"Ha! Lily, I just yankin' your chain. You're taking it too seriously. Like this thing with the bank," she said, tapping the phone with a bright orange and green candy-cane-striped fingernail.

Mina snatched it away from her. "How can you say that? They own my house, you know. They want us to pay and they've said if we don't . . . " Mina trailed off. When she spoke the words out loud, they started to sound absurd even to her.

"Yeah, that's what I thought." Char pursed her lips and let out another laugh. "They ain't gonna do shit," she said. "It's just a credit card."

Mina refocused herself. Of course this was serious. "You don't understand. It's the same bank. They hold our mortgage. They said if we don't pay—"

"What? That they gonna throw you out onto the street? That they gonna take your house?"

"They're very powerful."

"They just like anyone else. They only as powerful as you let them be. And besides, you got your car back didn't you?"

Mina was speechless.

"She's got a point, Mina," said Alex, and she realized that until that moment she'd forgotten he was with them.

"No, you guys don't know what you're saying. This isn't a game. They hold the power. They said—"

"They can say whatever they want. Don't make it true."

She looked at Alex.

"No. It sure don't," he said, and Alex and Char-a'tee both laughed.

Mina was getting pissed off. What was she thinking, confiding in this woman? This woman she barely knew, who was clearly trouble, squeezed into a turquoise Juicy Couture tracksuit two sizes too small.

"Give me your phone," Char-a'tee said, and she held out her hand, nodding insistently. "Come on, girl. Hand it over."

"I think you should listen to her," Alex said. "I think she can help you."

"I can help you, Lily. Hand it over to sweet Char-a'tee now and let's be done with it already."

Mina looked at Char, then back at Alex. No, she didn't know the woman that well—or barely at all. And she still didn't remember how she knew Alex. But that's why they were here. Alex was going to do some talking and Char-a'tee was here to look out for her. So it had to be alright. Right? Alex smiled reassuringly and it put her mind at ease. "Just sit back and learn something," he said as Char snatched up the phone.

She flipped it open with a sly smile. "Now . . . let me see," she said, scanning the screens. "Missed calls. That's what I want." She pressed the call button and waited. Mina started to have second thoughts and reached for the phone, but it was too late.

"I wanna speak to your supervisor, please," Char-a'tee said into the phone, sweet as could be. She looked up at Mina, covered the phone with her hand, and whispered, "You gotta start being polite with these people, else you get nowhere," she said. Then, as almost an afterthought, "You got your car back, right?"

Mina started to speak but Char-a'tee waved her silent. "I don't fucking care if she's out shooting her dog in the yard because the damn beast swallowed her son. Get dat bitch on the phone!" She smiled smugly.

"This was a terrible idea," said Mina, shaking her head.

"Trust me," said Alex. "Trust her. She's going to fix this for you. I believe she will."

"How do you know?" she asked.

He smiled calmly. "I know. Just watch."

Char's eyes took on a whole new light as she got the party of interest on the line. "You da boss?" she asked, nodding at Mina. "Well, I got something to tell you," she said, and broke into a colorful rant. While she talked, Mina nervously sipped her drink and Alex spoke.

"Your mother was my sister," he said, just like that, and the information seemed to warm her in the same way the vodka from the Bloody Mary warmed her from the inside when she drank it in. And it also enraged her. And it confused her.

He took a deep breath. "So when I told you at that park that I'm looking after my niece, I wasn't lying. The connection you feel to me is because I am your uncle," he said, and waited for her to reply, but she couldn't speak.

He nodded, knowingly. "You asked me when we first met. It was the day you were born. My sister—"

"Well, you call off your goddamned dogs now and stop harassing my girl or you're gonna have some Char-a'tee without mercy to swallow!"

Alex's eyes filled with tears. "My sister was very dear to me. I almost died when she . . .when we lost her . . .It nearly killed me. I didn't know what to do . . ."

"What about my father?"

"You didn't know your father. Not really. None of us did. He didn't, well, he didn't stick around when your mom told him she was pregnant."

"Oh."

"I tried to find him, I did. But, you know. If people want to disappear, it's actually surprisingly easy."

"I don't know what to say. Maybe if I told Jack—"

"Oh, I would be careful about what you tell Jack. I'm not sure things were, well, I don't know if we were all on the best of terms when last . . ."

"But I can't keep this from him. He's my husband."

Alex took a deep breath. "Well, okay. I have to respect that. But you're going to have to prepare yourself then. Because he might not take it too well. He isn't . . . well . . . he's not quite . . ."

"Oh, I disagree. I think Jack would be happy to know I'm putting the pieces together," she said, thinking of how he'd spoken about her being ill on the phone that morning. How badly her illness must be taxing him. Draining their lives. If she was well, she could work again. She could help with the bills. She could make the calls stop. And then she thought about the night. The wonderful, blissful night she actually felt married to and in love with the man who shared her life. "Just the other night I remembered—"

Mina was interrupted when Char flipped Mina's phone shut. "And that's how you handle that shit! They ain't gonna bother you again," she said, and took a long sip of her drink. "Now what did I miss?"

Alex looked at Mina, great concern in his eyes. "Look, now that you know what you know, there's a chance you're going to become overwhelmed, Mina. You may get angry at me. You may, well . . ."

"Well, come now. Spit it out, white man."

"Just try and take it slow from here, okay? Because there's a really good chance things will flood back to you quickly and without mercy. And there's a lot you're going to have to face when it does."

"Everyone always said it was bad, what happened. But just how bad . . ."

He shook his head. "I won't say. I can't say. Just know that you are precious to me, okay? And as you begin to remember things, please also know this. I no longer harbor the intensity of resentment I did over anything that may have gone down between us. It would be foolish and trite of me to say that all is forgiven. But underneath it all, that sentiment, if you're wondering, is there."

"Uh, okay?" she said, and downed the rest of her drink.

"I am here for you, peanut. It may not seem like that all the time, but I am here now, as I have always been."

"Well, I'll be damned," Char-a'tee said.

Mina drove at near-light speed on her way to pick up Emma, her head spinning wildly from the events of the morning, and probably also a little bit from the vodka. An uncle? She has an uncle! A real blood relative. Someone who knew her from the beginning. Someone who could help her figure out the missing pieces of her memory, the loose, jumbled fragments that floated in her mind.

There were so many emotions racing through her as she drove. Excitement at finding a link to her past at last. Joy at knowing she could now discover secrets about herself so long buried. Rage that he'd only revealed himself now. Hurt that he'd let her be raised by someone else after her parents died. So much conflict. So much confusion. And so much curiosity.

She pulled up at the Acela Academy as early dismissal was ending and Emma, standing with Miss Rosemary, was the only child who hadn't been picked up yet. They held hands in the parking lot, Emma desperately trying to squirm away; Miss Rosemary, who could not have been older than twenty-five, looked about sixty, as she did every day at this time, after spending a morning with Emma and nineteen other darlings. Mina knew Emma saw the car as she nearly tore off poor Miss Rosemary's arm to get to the car.

Mina threw the car into park and raced out, sure Emma had the strength to make the nursery teacher an amputee if she wanted to get to Mina badly enough. She jogged over to where they stood.

"Hello, Mrs. Clark." The teacher's voice was saccharine-sweet; Mina knew the only reason Miss Rosemary was happy to see her was that she had been alone with Emma for at least ten minutes, against Emma's considerable will. "So nice to see you today."

"I'm so sorry. I can't believe I'm so late," Mina tried to be sincere. The teacher's artificially sweet outer shell never cracked.

"That's okay, Mrs. Clark. I was just worried about standing out here in the cold. Emma told me she was quite sick yesterday. That she went to the doctor and took pink medicine."

Emma pulled away and ran to Mina. Mina felt guilty because she knew she'd violated the school rule of twenty-four hours at home before returning to school.

"I know how it goes," said Miss Rosemary. "Don't worry. The imagination, it's so rich now, at this age. I don't believe most of what they tell me about what goes on at home, as long as you don't believe most of what they tell you about me," she sang.

Emma snarled at Miss Rosemary. "I wanna go home, Monny."

"Just say good-bye and thank you to Miss Rosemary."

Emma scrunched her face into a fresh new scowl. "I don't like Miss Rosemary."

"Sorry," Mina said as she scooped up Emma and began walking away with her. Then she stopped. She put Emma down, grabbed her by the hand, and pulled her back toward the school. "Miss Rosemary," she called, just as the teacher was heading into the school. "Sorry, Emma has something she wants to say to you. Emma?"

"I don't like you!"

"Emma! I want you to apologize to Miss Rosemary right this instant," she said with a firmness that shocked even her. "Or no *Blue's Clues* for you tonight. Come on. Let's go."

Emma was quiet and Mina gave her little hand such a tight squeeze, Emma cried out. "I said, say you're sorry."

"Sorry," said Emma, another thing that astonished everyone present, including Harriet, who somehow appeared out of nowhere just that minute.

Miss Rosemary kneeled down to Emma. "That's okay, sweetie. See you Thursday," and she headed into the school.

"Good for you!" said Harriet. "That was great!"

"Oh, hi."

"I always say, you have to be firm with these kids or they'll get out of control. You have to be firm and use good discipline and let them know where the boundaries are."

Both Mina and Harriet then turned to find Harriet's brood racing manically around the parking lot, the oldest one climbing a drainpipe leading to the roof. Harriet rolled her eyes. "Except when you have too many of them," she said, not a trace of regret or remorse in her voice. "Come on, William," she called, half-heartedly. "Down from there."

"I want to get to the roof. See if I can see our house!" he called back.

Harriet turned to Mina. "So you want to come over?" Emma ran off from Mina to chase Brittany around.

"I guess, for a little bit. Emma got really sick yesterday so I don't want to push it."

Emma screamed at the top of her lungs as she chased Brittany down and knocked her to the grass. "Looks fine to me," Harriet said. "Excuse me for a second," she said, shading her eyes from the sun with her hand as she addressed her eldest. "William. Down."

"Not yet, Ma. I'm almost there!"

"My husband's home but you'll never notice him," Harriet said. "What do you say?"

"Why not."

The next thing they knew, there was a crashing noise at the side of the building.

"The bigger they are, the harder they fall," said Harriet, shaking her head.

Mina was terrified. "Do you need me to call an ambulance?"

Harriet chuckled. "Are you kidding? Nah. This happens all the time. Sometimes I wish he would hurt himself for once, get a free tuition, if you know what I mean. But there's a giant azalea bush over there he always lands in so—"

"Are you sure?" Mina was horrified.

Harriet put up her hand. "William? William!"

"Yeah, Ma," said William, walking over to them, unscathed.

"You have to get your right leg up on the roof first. It's stronger. It will anchor you. How many times do we have to go through this?"

"Sorry Ma. Next time," he said, brushing twigs and dirt off his uniform.

Mina followed Harriet back to her house. As she walked up the driveway with Emma, she noticed there were no flowers in Harriet's flowerbed at all. Just a patch of mangy-looking, twisted weeds.

"If you don't mind me asking, how do they allow this? I mean, Charlie . . ."

"Chuh. That Witmore's such a pig. You never heard the story? Of how he got wasted and hit on me at the homeowners' association annual party? How my husband punched him in the face?"

"Uh, no. That I would have remembered," said Mina. "But I guess as a widower . . ."

Harriet punched her in the arm. "Wifey was still around, dearie."

"Ewwwww," said Emma, who was watching William poke a slug with a stick.

"Anyway," Harriet said, "because we're all the way in the back here and no one sees our house, except our neighbors on both sides, and they had these huge hedges planted to, I guess, block us. Well, no one forces anything on us."

"I see. So no one lives across from you," Mina said, feeling unreasonably suspicious of Esther for maybe having a role in Witmore's aggressive flower-planting antics. Then feeling incredibly guilty for entertaining such an insidious thought.

"You got it," Harriet said, looking over her shoulder, and finished with, "Thank God for that" as she pushed open the front door.

The chaos of the Saunders home was almost disappointingly predictable. Mina knew the destruction Emma alone was capable of; here, in this home, it was like a flood had washed through, upending tables and chairs, pulling toys and books from shelves. From the ground to about four feet up, the scene was pure devastation.

Harriet kicked a pathway through a pile of laundry, dirty or clean, or perhaps both, to the living room. She gestured to a figure on the couch with her thumb. The figure, wearing a Black Sabbath concert T-shirt and a pair of torn jeans, was tapping wildly at a game controller. "Sammy," she said, with an affectionate smile. Then she turned to Sammy. "Sammy! We got company!"

Sammy didn't look up. "One second . . . Almost . . . Got it . . . Got it . . . YES! Done! Ha! Take that, she-beast!"

"Sammy's a video game designer," Harriet said. "He 'works from home.'" She shook her head. "Some job for a grown man, huh?"

"Job pays Acela," Sammy said, putting down the game control and rising from the couch. "And the mortgage. And the—"

"Okay, smartass. We got it," said Harriet, as he pulled her from behind into a tender hug and planted a soft kiss on her neck.

"Who's this?" he smiled brightly at Mina.

"Mina, Sammy. Sammy, Mina. She lives here."

"Really? I thought we knew everyone . . ."

"She kind of keeps to herself. Or she did. Actually," she giggled, "she hangs out with the old fogies."

"That's not—" Mina defended.

"Oh no?" Harriet teased. "Esther Erasmus?"

Sammy made a noise like he swallowed something gross. "Esther? She's the worst!"

"Esther's a lovely woman. She—"

"She and her mahjong cabal have it in for all of us," said Sammy. "Don't be fooled."

"Let's agree to disagree, okay?" Mina snapped.

Harriet and Sammy shared a silent look that spoke quite loudly, signaling that the conversation would be dropped but wasn't over.

"So what did you do today?" Harriet asked, scoping the room and its untouched chaos. "Did you miss me? More importantly, did you miss the kids?"

"I miss them because I have poor aim," he deadpanned, then broke into a fit of laughter. "Get it? Missed them? Poor aim? Get it?"

"Oh, very funny," Harriet said, sarcastic, shaking her head at Mina, then looking back at Sammy. "Seriously. How was your day?"

"I defeated the she-beast!" he said, triumphant.

"What about in the *real* world?" she chided.

"Your reality bores me, woman."

She looked back at Mina. "You see what I have to put up with?"

Sammy leapt into the kitchen and came out balancing a platter piled high with tiny pigs in blankets. "Kids! Lunch!"

"Not bad," said Harriet, and she helped herself to one. "Go ahead," said Harriet, motioning to Mina.

Mina took Harriet up on her offer. One bite and she had to admit it was pretty delicious.

"That's pure beef, baby," Sammy said, and winked at Harriet, who rolled her eyes. "And I also slathered a little Dijon mustard on the crescent dough before rolling the dogs in them. Kids think they don't like mustard but they don't know anything."

"He does this all the time and they gobble it right up. They're probably going to be mad when they grow up and we tell them how we tricked them."

"To hell with that. Let 'em figure out their own tricks for their own kids."

"Huh," said Mina, finishing her hot dog and taking another. "So you work from home?" she asked Sammy.

"My God. He's here all the time. I can't shake him."

"Sometimes I'd like to shake her," he said playfully and Harriet rolled her eyes at Mina. "See what I mean. You're lucky your husband works so much. What did you say he does again?"

"I didn't, actually," said Mina. "But I don't know. I think you're the lucky one. I mean, I never see Jack. Like, never."

"That sucks," said Sammy, wrapping his arms around Harriet and pulling her close. Harriet snuggled the back of her head into his shoulder.

"It is what it is," said Mina, and she helped herself to another hot dog, pained and deeply jealous of Harriet for having her husband in her life.

# 9

Two hours later, Mina and Emma pulled up the driveway of their own house, terrible heartburn making it impossible for Mina to ignore the fact that twenty pigs in blankets was probably too many.

What she did try to ignore, though, were the new mums that had been planted over the forty-eight hours since she and Jack had done away with their predecessors. This new batch seemed to mock her as she walked by them. She wondered if she could get Witmore to hit on her, and if Jack would punch him in the face if he did. Though she felt that, unlike Sammy Saunders, Jack wasn't a punch-him-in-the-face kind of guy. What about her uncle, then? Maybe this newly discovered uncle was that kind of man. But who knew? So many questions.

Upon entering the house, Mina took a deep breath before pressing the "play" button on the answering machine. Only three messages—couldn't be so bad. Except one of them was Jack, who would be detained one more day, but was looking forward to spending Saturday with her and Emma.

Just beyond the entryway, she could see the basement. There was something amiss, she could feel it and she could see it. It looked as if the door was open—not just unlocked, but open. Had Jack forgotten to lock the basement door? She moved closer.

Excitement now rose in her. Maybe if she just went downstairs for a few minutes, she could find something. Another clue to help her put the pieces together. To make more sense of everything.

But with the excitement there was fear. There was always the fear. The door had been locked on Barsheed's orders. What was down in the basement might be too much, might overwhelm her. She didn't have much faith in Barsheed; she found it hard to believe that what he told her could be true—that by remembering too much too soon, she might "check out" for good . . . But what if he was right?

Mina struggled with the frustration of not knowing and the fear of what knowing could do to her. Finally, curiosity won.

"Why don't you go play in your room for a little while," Mina said. Emma ran up the stairs and Mina headed for the basement.

Mina took a deep breath before switching on the light and walking down the stairs. Once in the basement, she looked around and spotted a stack of boxes. She headed over to them. Glancing through the labels, she noted how they were marked. And then she found one with "Wedding" scrawled over it in her handwriting.

The box wasn't sealed. The thought of Jack coming down here and looking through this box made her feel at once sad, because it made her begin to understand how lonely this marriage must be for him, living a life with a woman who only remembers the last several years. But it also comforted her, because how could a man who visits boxes of treasured memories be cheating on his wife? Unless guilt drove him to it . . . She pushed the idea out of her head.

Mina lifted the cardboard flaps and took out a white satin-covered book with "Wedding Memories" pressed in gold foil cursive letters on the cover. She opened it.

There she was, Mina—she was sure of it. But her hair was different. Long and dark. Her face was hers, sure, but it still seemed a stranger's face staring at her through a gauzy, ivory veil. Dark lipstick. Dark eye makeup. And a devilish fire in the eyes. She flipped through various pages, looking at the strange bride that had been her. At the strange woman with other women she didn't know, dressed in matching aubergine dresses. Friends she'd had. Friends she didn't have anymore.

She turned another page, and the next image took her breath away. Here the woman stood with a man. An older man. A man who was not Jack, but a man she knew. He had kind eyes and a thick shiny mane of silver hair. There was no salt-and-pepper beard, and he looked considerably younger in this picture, but she would still know this man anywhere. This was Alex, for sure. The picture confirmed that he'd told her the truth about who he was. This was all very real.

In the picture, the man was placing a necklace around the woman's neck. Mina pulled the album closer to her as she squinted to see. A pendant. A dragonfly. She was sure. Alex had called her "peanut," just like the man in the marsh. It was all coming together. At last, her life was starting to come back to her.

Just then, the phone rang, making her jump. It rang again, and she placed the book back in the box. Thinking it might be Jack, she wanted to answer it, and she ran up the basement stairs, turned off the light, and closed the door. But the phone had stopped ringing. After only two rings. Which was weird because the answering machine never picked up before four rings.

Realization hit. "Oh shit!" she said, and ran up to her bedroom. There she found Emma, holding the phone up to her face. She took the phone away from Emma and gulped, "Hello?"

"Mina Clark, please," came a curt yet familiar voice on the other end. Mina was somewhat relieved as she joined in the regular dance.

"This is she," said Mina, just as businesslike as the caller.

"By acknowledging that you are Mina Clark, you are acknowledging that you are able to speak about this matter. This is a private business matter. If this is not Mina Clark, please hang up—"

"Kim, you know it's me."

"Please be advised that this is an attempt to collect a debt, and any information . . ."

Mina pulled the phone away and counted to seven, which she knew by now was how long it took Kim to deliver her speech. She pulled it back to silence. "You're done?"

"I'm done."

"Good. Well how are you?" Mina asked.

"Your payment bounced," Kim snapped, somehow taking it personally.

"I know," said Mina, shamed.

"Well, if you knew, why didn't you call us to make another arrangement," asked Kim, still terse.

Now Mina could feel fury rising in her. Why was she on the defensive here? Why was she feeling guilty for having been forced to make a payment she knew, and had told this woman, she couldn't make? "Yes, like we haven't been through this before. Like if I don't make a payment when you want it, you threaten to sue me, so somehow the money's just magically supposed to appear and—"

"Look Mina—"

"Mrs. Clark, thank you."

"You gonna be like that?"

"You bet I am."

Kim let out a long sigh. "Okay, baby. That's your right. Can we set up another payment at least?"

"Oh, sure. Just set up—"

"Okay. Well, look. I want you to hang up the phone now and I'm gonna call you from another number. Promise me you'll pick up."

"What's the matter?"

"I'm goin' out for a break and I'm going to call you from my cell phone—"

"Why . . ."

"That's all I can tell you now. Count to thirty. When the phone rings, pick it up." And Kim hung up. Mina counted in her head as she walked over to check on Emma. Emma had trashed her room. Mina walked back to her own room just as the phone rang. She picked it up right away.

"Hello?"

"Look, I only got like five minutes here, and then I can't call you again, understand? So you gotta listen good. Okay?"

"Okay."

"Cuz they're not only gonna fire my ass if they know I'm telling you this. It's gonna be much worse than that," she said.

"Okay, okay. What is it?"

"Girl, you in trouble. You better start watching your ass."

"What do you mean?" Mina was more than a little taken aback by Kim's foreboding tone.

"Have you made any new friends lately?"

Mina had in the past several days made more new friends than she had in years, but she gave no reply.

"I'm gonna take that as a yes. Okay, well, here's how it goes. Don't trust anyone. You hear me, girl? No one."

"What do you mean—"

"What I mean is, the bank's watching you. You know this. And they got folks working for them. Out in the field and such. Spies, I guess you could call them. Special agents. Could be anyone—"

"Kim, are you drinking?"

"Look, I'm not shitting you here. They're around to keep tabs on you. They're gonna tell you all kinds of stories, like they're looking after you—that kind of thing. So you gotta know this. It's gonna get much worse for you soon, especially if you keep bouncing your payments. You and your family are gonna be in some serious trouble. You gotta watch your ass—"

The connection cut out. Mina checked the caller ID and tried to call Kim back. She was greeted by a few shrill siren-like noises and an automated message. "The call you have made cannot be completed. Please check the number—"

She hung up and dialed again. "The call you have made cannot be—"

Mina hung up again. Now she had to pull herself together. This was not adding up. No phone gets disconnected that quickly. Why *did* she have so many new friends in just a short time? Coincidence? Maybe she had decided to open herself up to having new friends. Although all of them . . .Harriet and the other mothers, Char-a'tee, Alex . . .they'd all seemed to steamroll her into being friends with them, hadn't they? And what of her old friends? She hadn't heard from Esther in days. Was Esther still angry with her? Was she pushing Esther away? And how the hell did she get her car back?

Mina couldn't think clearly and she began to fear the worst. That Dr. Barsheed might have been right. That knowing too much too soon could take her mind, and now she was in the midst of losing it completely. Was anything any of these people told her even true?

Mina found Emma in her room, sitting in the middle of the floor, naked. She had managed to find and open a set of magic markers, and had completely covered the entire surface area of her hands in bright green. She had also drawn a giant green circle around one eye. With a red magic marker, she'd colored in her belly button, spilling over to her tummy. It looked like she'd been stabbed.

Mina sank against the doorjamb and cried. Emma came over to her, snuggled her mischievously marked-up naked body into her mother's lap, and said, ever so sweetly, "Don't cry, Monny," before peeing all over Mina's pants.

Mina pulled them both into the shower and afterward heated up a can of soup for dinner, which Mina barely touched. She couldn't stop thinking about her conversation with Kim. How completely weird it was. So weird, it was like it could not even be real. And that's what worried her the most.

After dinner, Mina gave Emma her medicine and put her to bed. Emma clutched PP to her, sniffing gleefully at the bunny's filthy ears, and dropped off into an easy sleep. Mina envied her so much for that. That something so small could take all her cares away.

Mina headed downstairs and opened a bottle of red wine. She filled a glass, intending to close the bottle before heading to bed, but decided instead to take both the glass and bottle upstairs with her. Stinky ears for grown ups.

Mina placed the glass and bottle on her nightstand. The remote in hand, she turned on the TV and realized the cable had been turned off. Again. She switched off the TV and decided she'd look for her tapes. She reached into her purse, and even turned it over on her bed when she couldn't retrieve them. Nothing. "Dammit!" Mina said when she remembered she'd left them in Jack's car, which was now parked God only knew where. In front of God only knew which hotel or sleazy motel . . .

She now had a vision of Jack, her Jack, naked in a by-the-hour room, splayed out on a heart-shaped bed next to a leggy brunette, also naked. Amber. Maybe she was a leggy redhead? And they seemed to be reviewing meeting notes.

She shook that image away. Just because she hadn't heard from Jack didn't mean he was cheating on her. Kim said he wasn't, and the bank would know. But Kim also said to trust no one. Did she mean not to trust Kim either? And about what? About Jack not having an affair with this bosomy boss, Amber? About not trusting anyone else? It was all too confusing.

Mina poured more wine into her glass and noticed her notebook among the debris she'd spilled from her purse. She shrugged her shoulders and picked it up. She sat back in her bed, the soft down pillows sucking her into restful comfort. Her eyes felt heavy as she sipped her wine then flipped through the pages. The meaningless scribbles. The doodles. The dragonfly . . .

Mina was asleep, she guessed, for the next thing she knew, she was sitting in a large auditorium, lights flashing and music blaring. She could feel the light and the music pulsing within her, like it was all her very blood.

She sat by herself in an ocean of strangers. She didn't recognize anyone else in the audience. The seat on her left was empty. To her right, a young woman was dancing and singing and started to jump wildly around, flailing her arms as if at a Grateful Dead concert.

Suddenly, the music changed. The seating area went completely dark and the audience began to cheer loudly and wildly. Then all the lights in the auditorium faced the stage, which exploded in a burst of smoke and light. A platform in the middle lifted as the form of a man who'd been curled into a fetal position rose to prominence on the stage.

The crowd erupted in frenetic chants: "ZANDER! ZANDER! ZANDER!" Zander? Mina, thought. Zander? Of course. The tapes. She was missing the tapes. Of course.

Then the whole auditorium, including the stage, went completely dark, and, oddly, also completely silent.

"What'd I miss?" came a voice from her left. Mina turned to find Char-a'tee there.

"What are you—"

"Shhh!" came an angry hissing whisper from the young girl on her right, whose face had now changed to become Emma's face. Mina rubbed her eyes and looked back at the girl, whose face remained that of her three-year-old daughter.

"Oh, you gonna love this, Lily," said Char, whose face flashed as Mina's, the face Mina had worn in the wedding album, and then back again to Char's. "I know how much you love yourself some shit like this, Lily. Oooo-weeee!"

The man on the stage popped up into a standing position, like a jack-in-the-box, and the crowd went wild at the sight of him in all his shiny-suited glory. The rock star preacher.

*"You are the light of the world!"* he exclaimed, and the audience was flooded with light.

"You are the light of the world!" the frenzied mob parroted back.

*"No! Not Me! It's You! All of you! You! Are! The! Light! Of! The! World!"* he shouted back at them, before swirling lithely down a fireman's pole onto another platform on the stage.

Mina was absolutely enthralled by the energy of this man. The excitement exploding in this theater, this space. This following. She'd never experienced anything quite like it, yet she also felt this was a lie she was telling herself. Because this was all familiar to her, of course. Because she listened to the tapes of Zander Randalls almost daily. Though the tapes had never seemed quite like this. Quite so . . . electric.

The man called Zander had the audience under his spell, for saying not much, for doing so little. For shouting out words that weren't even his, it occurred to Mina.

But it didn't really matter to her at all because like the rest of the crowd, she was hooked. And they didn't notice or care even a little bit. They cheered and screamed and jumped and danced as Zander continued to bounce around on the stage, throwing his fist in the air as he chanted into a microphone that seemed to have appeared in his hand magically.

*"YOU are the salt of the Earth!"* he belted. *"YOU! ARE! THE! SALT! OF! THE! EARTH!"*

Char-a'tee shouted back at him, along with the others in the audience, throwing her fist up, with what seemed a thousand gold dangling bangles shaking up and down as she waved her hand wildly around in the air.

"Come on, Lily! Let yourself go!"

The woman to Mina's right, who was still wearing Emma's face, was now standing on her chair. She began tearing off her top.

"No!" said Mina, protectively. But when the woman pulled the blouse over her face, it was Esther's face she wore.

"Holy shit," said Mina, trying desperately to tell her conscious self, from this wacko dream-place she was in, to please lay off the wine before bed on days that were as strange as this one had been.

"Pretty fucked up shit, huh?" Char-a'tee shouted back at Mina. Mina nodded.

"Well, you think that's crazy, check out the stage," she said, and Mina did as she was told.

The man was still dancing and prancing, preaching and panting, and a tunnel now formed between Mina and him. A passage as clear and quiet as a pool in a country glen, with everything that surrounded it a blurry swirl of color and light and intense sound. Mina felt herself flying through the tunnel, though she was very aware of her body staying firmly planted in her seat. And she could feel Char pulling on both her arms, weighing her down. "I got-chu, Lily!"

Mina felt drunk and dizzy. Her heart raced and she couldn't bear the sensation. She closed her eyes in a vain attempt to protect herself. But she knew she had to look. Of course she had to look.

"Okay, Lily. You ready for this?" came Char-a'tee's voice just as Mina opened her eyes. "Brace yourself, baby . . ."

And now Mina was face to face with the man on the stage, though her body was still being held in her seat by Char. She could feel Char-a'tee's hands on her, and yet here she was. Her face to his. The face of Alex. The face of her long-lost uncle. Until the face changed, she surmised, as that seemed to be the pattern in this dream. Right?

Then he spoke.

"Here's where things are going to start to get weird," he said.

# 10

Mina awoke to the sensation of soft kisses on her face. She opened her eyes. "It's you," she smiled sleepily. "When'd you get back?"

"About three minutes ago," Jack said. "Traveled all night to get back to you."

"Romantic," she said.

"Red-eye."

"Ah. So how was the . . . whatever it was you were doing?"

Jack hesitated, Mina felt, just a second too long, and suspicion triggered in her like a switch. "Conference," he said. "I told you . . ."

"Not really."

"Of course I did. I was sure I did."

"Maybe it was Amber you told," she snapped.

"Amber was with me," he said, unthinking rather than insensitive.

"Of course she was," Mina jumped out of bed and headed to the bathroom. He followed her; she closed the door on him.

"You're mad at me?"

"No," she called from the other side of the door.

"I skipped the dinner last night. All I wanted was to come home to you. To Emma," he said, but she kept the door shut.

"And when do you leave again?" she called.

Again, a hesitation just a moment too long. "Tomorrow morning."

She threw open the door. "Tomorrow? Sunday? Are you fucking serious?"

"Amber—"

"Fuck Amber, Jack. And fuck you." She slammed it shut again.

"Don't be like that. You know I have to . . ."

She opened the door again and faced him. "You have to jump every time she snaps her fingers? What are you, her fucking dog? You can't tell her you have a life? A child who needs you around sometimes? Forget about me. What about Emma? Don't you know how your not being here affects her?"

"Mina, you know I don't have a choice," he said, trying to stay composed. "You think I like going to that cesspool all the time? Selling crap I don't give a shit about? I travel around the country to sell doorknobs, Mina. Freaking *doorknobs!* How would you like it if that was what you had to do all the time? Huh? But really, what choice do I have? Thanks to this fucking mess we're in. Thanks to—"

"Thanks to what? Huh? Say it. Say it, Jack!"

"Forget it, okay? I'm just sick of not having a choice, is all."

"Of course you have a choice, Jack. Just choose us."

His patience was slipping. "Right. And then what? Then neither of us will be bringing in any money." His words were becoming increasingly terse. "So then we'll, what? Move in with that horrible Esther after we lose the house?" His words sliced through her heart.

"Don't talk about Esther like that. At least she's around for us," she shouted. She slammed the bathroom door on him again. She sat on the floor and she cried.

"Mina," he said, and she could tell by the sound of his voice that he was also now on the floor. "I'm so sorry, Mina. I didn't mean it. It's just . . . Can you just try and understand what this is like? What I'm up against here? It's not always easy . . ."

He asked her to open the door, but Mina had stopped listening. She felt herself numbing to the frustration and the hurt as she stood up. She watched herself in the mirror as Jack continued to speak. She knew he was speaking words but she was numb to what they were.

*You are the bus driver of the route of your life. Why aren't you driving! Your passengers are waiting!*

The man's words—the man from the tapes. Zander Randalls speaking to her. The words resonated within her as she stood there, and for the first time she could feel that they were not mere words. They were a call to action that had finally manifested within her and, like a battery, charged her to life.

So instead of opening the door for Jack, she took a shower. She did her hair and brushed her teeth. She put on a light layer of makeup, then went back to the drawer where she stored her cosmetics. She burrowed through the various compacts and tubes with her fingers, producing a smoke-gray eyeliner and dark lipstick. Once on, she knew this makeup didn't go with her light coloring and hair. But now she looked more like the bride in the album she'd unearthed the day before.

When Mina finally opened the bathroom door, Jack was still sitting there. "What are you doing?" he asked, taken aback by her appearance.

"I'm going out," she said, and dressed quickly as she spoke. "I don't know when I'll be back."

"But where are you going?"

"To see some friends," she said. Mina slipped a light gray cardigan sweater over the white T-shirt she wore. She looked at herself in the full-length mirror. She frowned. She returned to the walk-in closet, dug around for a while, unsure of what she was looking for. Then she pulled out a black leather jacket with a faux-leopard collar. She didn't know how she knew it was even there or that she had it at all. She slipped on the jacket and walked past Jack without saying a word.

Finding the Queens neighborhood where Pearls of Wisdom was located via car was less of a struggle than Mina had thought it would be, though she couldn't pinpoint the exact location of the dental spa. Not that she needed to know where it was exactly. She felt that simply by being close, by being in this neighborhood and letting the Universe know she wanted to see Char-a'tee, she would run into her.

*Don't just sit there. Dance your dream! The Universe wants you to dance!*

That may have been a crazy thought, but not the craziest of the day, she well knew. After all, wasn't it just a little peculiar that she felt so compelled to see this strange woman she'd only met a couple of times? Why had she felt so compelled to see Char-a'tee? She had no idea, but she was hoping fate would be on her side as she parallel parked her car in an open spot.

*If you put it out there, what you want . . . Then what you want will come to you . . .*

Mina slipped into a run-down looking diner and ordered a coffee and a lemon-poppyseed muffin. As she took her first bite, her phone rang.

She looked at the caller ID. Not Jack, but not an 888 number either. It was a number with a 718 area code, which meant Queens. Had she given Char-a'tee her number after all? She was feeling a little confused. But she couldn't deny feeling a twinge of excitement as she picked up the call.

"Hello?"

"Mina," came the voice from the other end.

She had not remembered giving Alex her phone number either, but there had been so much to process the past couple of days. Of course it was possible.

"Oh, hi," she said, surprising herself at how crestfallen she sounded.

"Not expecting me," he said more than asked.

"Not really. No."

"Ah. Well, I just looked for you at the playground but you weren't there."

"No."

"Jack was there."

"Oh?"

"With Emma."

"Wait—you didn't . . ."

"What? Talk to him? No, no way. They didn't see me. But I do need to see you. I have to talk to you about something."

"What is it?"

"Where are you?" he asked, and she gave him the name of the diner, read from a nearby menu. "Stay where you are. I'll be there in twenty minutes."

It seemed only moments later that Alex entered the diner. He had managed somehow to find Char'a-tee, who sashayed behind him in a pair of gold spandex pants, zebra-print heels, and, oddly, a navy blue peacoat. Alex seemed not to notice Char-a'tee, who, once she caught Mina's eye, began walking behind him in the manner of a cartoon character, as Alex acknowledged Mina with a nod and a wave. Mina looked away and giggled as they approached.

Char spoke first. "I saw this guy wandering around outside," she said. "Figured he'd lead me to you."

"Ms. Pryce," Alex said, smiling warmly. "I didn't see you there."

"Hmph," said Char, with a sassy shrug of her shoulders that made her dangling beaded earrings, the size of children's hands, jingle. "That, and I don't trust him trolling around in my backyard, if you know what I mean."

"Oh, he's okay!" said Mina defensively, though how could she be sure? Alex gave her a warm, reassuring smile that relaxed her.

"Whatever," said Char, now turning her attention to Mina's plate. She scrunched up her face at the remnants of muffin that lay in crumbles there. "What kind of shit is that?"

"Breakfast," said Mina. "A muffin."

"That ain't no kinda muffin," she sniffed. "And a muffin ain't no kind of breakfast. Let's have some eggs and bacon—and whatever Vladimir over here wants."

Alex chuckled, seemingly charmed. "It's Alex," he said. "Vladimir isn't even a Russian name."

"Whatever you say, baby. As long as I get my breakfast, I'll call you anything you like." Now she turned her attention to Mina. "So what's your business here, Lily?" she asked, scooping up a clump of muffin and chomping it down.

"Actually . . ." Mina began.

Char spat. "Shit's dry!" she said and shook her head. She proceeded to take a sip of Mina's coffee, which she managed to spill on her coat. "Well, ain't that a sonofabitch," she said, taking off the coat and hanging it over the back of her chair. "Never liked that piece of shit coat anyway and . . ." she trailed off.

There was a silence as Alex and Mina waited politely for Char to finish her thought. But she never did. So Mina spoke. "Actually, I was trying to find you," she said.

"Well, I know you ain't here for the food," Char said with a giant laugh. "So what can I do for you, Miss Lily?"

Mina smoothed her hair with her hand and chose her words carefully. "Well . . . I wanted to know how you knew where I lived, for starters," she said. And then more forcefully, "And how you got my car back."

Char stared at Mina a minute and took a quick glance at Alex before she spoke.

"Baby, I didn't get your car back," she said.

"Why, yes you did. You even wrote me a note and—"

"Nope," she shook her head. "Not me. Why don't you ask Baryshnikov over there?"

Just then the waiter came over with Char's breakfast and she grabbed up a giant slab of bacon. Mina tried to catch Alex's eye, but he looked away.

"And while you're at it," Char said, chewing away at her food, "why don't you tell her why you keep planting cash in her purse."

"Is that true? Alex? Is what she's saying true?"

Alex let out a deep sigh. "Everyone needs a guardian angel sometimes," he said. "What's the big deal?" This last question he posed to Char. She just folded her arms across her ample bosom and clicked her tongue at him.

"I'm confused . . ." said Mina.

Alex put his hand on Mina's shoulder. "I told you the other day that I am your uncle. And that's true, a hundred percent true. But there's more to the story than that, I'm afraid. And I'm not sure you're ready to know . . ." he trailed off.

"I can handle it," Mina snapped, losing her patience. "Tell me."

He shook his head. "No. Not yet. Let's just say I owe you much more than some pocket change and a few car payments."

"I'll say!" Char said.

"What else then?" she said, joking but nervous. "How about Emma's school tuition? How about we throw that in and call it a deal?"

"Good one, Lily!" said Char, with a big laugh.

Alex did not laugh. In fact, his gaze turned dead serious. "No," he said, solemnly. "I kind of owe you my life."

"What? Oh, that's just silly," Mina said. "I mean . . . that doesn't make any sense at all. Does it?" she asked, looking to Char. Now Char looked away. "Oh my God. What do you know about this? About any of this? Who are you anyway?"

Char just shrugged her shoulders and sucked down her drink. "It ain't for me to tell," she said.

"I don't like being lied to," said Mina.

"You think I like keeping things from you?" Alex snapped.

They sat for a while in silence as Char finished her bacon and eggs and pancakes, and Alex quietly and deliberately sipped his coffee, glaring at Mina as he did. Once Char had mopped up the last of her eggs with her toast and licked her fingers clean, Alex summoned the waiter for the bill, which he paid. Then the unlikely trio headed out of the diner into the street, Alex walking a couple of steps ahead of the women.

Mina decided to amuse herself and Char by mocking Alex's gait, as Char had when she first came into the restaurant, and both women burst out laughing.

"You know, Char-a'tee," said Mina, gasping for breath between chuckles. "We're a lot alike," she said, trying to connect to the other woman.

Char smirked. "Shit, Lily. We ain't nothing alike."

"No seriously. Think about it. I know we come from different places and all but we—"

Char tapped her teeth with a long green and purple fingernail. "No baby. We different, me and you. You, you let the world bulldoze you. That kid of yours. Your husband coming and going as he pleases. Those damn banks. I would never take the kinda shit you take like it's a fucking vitamin every day. And that's a *huge* fucking difference, if you ask me." Now Char walked a few paces ahead, looking into store windows.

Mina was annoyed. Hadn't she just walked out on Jack that morning? Hadn't she been firm with Emma, making her apologize to her teacher? What did this woman know anyway? She picked up her pace to keep up. "I can stand up for myself," she said.

"Uh-huh," said Char, matter-of-factly.

"I can!"

Char crossed her arms over herself again. "Oh yeah?" she challenged. "Then why didn't you press your friend over there to tell you what the fuck he was talking about when he said you saved his life? Huh?"

"I . . ."

"You nothing. You just let it sit there in the air, like you were scared to offend him or something."

"I was trying to be polite."

"Yeah, well, sometimes you gotta get past that. Ain't no one being polite to you."

"But—"

"Look, Lily. Ain't no one looking out for you out there. 'Cept maybe me."

"And me," Alex called back over his shoulder.

"Hmmph," said Char. "Well, me at least. But I'm telling you this. You got to start looking out for yourself now. You gotta start going after what you want."

"But I do go after what I want!" Mina said. It was something she felt, but Char was right; there was no way she could prove she'd been anything but accommodating to everything and everyone else, and at her own expense. Jack. Her daughter. The school. Everything. Becoming aware of this was starting to make her incredibly uncomfortable.

"Prove it then," Char said. "Come on. In here."

Mina looked at the storefront Char wanted her to enter. "Smitty's?"

"Yep. Smitty's." Char looped her arm through Mina's, and cupped her mouth with her other hand. "Come on, Gorbachev. We're going in here," she called.

Char pulled Mina through the front door of what appeared to be a consignment shop. She was assaulted by the aroma of mothballs and age and dust. She felt like she had just climbed into a musty trunk in a neglected attic in a house the world had forgotten about.

The second assault was visual, in the form of a very ancient, yet very elegant woman wearing a silver silken turban secured in the front by a jewel-encrusted dragonfly pin.

"Ooo-weee. Bet-choo want that pin, Lily," Char joked. Mina felt embarrassed by this because Char was right. What did Char know? And why wouldn't she tell?

"May I help you?" the woman asked in a tone neither pleasant nor terse, just matter-of-fact. She fondled her turban pin absently while she awaited an answer.

Alex came up behind Mina. "Go ahead and ask her," he said softly, just for her ears. She found herself oddly aware of his cologne for the first time today. Had he just gone and doused himself with it?

She didn't ask. "It's not for sale," Mina whispered.

"Everything here is for sale," he whispered back.

"Nah, we just looking for now," Char told the woman.

"Okay, well do let me know when you're ready," she said, and she walked away.

Char and Mina started looking around; the shopkeeper hovered nearby.

"I said we're good now," said Char, loud enough to be obnoxious, and the shopkeeper disappeared.

There seemed no order or organization to the way items were laid out in Smitty's. Random old things, randomly placed, impossible to retrieve without considerable digging. Much like the state of Mina's own brain. An old pop-up toaster was placed between a stack of vinyl jazz records, some broken, and a pair of fuzzy slippers. An assortment of mismatched eggcups was surrounded by well-loved stuffed animals. Mina thought of PP and

Emma, and felt a pang of guilt about leaving the house without seeing her.

But then she was distracted by an item that caught her eye. Perched on a stack of old picture frames was a glint of beaded gold, the top of an ancient perfume bottle. Its delicate pink glass base looked like the bloom of a tulip; a dragonfly perched above it. Mina felt the same familiar warmth in her at the sight of the dragonfly. She looked at the price.

"Ouch," she said, and then started walking off.

"You know you want that, Lily," said Char, a disjointed voice from behind her. "You want that more than the pin."

"It's pretty," said Mina, trying to sound calm.

"But how much do you want it?" Char asked.

Mina shook her head. "I can't spring for it today," she said, feeling slightly embarrassed that she couldn't buy it, even if she thought the piece was overpriced at a hundred dollars.

"Use a credit card."

"I, uh . . . I didn't bring one," Mina lied, not wanting to admit she no longer had a working one.

"Maybe your boyfriend?" Char baited, nodding at Alex, who was admiring an old model sailboat.

Mina gasped. "He's my uncle!"

"Oh, sure," said Char, shaking her head. "Whatever he tells you."

Mina looked at Alex, who was surveying a cracked aquarium. She watched him knock on it and crane his neck to poke inside. She shook her head. "Why don't you think he's my uncle," said Mina. "What do you know?"

Char opened her mouth to speak then clamped it shut. "Nah. Forget it," she said. "You'll find out soon enough."

"Sure I will," said Mina.

"Hey, if you want this precious little bottle so much, why don't you, you know . . ." Char made a motion of slipping something into her pocket, while nodding and raising her eyebrows.

"Steal it?!" Mina shouted.

"Is everything alright?" asked the shopkeeper, who had glided mysteriously back into view.

"We're fine," Mina snapped, and the shopkeeper disappeared again. She looked at Char. "I can't believe you'd suggest I would—"

"Oh Lily, I was just kidding! Man, you got no sense of humor." Mina didn't believe her, but decided to let it go.

"Sure is a pretty piece, though," said Char.

"It is," said Mina.

"And don't you deserve something pretty like that? Weren't we just saying you gotta DO for YOU?"

"I guess."

"Then you gotta get it, Lily."

"But she wants a hundred dollars for it! I mean, I don't have a hundred dollars to just—"

"Yeah, we all want things. I want to wake up in the morning shitting diamonds. Don't mean we get what we want. But I bet she ain't sold nothing for weeks. Look at all this crap."

"You have a point."

"And I bet she's tracking us like the little old buzzard she is because she's hungry and she's got no money to eat. I bet she'd sell you your pretty little bottle for the price of a steak."

"Well, she does look a little gaunt . . ."

"So make the old swami an offer!" Char yelled.

"I heard that!" the shopkeeper called from the next aisle.

"Come on, Lily. You can do this. I got'cher back."

Mina nodded. "Sure. I can do this. Sure." Mina felt a new confidence rising in her. She looked over at Alex, who was smiling at her. She smiled back. She picked up the perfume bottle and brought it to the counter.

"Excuse me," Mina said, and the shopkeeper turned around.

"Yes?"

Mina stood there dumbly until Char elbowed her in the ribs. "Excuse me . . ."

"Yes . . ."

"I would like to buy this perfume bottle," Mina said, and smiled stupidly at Char.

"One hundred dollars," the shopkeeper said. Mina froze and Char nudged her again. Mina cleared her throat. She looked the woman right in the eye. It felt so good, so empowering, to hold her gaze in this way. As if Mina's gaze were a cage she held the other woman in. She felt, for the first time in who knew how long . . . perhaps ever, in complete control of the situation. "Thirty dollars," she said, never breaking eye contact.

The woman was quiet a moment. "Fifty dollars."

Mina felt a strange sensation rising up in her. It was both supernatural and highly natural. She could feel it like molecules vibrating within her. Molecules of strength and power and control all now coming to life in her.

"Thirty dollars," Mina said in a cool, measured tone that she never remembered using before. She pulled a ten and a twenty out of her purse and placed them on the counter.

The air was tense with the negotiation, and Mina was sure she could stand her ground till the following Tuesday if she had to, and she would not be backing down.

The woman behind the counter let out a big sigh and looked away. "Fine. Thirty dollars. It's yours. Just leave and don't come back," the woman said. She snatched the bills from the countertop and stormed to the back of the store.

"And that's how it's done!" Char beamed. "How do you feel, Lily?"

Mina felt like she'd just had the best sex of her life. "I feel pretty good, actually," she said, also feeling slightly flushed and even a little bit sweaty.

"Good. Good girl. Now you gotta take that and use it, baby. You know you got it in you now, Lily. Now you do it."

"She's right, Mina," said Alex, who was clutching an old Batman comic book. "Well, I guess I won't be getting this today," he said, putting it down. Mina felt a little guilty about that, and then Char tugged on her arm and distracted her. "I gotta go now," she said. "Come on."

The three slipped out through the front door. "A pleasure doing business with you," Char called over her shoulder as they headed out into the street.

"Nice work in there," Alex said.

"Thanks, Stalin," said Char.

"I was talking to Mina," he said, and he gazed at Mina with a look of deep, genuine sincerity. "You're really coming more and more into your old self every day."

"What does that mean? What does that—"

Char burst out laughing. "He's right, baby. I guess you and me are kind of the same after all, Lily."

Mina walked between her friends, so many emotions coursing through her. They strode in silence until they ended up back in front of the diner.

"Time for me to go now," said Char. "I think the two of you got some talking to do. Lily, you take care, girl. Stalin, try not to—"

"I think we all know I'm not Russian now. Joke's getting old," said Alex, annoyed but charmed all the same.

Char shrugged her shoulders. "Well, I can stop yanking your chain. And maybe now you can start being straight with our girl here. Okay?"

"Okay," he said. And with that Char-a'tee Pryce took her leave. As they watched her waddle out of sight, the waiter came out of the diner. "Someone left this?" he asked. He was holding Char's peacoat.

Alex reached out for it. He handed it to Mina. "You take it."

"Oh, but I have no idea how to get in touch with her" said Mina. "Maybe we should just leave it?"

He shook his head. "I think she wanted you to have it," he said. "Look." Alex reached into the breast pocket of the coat and pulled out a photograph.

It was an old photograph from the 1970s, edged with white. In the picture was an older couple. Alex asked, "Recognize them?"

"I don't think so," Mina said, squinting at the image and trying to make sense of it.

"You will," said Alex. "Please just hold on to these." And Mina complied.

"Can I ask you something?" Mina said.

He nodded.

"Why did you say that before? That I saved your life? Were you just being dramatic?"

"Oh no," he said. "Not in the least." And he smiled that smile again. A full mouth lost in a salt-and-pepper sea of beard. Kind eyes crinkling under the edge of the black wool hat. She couldn't decide if she thought he was attractive or not, but there was definitely something . . . something about him that compelled her.

"So?"

"Can you give me a ride home?" he asked. "I promise I'll tell you more when we get there."

Mina hesitated. Ever since this man had come into her life—or rather come back into her life, apparently—things had started getting strange. And yet, things were also feeling more normal than they had in years. She put her hand in her pocket and felt her new small dragonfly treasure with the tips of her fingers. It put her at ease. Now she smiled at Alex. "Okay," she said. "Sure. Let's go."

In the car, Mina placed the peacoat in the back seat. Alex turned to her and placed his hand on hers as she drove through the neighborhood. "Did it feel good to you, Mina? What you did in the store back there? Did it feel . . . you know . . . *normal?*"

"Honestly . . . It felt a little weird that it felt so normal. I can't really explain it I guess . . ."

"I wasn't kidding about what I said back there, Mina. You used to be more like that. You know. Before . . ."

"You mean when I had the black hair?" she asked him.

"You remember?" he asked.

She shook her head. "I saw the wedding album."

"Ah," he said, and they sat in silence for a while as Mina drove.

"That's how I knew you weren't lying, Alex. I saw you in the album."

"It was a beautiful day," he said wistfully.

"You gave me away."

"I did."

Mina pulled the car over to the curb. She threw the gearshift into park and she looked at him. "Are you being straight with me, Alex? Are you *really* my uncle?"

"Of course. Why would I lie?"

"*Are* you my father?" she asked, shocking herself, as it was a question she hadn't planned to ask him again, but it popped out of her mouth all the same.

Alex seemed distant now. He stared out the window on his side of the car. "I told you. Your father disappeared a long time ago. God only knows. He's probably dead by now." Alex looked at her now, tears forming in his eyes. "I hope he is anyway . . ."

"I'm sorry . . ."

"You shouldn't be. I'm sorry to say it but your father was an ass. I hope he burns in hell."

Now Mina was uncomfortable—with the discussion, the emotion. She slammed the car back into gear and kept driving until she pulled up to a house.

"So you do remember where it is," he said. "You notice you didn't ask me for directions at all? Not even an address?"

"I have no idea how that happened."

He chuckled. "You spent a lot of time here. When you were young. I mean, when I was around for you, you did . . . Do you want to come in?"

There was no way her curiosity would let her say anything but yes.

Alex grabbed the coat from the backseat and waved for her to follow him. She followed him up the driveway to a flagstone path that led to the back of the yard. There was nothing particularly impressive about the yard; it was neither well-manicured nor overgrown. In fact, nothing seemed to grow at all but grass. For some reason this made Mina sad, though, she rationalized, at least there were no mums.

Inside, it was as if she had stepped into a dream of her creation, with every stick of furniture, every picture, every throw pillow, just as she thought it ought to be. It wasn't a grand space by any measure. It wasn't elegant or chic or even well-designed. It was just . . . homey. The home had the thing her house in Easton Estates lacked most: a soul.

"Can I get you a drink?" Alex asked.

"No thank you," she replied, her eyes darting to various elements that drew them. A small piano. A Victorian mirror. A framed photo on a dark wood demilune table of a woman with blonde hair who wasn't Mina but could have been. She started to walk toward the photo but Alex jumped in front of her and turned it face down. "Not yet, Mina. Soon. But now . . . now that would be too much I think."

"Okay," she said, trusting him. Why did she trust him like she did? And then, in other moments, why did she trust him so little?

He pulled out the photo from the peacoat again. "This is Stan and Tanya," he said. "They raised you."

She snatched the photo away. "My parents? They're so old . . ."

"Your foster parents. They took you in, you know, after your mother . . . After she was taken from us. Eventually. There were a few homes before and . . ."

"Not you?"

"Me?"

"You're my uncle. Why didn't I live with you?"

He shook his head. "Things were different back then. I couldn't take you. I couldn't raise you—I couldn't give you the life you deserved. I had my reasons. Anyway, they took care of you. Russian immigrants. Good people. Loved you like their own."

"Russian? So that's why I know Russian?"

"Yes."

"Huh."

"What? Are you disappointed? Did you think there was more intrigue in your life? Before suburbia?" he teased, but his tone was not really playful. In fact, it was even a bit snide.

"What's wrong with my life?" she asked. "What's wrong with—"

"Don't get me wrong. You married a good man. Maybe a bit of a soft man, but a good man all the same. You have a beautiful child.

It's just a life I never imagined you living. I mean, I guess I encouraged you and . . ."

"And . . .?"

"Don't worry about it," he said.

She turned her attention back to the photo. "So I guess they're not around any more then?"

"I'm afraid not. I'm sorry. But they were very old even then."

"I see."

"But they were very good to you, very good to you. They were just limited in what they could teach you. In what they could do for you. I sent money. I made sure you went to the best schools possible. That your needs were met. But this neighborhood," he said, shaking his head, "it was a little different then. A little rough around the edges, to put it mildly."

"I still don't understand. Where were you?"

"Well, when I was around, I actually lived in the apartment upstairs. This part of the house was yours. And theirs. So, like I said, I could look out for you when I was around. But I traveled so much."

"For what?"

"Business."

"Like Jack," she half laughed.

"Something like that, yes," he said. He took the framed photo he'd placed face down and stuffed it into the table's small drawer.

"You always had an edge about you, Mina. Just like your mom. A feisty little thing you were. You definitely always had it. But this neighborhood, this life. It really brought it out in you."

"Good to know I used to be a pain in the ass," Mina smiled.

Just then Alex startled her by pulling her into a hug. She reluctantly hugged him back, more due to shock and surprise than anything else, but it felt nice to her to be in his arms. It felt good to be there. Except when she relaxed more into the hug, he pulled her closer. Her face, turned, rested against his chest. His chest hair pricked through his thin shirt and tickled her face, and she could smell now very clearly that he wore Old Spice.

The moment, it was so familiar. It was eerily familiar, in fact. She could not quite understand why, but all of a sudden, the secure, warm feeling she had in her uncle's arms turned. All of a sudden, she felt a deep foreboding. A tremendous sense of fear. In her head, words repeated over and over again, *Get out of the house! Get out of the house now!*

Mina squirmed free of Alex's embrace. "I have to go," she said, feeling deeply panicked.

"Oh, Mina, I'm sorry. I freaked you out. Too soon. You just . . . I just . . . I just missed you so much and . . ."

The voice in her head grew louder, more insistent. *Get out of the house! You are in danger! Get out of the house!*

She had no idea what the hug had triggered in her, what deep-buried dark secret this moment had brought to the surface, but there was no way she was sticking around to find out. All she knew was that she had to run. She had to run, and fast. She had to get away from the house! And, as deep as she could feel inside of her, she knew that if she didn't get out of the house, she would surely die.

"I have to go," she said, and she ran.

"Can I call you later?" Alex called after her. "Mina? Please, there's still so much more to talk about. I—"

Mina raced through the front door as fast as her feet could carry her. She drove home quickly and intently, her mind racing with questions and doubts. What the hell was going on? Why were things making so little sense? Fuck, nothing seemed to make sense anymore.

# 11

The sun was starting to set as Mina pulled into her driveway. She wondered where the day had gone. But even in this light it was easy to see that her satisfying patch of unplanted earth had again been replaced by an obnoxious new profusion of mums, these ones fiery orange and yellow. "What the fuck!" Mina scoffed as she walked past them. She clicked her key in the lock and opened the front door.

"Witmore returned," she heard Jack call from the other room as she entered the house. There was something not quite right about the house, she felt. Something about it was just too quiet.

"How are you doing?" Jack asked, and he entered the foyer. "Feeling any better?"

"I was," she snapped, more harshly than she would have liked. She wasn't angry at Jack, not anymore. But she wasn't about to tell him what had just transpired in that house in Queens and why she was as worked up as she was.

"I'm sorry Mina. You know I didn't mean—"

He looked so good to her right now, casually dressed in jeans and black *Star Wars* T-shirt, his feet bare. It was so rare she saw him when he wasn't buttoned up in a suit, but the other night and today . . . It was a good look for him, she supposed—there was something about this look, the five o'clock shadow, the mussed-up hair and bare feet. This was the Jack she knew she really loved, and, seeing him now, she felt it was impossible to remain angry.

"It's okay," she smiled. "It's forgotten." After the insane events she had just endured, she truly meant it.

He took her into his arms. And then it struck her why it was so peaceful. "Where's Emma?"

"Esther," Jack said. "She took her for the afternoon."

"Oh," Mina said, now feeling slightly annoyed that Jack couldn't handle hanging out with his kid even for a few hours.

"I was just about to pick her up. Wanna come?"

"Not really," Mina said. "I'm a little tired."

"So where've you been all day?" he asked.

"Out," she snapped, defensively.

"Just out?"

"Just out," she said.

"Okay, I won't pry then," he said, leafing through a stack of unopened envelopes on the hall table. "So were you alone?" he tossed the mail into the cobalt blue bowl with the silver dragonfly.

"I thought you weren't prying," she said, but before she even got all the words out, the phone rang.

"That thing never stops, you know that?" Jack said.

"Uh, yeah. I'm home all the time." He walked over to the phone. Mina panicked. "What are you doing?"

"I'm going to answer it."

"Why in God's name would you do that?"

"Because . . . it's ringing?"

"That doesn't mean . . ."

"Hello?" Jack said, and his face immediately fell. "This is he."

"Jack, just hang up."

Jack did not hang up. "Oh yeah. Sure. Okay . . ."

"Jack!"

"Well, I guess I could sell my car, sure, but then how would I get to work?"

"Dammit!" said Mina.

"My kid? What do you mean, I better watch my kid?" Jack said.

A wave coursed through her as it had in Smitty's. That sense of power rose in her again and she charged across the room, over to Jack and to the phone. She pulled it away from him with a force she didn't know she had.

"Who is this?" she shouted into the receiver.

"Ma'am, this is Bob from—"

"Are you threatening my husband? Are you fucking threatening my husband?" she shouted into the phone.

"This matter is between us and your—"

"Are you threatening my husband with my kid's safety, you fucking vulture?"

"Look, he owes us money and—"

"And what? You're going to kidnap his child if he doesn't pay you, you fucking viper?"

"Mina . . ." Jack stammered, and Mina waved him away.

"Put your supervisor on the phone, you bloodsucking pig. Do it now!"

"You are not authorized to speak—"

"NOW!"

There was a click, and then the sound of muzak.

"Mina, you really shouldn't be . . ."

"Jack, let me handle this." The muzak stopped and another voice spoke.

"This is Mr. Templeton. How can I help you?"

"Look, Templeton. I know we owe you money. But we have no money. And if your fucking minions ever call here threatening my family again, I'm going to come to your offices and I'm going to rip your balls off with my bare hands, and then I'm going to feed them to you!"

"Mrs. Clark . . ."

"Mina!" Jack gasped.

"Because I'll tell you this, you shit-sucking low-life. I know we have rights. We have the right not to be threatened, and we have the right to report you if you so much as suggest doing any kind of bodily harm to anyone in this house!"

"Yes, but the fact remains . . ."

"And I also have the right to tell you to stop calling this fucking house. And you know what happens if you don't respect that request and you keep calling? Do you?"

"Are you *threatening* me, Mrs. Clark?"

"Nothing in the rules says I can't," she said, having no idea if anything she was saying was even true, but it felt so good to say it, she couldn't stop herself.

"And I'll tell you another thing. Not only should you *not* be threatening me and my family, you disgusting, usurious troglodyte—"

"Troglo-what?" Jack whispered.

She cupped the phone and whispered back. "Cave dweller."

"Oh . . ." he said. "Huh."

"You should be getting down on your fucking knees every night and thanking God that we don't pay our bills so that you can keep your pathetic, beggarly job, without which, you would be just like us. Except we're better than you. Because I tell you this, I would never do your disgusting job. I would eat my family before I'd stoop to your level!"

"Mrs. Clark—"

"And you know what, fuckwad? I'm going to get down on my knees and pray tonight. I'm going to pray that the tides turn and people do get to start paying their bills again and that you lose your fucking vulturous job and end up in the fucking street. And my dearest wish is that if anyone you ever harassed is out there with you, they tear you to shreds. Like they do to child molesters in prison." Her uncle's face flashed before her in that instant and she felt equally sick to her stomach and angry, more angry than she'd ever felt in her life.

Now there was only silence on the other end of the line. "Call my fucking house again and I will find you. Now good day!" she screamed, and she slammed down the phone.

Mina's heart was racing. Sweat formed on her brow. She was short of breath, like she'd just run a mile or had an explosive orgasm. She felt empowered. She felt invincible. She was exhilarated. Alive!

Jack approached her, an incredulous look on his face. "What was that?" he asked, not breaking his stare.

She blew her bangs up out of her eyes, her breath cooling her forehead.

He grabbed her by the shoulders and pulled her into a smoldering kiss. Her whole body was on fire as she returned it. "Oh Mina!" he gasped, as he pulled her into another deep, intense kiss. "You're back. It's you. You're back."

Mina's clothes became constricting all of a sudden and Jack, as if sensing this, began tearing them away. He pulled up her shirt and ran his mouth all over her body. He unzipped her jeans and slid his fingers into her as he kissed her. He took her into his arms and carried her to sit on the hall table. He pulled off her jeans, pulled her panties to the side, and entered her, every thrust more intense than the last, until the act culminated in a tremendous climax for them both.

"Holy shit," said Mina.

"Holy shit, indeed," said Jack, wiping his brow and zipping up his pants.

Mina hopped off the table and repositioned her clothes in the "on" on position. "Jack?"

"Mina?"

"Jack, what did you mean? Before? When you said I was back?"

Jack looked away. "Sorry. I wasn't really thinking—"

"Tell me."

He smiled sheepishly at her. "You seemed a little more like you, you know?"

"Not really," she said, shrugging her shoulders. "I mean . . . I'm starting to know things again, but . . ."

"What came over you, Mina?"

She wanted to tell him everything then. About Char and her perfume bottle. About the events of the afternoon—and even the past week. About venturing down into the basement. But something stopped her. Instead, the words "I saw my uncle" popped out of her mouth.

Jack's curiosity quickly switched to alarm. "What did you say?" he asked her.

"Why? What's wrong with my uncle? Actually, I was hoping you could tell me what happened with him, because I got a very creepy feeling before, when I saw him and . . . what?"

Jack sat down on the foyer bench, his face buried in his hands.

"Oh my God!" said Mina. "Is that it? Did he attack me? Or molest me when I was a child? Is that the crazy bad thing that happened to me? That's what I can't remember?"

Jack looked up at her. He pursed his lips, then looked around the room for guidance that wasn't going to be found. "Esther said you fired Dr. Barsheed," he said.

Mina pulled the unopened mail out of the bowl. "I did," she said, and she also began shuffling through it. Envelopes more ominous than bills, with words like "Final Notice" stamped across them.

"Mina, why?"

She tossed the envelopes back into the bowl, unopened. "I had to."

"But *why*? I think it was a mistake. This business with your uncle," he shook his head softly. "This isn't good. I mean, it really isn't good."

"What? What did my uncle do that was so bad? I need to hear what he did!"

"You mean aside from getting us into this mess?" he said, waving his hand around the room.

"What does that even mean?"

"I mean he talked you into buying this fucking trap and it's killing us! Him and his new-age nonsense. Fucking brainwashing bastard."

"My uncle . . .?"

"Look, that's not the point, okay? Dammit, I should have been more on top of this," Jack said. "Fuck!"

"Jack?"

"I know you found the tapes, Mina. You left them in my car."

Mina felt her face flush red. "You mean the Zander Randalls tapes? What do they have to do with anything?"

"What do they have to do with anything? I may as well tell you that Zander Randalls is your uncle. Do you know that yet?"

"What? Alex is Zander? Alexander . . . Alex-Zander! Oh God!" She put her hand to her mouth.

"Yeah, but that's not the worst of it," he said. "His brainwashing and all. Making us think we could pull all this off and all that other bullshit. Oh no. Not *nearly* the worst."

"Jack, what are you saying?"

Jack paced the room, speaking to the air, not looking at her. "Dr. Barsheed said this might happen to you. Like when you were a kid and you lost your mother. The first time you got amnesia. He said this might happen again."

"First time? Barsheed mentioned that too. What are you talking about? What are any of you ever talking about!"

"Just that . . . Well . . ."

"Jack, please!"

He sighed deeply. "I shouldn't . . ."

"Jack!"

"Okay. When you lost your mother like that, when you were a kid, lost her so horribly . . . . Well, you had no recollection of what happened, but you kept, well . . . seeing . . . You started to see . . ."

"Kept seeing what? Jack, tell me what you're trying to tell me already!"

Jack walked up to Mina and gently placed his hands on her shoulders. He looked intently into her eyes, and he stroked her face with his hand. "Mina," he said, and then paused. "Your uncle is dead."

At just that moment, the cobalt blue bowl with the silver dragonfly and the ominously stamped pile of unopened mail fell to the ground with a terrible crash.

Mina felt a hot flash tear through her and then everything went dark.

The next thing Mina knew, she was lying face down on the floor. Not the cold, hard floor of her foyer, where she expected to be, but on a plush, pink carpet. The surface was soft and warm, though she felt anything but. Somewhere in the distance she could detect a pleasing aroma, of strawberries and cream. The faint whiffs of that scent were the only things about this situation she found even remotely soothing.

Mina lay trembling, and soon realized that she was away from her house. Away from her time. Another dream. She was a small child again. A small child hiding under a bed.

A shadow passed through her room, and she could feel a deep sense of terror course through her at the sound of the heavy steps that accompanied the shadow. The rancid smell of stale gin and anger.

"Where are you, Ali?" a man's voice called. "Damned kid," he muttered, and he turned to leave. Only when his footsteps became faint again did she realize she had stopped breathing.

# 12

When Mina awoke, she was *in* her bed, her adult bed. In her adult body. *Just a dream*, she thought. She turned toward her night table to see her new perfume bottle, pretty and perfect. It made her happy to see it there. Jack must have found it; she briefly hoped this little extravagance wouldn't annoy him. Then she read the clock. "Nine o'clock! Oh fuck! Emma!"

At that moment, Jack raced in, a glass of water in hand. "Hey, you're up. It's okay. Emma's home."

"What happened?"

"You kind of passed out. I guess the news was too alarming. I guess I probably should have—"

Mina clasped her mouth and gasped. "My uncle!"

"Yes."

Mina slumped back into the blankets. "I'm so confused."

"I know," Jack said, and he sat beside her and took her hand in his. "I think all this remembering . . . the honeymoon . . . I think you remembered too quickly. Just like Barsheed said."

"But Alex. He looks just like the man in the wedding album. The man who gave me away?"

A look of panic came over Jack's face. "What do you mean, wedding album?"

Mina felt embarrassed and guilty and annoyed all at once. "Wedding album," she confirmed. "I found it in the basement."

"Basement!"

She looked away. "You left the door unlocked."

"Oh no. Are you kidding me? Dammit! Dammit! How could I be so stupid!"

"It's not your—"

"Too much too soon. Too much too soon! It's my fault. Oh fuck. It's all my fault."

"It isn't your fault, Jack. I could have locked the door when I saw it open. I didn't have to go down there."

He shook his head.

"I could have listened but I didn't."

Now he took a deep breath. "What else did you find?"

"Just that," she said, and a look of great relief washed over his face. "Okay."

"This guy, Alex? He looks just like the man in the album."

"Of course he does."

"Just older and . . ."

"Older?"

"Yes, older. I'm guessing it was some years ago . . ."

"Barsheed said you'd probably see him the way you remembered him. That's weird that he looks older to you. But he also mentioned that sometimes hallucinations—"

"Hallucination? He's not a hallucination!"

"Mina—"

"An impostor, okay. But I swear to you, Jack. He's real. As real as you sitting there. He hugged me for Chrissakes! I know what he feels like. What he *smells* like. Dammit, Jack, I was just—"

He tenderly put a finger to her lips. "You need rest, sweetie. And you need to see Dr. Barsheed. Tomorrow morning. I've already made the appointment for you."

Mina felt deflated. She didn't want Jack to be right, but she kind of knew he was. "Are you coming with me?"

His face dropped. "You know I can't . . ."

"Right. Amber."

"Come on, Mina. That's not fair. You make it seem like an affair. It's a job and if I want to keep the job, I have to go away for a couple of days. Please, don't make this harder than it has to be."

Mina didn't want to get into that drama again, and could read in Jack's face that he didn't want to either, so she let it go. "Wait. I can't. I have to take Emma to school in the morning."

"Esther will take her there, Harriet will bring her home. It's all been arranged."

"Oh. Okay. Where's Emma now?"

"Asleep. And so should you be," he said, and pulled a small pill out of his pocket, which he handed to her, along with the glass of water.

"Stay with me?"

"Okay," said Jack, and he slid into the bed next to her and spooned against her.

"Nice perfume bottle."

"It wasn't that much . . ."

"It's okay," he whispered into the back of her neck. "I just wish it wasn't a dragonfly."

"What does that mean?"

"Shh. Let's not talk about it now, okay?"

"Okay," she said. Within ten minutes, they were both asleep.

It was pouring rain as Mina pulled into the parking lot of Dr. Barsheed's office. A deep sense of dread weighed on her as she tried to find someplace close to the building to park. Mina wasn't convinced Barsheed was the answer, but what else could she do? What choice did she have? She was hanging out with her dead uncle now; clearly, her mind was slipping, which would make her a danger not only to herself, but to her family. What about Jack? Emma? Emma especially. She couldn't put Emma's safety in jeopardy just because she didn't particularly enjoy the company of her shrink.

She found an open spot just to the right of Barsheed's office window and she pulled in. She turned off the car.

Had Barsheed even helped her at all though? Maybe she wasn't getting better when she saw him, but it's not like she had been getting worse—as she apparently had been since she'd stopped seeing him. Before Mina stopped seeing Barsheed, she hadn't been "seeing" things. "Seeing" people? Had she?

She stayed in the car, telling herself she would just wait until the rain died down a little but knowing full well the sun could be shining bright on a seventy-degree day and she'd probably still be sitting there in her car, making any excuse she could find to avoid Barsheed.

As she sat, she tried to reconcile when she fired Barsheed and when she first met Alex in the park. Was there a correlation? She knew the day she fired Barsheed was the day Emma got so sick at the playground and Alex had to take them to see Dr. Swenson. No, she had met him at least a couple of times before that! Of course she had. The first day, when she thought he was stealing her things. The second time, when he spoke Russian to her—and she responded. No. Not only was she still seeing Barsheed then, she wasn't remembering anything . . .

She looked out her car window and up to the second floor, to the windows of Barsheed's office. Now she saw him standing there, peering down at her car. He held a phone to his ear with one hand; with the other, he fondled his beard. She imagined he was calling Jack, and the thought of that made her chuckle as she watched him pull the phone away and dial another number. "Yeah, good luck with that, pal," she said aloud, but still only for her ears.

She continued watching him from the car, trying to piece together the events of the last couple of days. Maybe, just maybe, she rationalized, Alex was not a hallucination. Char-a'tee would know for sure, if she could find her. And Char also seemed to know things about Alex. Other things. Mysterious things. If she could confirm that Alex existed, even if he was just someone pretending to be Alex, then she wouldn't need to see Barsheed at all. Because it wouldn't be about her hallucinating anymore. Then it would be another issue. If Alex wasn't a hallucination, what was he? Why was someone pretending to be Alex? Why was this stranger hiring cleaning ladies and making her car payments and slipping cash into her purse? What did he want from her?

And then there was the whole last mindfuck about Alex being Zander Randalls. Her uncle, the schlub in the ski hat, was the world-acclaimed motivational speaker whose tapes had been the only thing of late that had made any sense to her.

Was Jack right? Was Zander Randalls really dead? Why didn't she know that he was dead? She decided she had to find out. And *not* after her appointment with Barsheed. If she was going to remember anything else ever again, she'd definitely have to stop seeing Barsheed.

She looked up to find him still standing at the window, still on the phone. She started up her car, gave him a quick wave, and peeled out of the parking lot and into the street before the men in the white coats came for her—because surely it was possible that the mental hospital was on the list of places Barsheed was calling.

By the time Mina got home, the rain had stopped. As she walked to her front door, she found the mums drowning in an enormous puddle of water that hadn't drained properly from her garden, and she found herself filled with glee. She looked down at her watch. Ten o'clock. Good. There was time to start figuring things out before Emma came home.

Mina rationalized that Esther could help her look for clues in the boxes in the basement, so when she walked into her house, the first thing she did was call Esther. Of course Esther would want to help now that Mina was starting to remember things on her own. In fact, she was sure Esther would be excited by the prospect once Mina told her everything she had been discovering! But no one answered the phone at Esther's house.

Then she got another crazy idea. Maybe, just maybe, she thought, Zander also owed some huge international bank some money. Maybe even her bank! Of course it was possible, right? It seemed like lately anything was possible. Maybe it was a long shot, but if he did do business with her bank, Kim would help her for sure.

Or maybe not? Mina recalled her last conversation with Kim. What had it meant? Why would Kim tell her those kinds of things? Maybe she was starting to come undone from wedding planning.

Maybe the things Kim was telling her were right, though . . . And if Kim was right . . . No. It was impossible. Kim had just been acting paranoid. She decided to take a chance. She called Kim, but all she got was voicemail and she hung up. So, it looked, at least for now, like Mina was on her own.

Mina peeled off her jacket. She headed into the kitchen and put the kettle on the stove. She slipped a pouch of chamomile tea out of a drawer and waited for the kettle to boil. Then she poured herself a cup.

Mina glanced over at the basement door and couldn't help but notice that it was open. Again. Although this time it appeared that the doorknob had been removed. Poor Jack, she thought. He'd probably gone to change the knob and gotten distracted.

Despite the events of the past day or so, however, Mina couldn't help but feel intrigued by the prospect of learning more about herself and her life. She grabbed her mug of tea and headed to the basement.

Mina flipped on the light switch and a city of cardboard boxes came into view. She had no idea where to begin.

She stepped over the open box of wedding memories and positioned herself comfortably on the floor in front of a box labeled "Clippings - 2." The box was taped shut and she dug her finger under the flap to peel off the tape. Her heart was racing in anticipation, though that crashed into disappointment when she opened the box and all she found inside was a stack of old newspapers.

She grabbed a few off the top and pulled them into her lap. She sat back and glanced through the headlines, but nothing jumped out at her. The newspapers were more than five years old; she couldn't imagine that she had been a packrat, but she knew, of course, anything was possible.

And then her eye caught an image, an image of the woman with the black hair who lived in her wedding album. Her face. Her unsmiling face. Frantically, she pulled the paper closer and read the headline that appeared next to her picture:

## BANK CEO OUSTED IN TERRIBLE SCANDAL

After glancing through the opening sentences, she knew she hadn't been the CEO, as she was sure she was not Phil Quinn, described as a man in his early sixties. Her eye went to the byline. Lexi Randalls. Lexi Randalls? Was that her? Her real name? Lexi Randalls . . . She thought: Jack had told her Zander Randalls was her uncle. If she'd never had a father, and her mother was Zander-Alex's brother, her last name would likely have been Randalls. Before she married Jack.

But then who the hell was Mina?

Mina scanned the article, then picked up a stack of others. Soon she knew something about herself, something real and tangible that she could grab from the time she couldn't remember. She was a journalist! An investigative journalist! Apparently a good one. There were all kinds of stories in the pile. All about her bringing down the bad guys. Exposing the bad guys. Ruining people who ruined other people.

Mina was filled with excitement and pride as she popped open "Clippings - 1," a collection of local stories from the old Queens neighborhood she had been raised in, if she believed Alex (or, rather, the man who called himself Alex). Turning her attention to "Clippings - 3" and digging deeper into the offerings, she found articles that were broader in scope, covering international topics and other interesting things. She wasn't just a journalist. Apparently she was a known, established journalist. There was Mina's old look, the dark hair and makeup, in photographs with luminaries and dignitaries.

And Mina's face with Zander's . . .

Mina stopped on an article she had apparently written about her uncle. A praise piece. She looked carefully at his face. It was younger but it was definitely the face of the man who called himself Alex. She believed, she had to believe, that the man she had been seeing was her uncle. This man in the photo. Jack had to have been wrong, she rationalized. There had to be more to it. This was clearly the same man.

Mina stared at the photo. She examined every one of Zander's features. His kind eyes beamed with sincerity. Looking at him warmed her heart. And then filled her with guilt. She must have misunderstood him. There must be some explanation for why she needed to get away from him so terribly . . .

She looked at his eyes. These were not the eyes of a monster. But what had he done that had terrified her so? The pull to get away from him, to get out of the house . . . it had been so indescribably strong. What could he have done?

"Mina? Are you here?" Esther calling from upstairs broke Mina's reverie. She took the clipping with the photo of Lexi and Zander and shoved it into her pocket.

"Down here!" she called up the stairs.

"Whatever are you doing down there?" Esther called down.

"Cleaning," Mina lied.

"Ha! Good one, dear," Esther replied.

Mina closed up the boxes, frustrated she hadn't gotten to "Clippings - 4," and raced up the stairs.

"Monny!" Emma yelled, and she wrapped her little body around her mother's legs.

"What are you doing here?" Mina asked Esther. "Jack said Harriet was going to bring Emma home."

"Did you really think I was going to let my precious ride with that maniac and her brood? I mean, where was Emma even supposed to sit in that filthy car? Oh, no. I cancelled my hair appointment and waited for her myself."

"You didn't have to do that," Mina said. "Harriet's fine. And I would have picked her up myself even, except . . ."

"Except you went to see Dr. Barsheed," Esther said, her suspicion apparent.

Mina looked away. "Yes."

"Hmm, mmm," said Esther, and she cocked her head at Mina. "You know I know you didn't go to see Dr. Barsheed today, right? He called me."

"When?"

"When you didn't get out of your car in the parking lot."

"It was raining," Mina excused herself lamely. She craned her neck around to the window. "Is it still?"

"It is not. And that's not the truth."

"Look, Esther, with all due respect—"

"Now you look, Mina. I told you I would never let anything happen to my precious over here. You should feel the same. If you're not feeling well, you're putting her in danger. You do realize—"

"Thank you, Esther. But this is between me and my *family*." For a second, an image of Alex's face flashed in her mind. She shook it away. Mina knew it was obnoxious to emphasize the word "family" as she had, but who the fuck did Esther think she was anyway?

Esther looked like she'd been kicked in the face at Mina's words, and Mina felt terrible. "Oh Esther, I am so sorry. I didn't mean . . . I'm just not feeling myself . . ."

"Which is why you need to go back to Barsheed," Esther said with an unusual firmness, and she glanced at the basement door. "Does Jack know you were down there?" she asked, and Mina looked away. "Honestly, Mina. I don't know why you're looking to put everyone at risk like this."

Mina tried to make nice. "Can I call you later? I did find out some things. I was hoping I could talk to you about it . . ."

Esther turned to answer Mina, and Mina knew from the look on Esther's face that she had crossed a line. "Sure, dear," Esther said with a saccharine smile, and she left.

Mina bent down and picked up Emma. "How was your day, sweetie?"

"I go potty!" the child beamed.

"You did? You mean at school?"

"I did!"

Mina pulled Emma into a warm hug. "I'm so proud of you, baby!"

Emma scowled. "I am not a baby."

"No, of course you aren't," she said. "What do you say we go get you some big girl underwear and then go to the playground?"

"Yay, Monny!"

Mina pulled open the drawer where she'd stashed her gifted cash and pulled out several twenties, which she slipped into her wallet. She felt kind of bad about using the money, considering how things weren't exactly copacetic between her and Alex. But this was a giant milestone.

"Let's go!" Mina said, and they headed out to the car.

After their mother-daughter shopping trip, which concluded with ice cream cones for each, Mina and Emma headed to the playground. When she spotted Harriet with the other mothers, she didn't feel her usual dread. In fact, she was almost happy to see them—at least to share the happy news! But as she approached and waved, not a single one of them waved back. In fact, they all turned their backs on her.

Mina felt a slight panic rise up in her. What had she done? She had an urge to run back to the car, just take Emma home. But Emma was already engaged with the other children, her dress up over her head as she showed off her new Ariel the Mermaid underwear. Mina forced down the panic and worked to bring back the other feeling. Those tingles of empowerment she had felt at Smitty's. When she took the phone away from Jack and tore the collector a new one . . . She concentrated hard to get that feeling back, and once it came, washing over her, washing through her, strong and powerful and ready, she walked right up to the mothers and proceeded to speak.

"Good afternoon!" she said, trying not to sound artificially sweet.

No one acknowledged her.

"What's going on?" she tried again. "Did you see Emma? Isn't that great news?"

The mothers shot Emma a bored look and continued to ignore Mina. Mina realized it still might not be too late to pull Emma away, but decided instead to stand her ground as the small molecules of empowerment coursed through her.

"What?" she said. She lightly grabbed Claire by the shoulder. "What did I do?"

Claire looked at Ellen before she spoke. Ellen nodded. "I can't believe what you said to Esther," she said. "About poor Harriet. How you could be so, well . . ."

They all shook their heads.

"What do you mean?" asked Mina.

"Mean? Yes, mean. You are mean and you don't care about anyone but these vicious old people. You're no better than them. You're one of them," Ellen fired off the verbal shots like machine-gun fire.

"To say that she was unstable!" Marie chimed in.

"And a drunk!" said Harriet.

"Wait a minute. I never said—"

"And that you would never let her drive your kid around in that lunatic mobile," said Claire.

Mina was confused. "But I never said—"

"I knew she was one of them," Ellen scoffed. "I told you and told you and told you, but no one wanted to listen to me. You all said, 'No, she's okay' and 'Don't judge her for her ratty old clothes,' but I knew there was something wrong with her. I always knew she was off," said Ellen.

"Just a total traitor," said Claire.

"I thought she was my friend," said Harriet, who now burst out crying. Marie shot a look at Ellen, who pulled Harriet into a tentative hug.

"I'm telling you I never said any of that," said Mina. "I didn't even make any of the arrangements for today. Jack did. I was as surprised as anyone else that Esther picked up Emma. Harriet, you can't honestly believe . . . and why would Esther say such a thing? It doesn't make any sense."

"It does make sense," said Claire. "She's against us, just like the rest of the old codgers and bats."

"I bet she's even playing mahjong with them now," said Ellen.

Mina shook her head. She looked at Harriet and tried to give her the kindest "What the fuck" look she could muster. "If you guys all believe the old people are against us, what makes you think they're not trying to turn us against each other? Maybe Esther made all that up. Did you ever consider that?" Mina was shocked at herself for the thought even entering her mind, but now it was there. "In fact, it's what she told me when she dropped off Emma. That Harriet was irresponsible. That she didn't trust her. Did you ever consider that? Did you?"

Harriet pulled away from Ellen. "You know? I think Mina may be telling the truth," Harriet said. "I mean, she isn't exactly sane, but it makes less sense that she would make that kind of thing up."

"Oh, thanks," said Mina, equally happy to have someone on her side and annoyed that Harriet had "outed" her condition to people she really didn't know at all.

Ellen stood with her arms folded. Claire shook her head. "Well, that's your mistake then," she said, and the others walked off, leaving Harriet and Mina on their own.

"Bitches," Harriet said.

Mina just shrugged her shoulders.

"Well, how did it go at the doc's?"

Mina looked away, guilty.

"You didn't go, did you?"

"No. And I don't need a lecture or—"

"Cool your pits, dude. It's none of my business, okay? Jack just seemed unnerved when he called. Like something crazy happened or something. Look, I have enough of my own crazy," she said, and, as if on cue, her oldest pulled down his brother's pants and ran, laughing, to the other side of the playground. Without saying a word, Harriet pointed a finger at William, who froze, turned around, headed back to his brother, helped him pull his pants back up, and hugged him. "Trust me, I don't need any of yours."

"Can I ask you something?"

"Maybe . . ."

"When did we meet?"

"You're really not faking with the amnesia, are you?"

"Why would you think I was faking?"

"Dunno. I guess this lifestyle, all of this," she said, with a wave of her hand. "It can get a little excruciating. And with you as a writer and everything—"

"You know I'm a writer!" she exclaimed. Maybe she was on to something here after all!

"Oh, fuck," said Harriet. "That's right. You don't know. Oh fuck. Sorry."

"It's okay! I found the newspaper clippings today," she said, and she pulled the one she had tucked into her pocket to show Harriet. "I *know* I used to be a reporter!"

"A reporter?" Harriet asked, her confusion evident as she half-heartedly glanced at the article. "Well, okay. If that's what you remember, just go with that."

"Wait, what makes you say I'm *not* a reporter?"

"I didn't say that, but you know I'm not supposed to tell you things. You're supposed to remember for yourself. That's what we've all been told. I think I've already blabbed enough, thank you. I hope to God you don't start flipping out now, here in the playground in front of my kids. That would be awful."

Mina ignored Harriet. She felt she'd gotten a door to open a crack and she was going to push hard to get it open. "What do you know about my uncle?"

"Mina, come on."

"The guy with the beard and the ski hat? Who's here with me at the park sometimes?" she said, pointing to the bench where she typically interacted with Alex.

"What guy?" Harriet asked, a look of suspicion on her face.

"The guy," Mina said, starting to lose patience. "The man. He was here the other day. He did a magic trick."

"A guy? Here? Sorry."

"You never saw him," Mina said, crestfallen.

Harriet shook her head. "I may be a shitty mother but I'm not that shitty. I mean, I think I'd probably remember a guy in a ski mask in a playground, don't you?"

"Ski *hat*."

"Same thing."

"Actually—"

"Mina, do you think maybe you should consider going to see that doctor again? That maybe . . ."

"What about Zander Randalls? This guy in the photo here with me? Do you know what happened to Zander Randalls? You know, the self-help guy. He was apparently pretty big-time once. I have his tapes, but I never hear of him being around anymore."

"That guy? Crap, he was brutally murdered like two years ago. Don't you remember, some guy—" Harriet clasped her hand over her mouth and gasped. "You know, that was really fucking sneaky, Mina," she said, keeping her face covered, speaking through her hand. "Really fucking sneaky."

"So something really bad happened to him. To my uncle. Is that why I can't remember?" she said to Harriet. And then out loud, but to herself, "Is that why I keep seeing him?"

Now Harriet was worried. "Mina, look, you gotta get back to the doctor. Okay? It's not just about you here. If you're seeing things, seeing this dead guy . . . that's just not normal. And it could be really dangerous, especially for Emma."

She put her hand on Mina's shoulder. "Please, Mina. Go back and see the doctor."

Mina cupped her hands and placed them over her face. "I guess I should," she said. "But Jack's away. I don't see how . . ."

"Leave her with me. With us," she said, nodding back at the mothers. "Kill two birds with one stone. You can get your head straightened out and earn some points with them."

"Why would I want to earn points with them?"

"Because you have to if you're going to survive around here. They may be bitches, but you never know when you're going to need them."

"Thanks, Harriet," Mina said. "You're a real friend."

Dr. Barsheed agreed to see Mina immediately—almost a little too quickly for a guy who's supposed to have been such a hotshot therapist and probably overbooked more often than not.

"Come in, dear," he greeted her, taking her gently by the arm as she entered his office. "Please. Have a seat."

Mina sat. She folded her arms over her chest and regarded Barsheed quietly. He sat across from her, his hands folded in a triangle cage over his nose. Finally he spoke. "So it was the rain before?"

"Sorry?"

"When you didn't get out of the car. Our morning appointment."

"Sure," Mina lied.

"Not something else?"

"No."

"No, of course not," he said, showing his teeth in what Mina imagined he thought was a smile. "It's not because you started seeing your dead uncle or anything then?"

"So Jack told you."

"Of course. Any chance you're seeing anyone else? How about Lucy? Any word from Lucy lately?"

Mina thought about the small girl in her dreams. "Why is everyone so obsessed with Lucy lately?"

"Like who?" Barsheed asked.

As the answer to his question was only the figment of her imagination known as her uncle, she said, "Forget it."

"Ah, your, uh, uncle," Barsheed said, and he sat back in his chair. "Well, why do you suppose he's asking you about Lucy?"

"You mean my uncle who isn't real? You want to know why my hallucination is curious about a friend I had as a child?"

"What makes you think Lucy was a friend from your childhood?"

Mina was taken aback by the question. "I guess because when I dream of her, we're children."

Dr. Barsheed nodded. "Excellent point," he said. "So you're dreaming of her now. That's interesting. Very interesting."

"Really only once or so. Why? Who's Lucy? What does it mean that she's in my dreams?" Mina pressed.

"Oh, you know I can't tell you that," he said.

"Okay, well, can you at least tell me why she keeps telling me my kid's in trouble? In danger?"

"She tells you that?"

"Yes."

"Interesting."

Mina rolled her eyes. "Honestly, either I'm on the brink of losing my mind here or I'm not. You're either going to help me keep my shit together or you're not. Why does it seem like you're not?"

"What makes you think you're on the brink of losing your mind?"

"I see dead people!" she said, exasperated.

"Good one!" Barsheed said. "*Sixth Sense*. Great movie. And talk about creepy kids. Actually, Lucy's nothing compared—"

"Doctor, please!"

"Lucy is kind of a creepy individual."

"So you've met her, then?" Mina said, feeling slightly relieved. "So she's *real*!"

"Oh," Barsheed said. "I didn't say that. But you believe she is, so that's where we might have to start. Let's try and talk about Lucy, shall we?"

"Not calling the nuthouse?" Mina asked.

"Not yet," Barsheed deadpanned. Mina started to cry. "Oh Mina, my goodness. I'm sorry. I'm just kidding with you. I forget sometimes that you have no sense of humor."

An hour later she emerged from Barsheed's office feeling more unhinged than ever. She headed to the playground to collect Emma. Everyone was gone now except for Harriet, whose husband had joined her. They were sitting on a bench together, snuggling and whispering to each other, in their own world together, as the kids swarmed around them. Why couldn't Mina's husband be around more? Why didn't she have the sense that she and Jack were in this together?

"Emma!" Mina called.

"Monny!" said Emma, and she flew into her mother's arms. "I missed you so much, Monny!"

"I missed you too, baby."

"Gowd tooft!" Emma chanted, trying now to pry open her mother's mouth. "Gowd tooft."

Mina complied and let Emma tap her little fingers into Mina's mouth; she could taste the dirt on Emma's fingers and regretted her compliance almost immediately. She delicately extracted Emma's fingers from her mouth.

"What is she talking about?" Harriet asked.

"I got a gold crown at the dentist the other day," said Mina, opening her mouth for Harriet to observe.

"Nice!" said Harriet. "Ghetto fabulous!" she joked, and Sammy and Harriet laughed heartily.

"Oh, very funny," said Mina, and her heart warmed thinking of Char.

"Where'd you go?" asked Sammy.

"It was the strangest place," said Mina. "It was a dentist office and a spa. Can you imagine?"

Sammy's face seemed to go white. "Not that place, Pearls of Wisdom? In Queens?"

"Exactly that place. Wow, you're good. But why do you look so . . ."

"I just read some fucked up shit on the Internet one night. Who knows, it was late. I was probably drunk and delirious anyway," he said, brushing it off.

"What did you read?"

"Don't worry about it," Sammy said. "I spend too much time on the Internet anyway."

"That he does," Harriet interjected.

"Just something stupid I read," he said. "That's all."

"Okay," said Mina, letting it go. "So how was the little monster?" she asked, squeezing Emma into a hug.

Harriet got up to meet her. "She was really good, Mina. I mean, really good."

"Emma?"

"This one?" said Sammy. "A total angel. And I would know," he said as his kids running amok all over the place.

"Seriously. I'm happy to take her whenever," said Harriet. "Just let me know," she smiled. "So . . . how'd it go?"

"Well, he doesn't think I need to be locked up," Mina said nervously. "But I'm going to have to see him a few times a week for a while—just until things level out a bit."

"Until you stop seeing the dead guy," Harriet nodded.

"I'm not seeing him anymore anyway," Mina said reassuringly—though she wasn't quite sure who she was trying to reassure.

"Oh yeah?"

"Got a little complicated anyway."

"Yeah, because hallucinating dead relatives isn't complicated enough!" Sammy laughed, interrupting.

"You told *him*?"

"I tell this asshole everything. He's too freaking nosy if you ask me, but whatever."

"She's stuck with me!" he said, wrapped his arms around his wife, grabbing her breasts with his hands.

"Sammy!" Harriet shrieked. "Sorry, Mina. He's just—"

"Don't worry about it," Mina smiled. "We're heading out now. Just try not to damage your kids too badly," she joked.

As Mina passed the mums on her way up the driveway, she noticed a cement mixer randomly sitting at the side of her house, along with a bag of cement. That gave her the quick thought that maybe, after she put Emma down to sleep, that maybe she *did* have a way to stop Witmore in his mum-planting tracks once and for all. . .

Except that she forgot all about it as soon as she got in the house and Jack called.

"How was your day?" he asked.

"Alright, I guess."

"Did you uncover anything with Barsheed?"

"We talked a little, but not really. I guess I have to start seeing him some more, but whatever."

"Well, that's probably best, don't you think? All things considered?"

"Actually . . . I did uncover something. On my own, though."

"What?"

"I found some things in the basement."

"How did you . . . Oh frack! I forgot to fix the damned—"

"Don't worry about it. It's okay."

"No, it isn't. I can't believe I messed up again like this."

"Do you want to know what I found?" she asked.

He sighed. "I guess. Yes. Let's talk about it."

"There were some boxes, with newspaper clippings."

"Oh," Jack said, sounding slightly panicked. "And?"

"Just some fluff pieces, I guess. A couple of exposes," she said. "I found out that I'm a reporter."

"Yes. You were. What else . . ."

"And that's about it. There was a story about a corrupt CEO, but that's hardly news," she joked. "Another one about a mayor in the Midwest who was robbing his town blind. Apparently, my stories took them down. Anyway, I'm just glad to know I used to be someone, you know. Maybe I can be *someone* again."

"I don't know about that," Jack said. "That might not be the best thing—"

"What? For me to be someone more than a housewife? More than a prisoner in this stupid complex ready to serve you whenever you decide to stroll in?" she snapped back.

"No. I didn't mean it that way. Sorry. Let's change the subject."

Mina took a deep breath and hesitated before she spoke again. "Okay," she said, but she didn't feel okay about it at all.

"So tell me about Barsheed?"

"I already did."

"Well did he give you anything?"

"What do you mean? Advice? Drugs?" she snapped defensively.

"Let's talk about it when I get home," he said, trying to sound sweet.

"Which will be exactly when?" she pushed.

"A day," he said. "Two, tops. I guess I can try to make it home tonight, you know, all things considered. Though I'd have to go back into the office tomorrow . . ."

Mina was quiet for a moment. "Emma used the potty," she said. "A couple of times even. You're fucking missing everything," she snapped, and she hung up on him.

Mina was surprised at how angry she felt at Jack, but he deserved it. She didn't care about his job anymore. She just wanted a fucking normal husband and a fucking normal life. Was it so much to ask?

She sat for a while, holding the phone in her hand, trying to cool down. But it wasn't working. She decided to call Esther, but strangely, Esther didn't pick up the phone. Mina looked at the clock. It was only 8:30, early for Esther to have gone to bed. She wondered where she could be, especially since she had told Mina she would be home that night. She started to worry about her, then pushed those thoughts out of her head. Esther was perfectly capable of taking care of herself.

She decided to try Kim. It had been quite some time since they'd spoken, maybe a week, which seemed like a long time between phone calls. Besides, she was still optimistic that Kim might be able to answer her questions about Alex/Zander/the ghost or the impostor who'd been hovering around her life.

Mina dialed the number, and quickly dialed Kim's extension. A man's voice answered.

"I'm looking for Kim, please," she told him.

"I'm sorry," he replied. "But she's no longer with the company." Mina was sure his voice cracked at the end of his statement.

"I'm sorry. Did you say she left? Where did she go?"

"I'm not really supposed to say . . ." the man said. And then another voice called to him in the background. A woman's voice, "Who is that?"

"There's been a terrible accident," he said. "She . . . she didn't survive it . . ."

"Hang up that phone!" the woman's voice called.

"I'm sorry, but I can't . . ." And then the phone went dead.

Mina was shaking when she hung up the phone. Kim was dead? How could that be? She pinched her own hand. Definitely not a dream. The ringing of the phone, still in her hand, made her jump.

"Hello?" she answered, but no one responded. "Hello?" she tried again, but still no one responded. She thought she could hear breathing though. Not pervy, heavy breathing, but someone was definitely there.

"Lily, I thought-choo didn't answer no phones?" Char'a-tee.

Mina checked the caller ID: *Unknown Number*.

"Why didn't you say something?"

"I'm saying something now," she said.

"Okay. So why are you calling?" Mina asked.

"Thought you could use a friend to talk to. Your uncle tells me you ain't speaking to him no more."

"You saw Alex?"

"How 'bout I just come over. You got Courvoisier?"

"I suppose . . ."

"Good. Meet me on your patio with the bottle and two glasses. And ice. I'll be there in ten minutes."

"Uh, okay. I'll call the security gate and let them know I'm expecting you. What kind of car do you drive?" But Char had already hung up.

Mina cracked opened the front door and noticed Esther's lights were still not on. Or maybe they were off already—maybe she had already turned in for the night.

The moon was full and it glistened on the rooftops. It was the kind of thing that should have evoked beauty, but Mina couldn't help but notice that it had no such effect in this soulless community of hers. And it especially infuriated her that it gave those stupid mums a sheen of iridescence . . . God she hated those mums.

Mina let out a sigh. How had she and Jack ended up here? What had possessed them to come here? She wasn't sure she would ever know as she headed into the kitchen to retrieve the booze and the glasses.

When she got back to the porch, she found Char sitting on one of the lawn chairs, her zebra-pumped feet resting on the arm of the other chair. She also noticed what she had forgotten: the bag of cement and the cement mixer, now both sitting right at the front of her house. "What the . . .?"

"This is some way you live, Lily. I can't believe how posh these digs are. You never struck me as no snotty little rich bitch. Especially because you always so piss poor when I see you. But now I see where all the money is."

"It looks a lot grander than it is, believe me."

"Though you probably lost that kid's whole college tuition with the market crash on these digs. Whoo-whee."

"Well, actually . . ."

"Nah, you right. Neighborhoods like this don't go down with the ship like everyone else's. Not like with the poor folk."

"Like I said . . ."

"Lily One Percent. Yep, I like the way that sounds!"

"Appearances can be deceiving, you know."

"You telling me! Aw shit, ain't it the truth! Well Lily One Percent, why don't you have yourself a seat and pour us some drinks and let's start talking about life now, hmmm? What do you say?"

Mina went to sit in the chair being occupied by Char's feet, and Char respectfully moved her feet to the ground. She poured out two healthy-sized drinks and slid the bottle down onto the table, next to a watering can and the shovels Mina and Jack had used to dig up the mums. Char lifted the glass to her lips and took a long, satisfying draw of warming amber liquid. "Damn!" she said. "Ain't that ever the shit?"

Mina took a small sip of her drink, just to be polite, but she had to admit it tasted pretty good to her and felt awesome going down, warming her from the inside.

"So what-choo gonna do about that old Ruskie?" Char asked.

"He's not Russian."

"No, but he's tenacious as fuck, just like a Russian."

"I didn't know Russians were supposed to be—"

"Oh, come on now, Lily. Let's cut the crap and tell Char what happened and what you plan to do about it."

Mina cleared her throat and took another sip, this one longer. "Jack says Alex doesn't exist. That he's dead," she said flatly.

Char laughed. "So Jack thinks we're both nuts then? That we both hanging out with this dude who doesn't even exist? Damn, that man of yours better be hot or good in the sack 'cause he's dumber than shit," Char said.

"Hey, that's . . ."

"Oh, come on. If he ain't dumb, where's he now?"

Mina looked away.

"Yeah. With some other bitch. You really believe he gotta travel so much, Lily? You really that naive?"

"Not that it's any of your business, but—"

"You right. That ain't none of Char's business. But this uncle of yours is. So what-choo gonna do about it?"

"I guess I first have to figure out why I keep seeing him and—"

"You seeing him because he's stalking you. And when he ain't, he's stalking me, looking for you."

"Let's drop it right now, okay? I've been having a kind of fucked up day as it is and I'd rather not talk about this anymore."

"Fair enough," Char said. "So tell me what else is going on wit-choo?"

Mina had no idea where to even begin until she felt a stab in her heart. The first thing that came to mind was the last thing she'd found out. "I lost a friend today."

"Lily, you ain't got no friends!"

"Of course I do."

"Well, besides me that is. And Uncle Ruskie, who—"

"And I would appreciate some sensitivity here. I didn't just lose her," she said, the words getting trapped in her throat. "She died."

"Oh, sorry, Lily. How did it happen?"

"I have no idea."

"Well, when then?"

"I don't know that either."

"Hmmm," said Char, and they sat in silence for a while.

"I think maybe it ain't that uncle of yours who's make-believe," Char said. "I think maybe it's this shitty make-believe story you're telling old Char-a'tee to get me off the topic of your uncle and your mental problems."

"Kim was not make-believe!" Mina snapped.

"Uh-huh," said Char. "Then what's her last name?"

"I . . . I don't . . ."

"Uh huh. I think you don't know her last name cuz she ain't got one. Because you ain't made it up yet in that crackpot brain of yours."

"I never knew her last name. They never tell you that. I just knew her from the bank. She worked there. She used to call me."

"Wait? You mean a *collector*, Lily? You sleeping with the enemy?" Char let out a big laugh. "Oh man, maybe you are nuts after all!"

"Hey! It's not like that!"

"Uh huh. You got Stockholm, baby. And you got it bad!"

"Stop it!"

"Come on, Lily. What's sadder than being besties with a person trying to shake money out of you?"

"Hanging out with your dead uncle?"

Char took a deep breath while she considered this. "Yeah, you in bad shape, Lily."

"Thanks," said Mina, and she took a big swig of her drink.

"So tell me about your friend," Char said, now with a hint of kindness in her voice. She drained the contents of her glass in one gulp. "You better hurry up if you wanna catch up, Lily!"

Mina downed her drink and then poured another. She clutched her glass to her. "I just can't believe it, you know. She was so young. She had her whole life ahead of her. I mean, she was getting married . . ."

"So what you really mean is that her whole life was *behind* her."

"Very funny. But . . ."

"But . . .?"

"The last time I spoke to her, I don't know. It was weird." Mina started feeling uncomfortable, that the booze was loosening her up too much, and that she really didn't want to tell Char what Kim had said. But she wasn't sure she was going to be able to hold back. She tried. "I'm sure it's nothing," she said.

"I bet it's something," Char said. "Spill it."

"Well . . . she asked me if I had made any new friends lately . . . And that I shouldn't be trusting . . ."

"Ha! That you shouldn't be trusting old Char? Shit! I'm the least of your dragons."

"Dragons? Why did you say that?"

"Say what?"

"Why did you say dragons? Not 'worries'—that you're the least of my *worries*."

"Girl, you ain't got worries. Worries means bullshit. Worries means something that ain't nowhere but in your head. But you, your troubles ain't in your head, baby. Not most of them. Your troubles are real and they're about to get a hell of a lot worse."

"Oh . . ."

"No, baby, *worries* ain't what you got. You got dragons. And you got 'em bad," she said, draining her glass again.

Mina took a cautious sip. "It's so weird that you say that. That you say 'dragons' like that. Because in my dreams, I see dragons in my dreams all the time . . ."

"Well, I'll tell you what I do think, Lily. I think you got a lot a dragons to fell."

"Fell?"

"You know what I mean. Those banks are crazy fucking places. The banks and the people that work in them."

"I don't think everyone is so bad. I mean, they're . . ."

Char slammed down her fist. "They're fucking crazy. Fuck, you know that don't you? Ain't nothing stopping them from tearing your heart right out. From tearing your sweet family apart."

"I think you may be overreacting a little bit here, don't you?"

"Yeah, well. Let's just say that old Char knows a thing or two about the bad in the world and about shutting it down. So tell me. Which one was it?"

"First Federal."

"Oh shit, girl."

"What?"

"They ain't just bad. They the worst. And I'll tell you something else. Your friend? You said she worked there?"

"Sure."

"Yep. I'd bet my life on it," Char said, and nodded her head.

"On what?" Mina asked.

Char stared pointedly at Mina now. "That I bet-choo they kilt her."

Mina was aghast. "What are you saying? That's impossible. That's insane!"

"Ain't it, though," said Char, nonchalant.

Just then, Mina's phone went off. Mina looked at the number and silenced the ringer immediately.

"Who dat?" Char asked, and then her mouth curled into a knowing grin. "Nah, forget it. I already know."

"I don't even know who this guy is and why he keeps calling me. I mean, if he isn't my uncle, what's he after? It's not like there's any money or . . ."

"Oh sure," Char laughed, looking around again. "Sure there isn't, Lily One Percent."

"Stop calling me that!"

"Alright, alright. But let me ax you something? What makes you think this guy isn't who he says he is?"

"Are you kidding? You're like the main person who tells me he's full of shit."

"Oh, he's full of shit alright. But that don't mean he's not your uncle. He's just your full-of-shit uncle."

Mina tapped her lip as she considered this. She noticed it had gone somewhat numb from the cognac. "I don't know. I mean . . ."

"Look, whoever he is, you can't hide from him forever. One way or another you're going to have to confront him. You're going to have to face what and who he is to you. So what-choo gonna do about his bullshit ass?"

"I don't know," Mina said, now feeling slightly queasy.

"Um-hmm. Okay. So what-choo gonna do about them damn flowers?"

Mina looked at the mums. "Those damned things. It's like I can't get rid of them. Every time I take them up or plant something new, they come and replant them."

"Ah. So more folks you letting push you around then?"

"You don't understand. It's a community thing. It's . . ."

"It's bullshit, that's what it is. So Char figured out how to fix your problem," she said, and walked over to the cement mixer. "And don't tell me you haven't thought about this either. Now you gonna get up and help or you just gonna sit on your lily white ass?"

Mina had no idea what she was getting herself into, but she followed Char's lead as together they tore out the mums. Once the flowers were out, Char wheeled the cement mixer over to the planting bed. They emptied a portion of cement from the bag and mixed it with water from the garden hose. Then they poured the entire contents of the mixer into the bed, covering every inch of plantable dirt. Then Char, seemingly out of nowhere, produced a trowel. "You do this part," she said.

And Mina complied. She got down on her knees and got to work. As she smoothed the cement over the surface of the flower bed, she couldn't help but feel that tremendous sense of empowerment tingling through her again. She had the feeling, as she pushed the trowel back and forth over the now solidifying planting bed, that Charlie Witmore would not be bothering her property or pushing her around anymore.

When they were done, they sat down and admired their work. Both Char and Mina drained their glasses now. They stared at each other for a good minute before Char spoke again.

"Whosan whit not withstanding who," she said.

"I'm sorry?" Mina said. "What did you just say?"

"Lily? For real?"

"It must be the cognac. I never drink this stuff. It just sounded like you said 'Whosan whit not withstanding who,'" she said. "But why would you say that? I mean, that makes absolutely no sense at all. Right?"

Char just stared at her. She put her glass down on the table in front of her, and she looked Mina in the eyes intently. "Crysome moretouch and denim blaster," she said, in a tone more sympathetic and sweet than Mina had ever heard her use.

"Oh fuck. I am crazy. I'm crazy now, aren't I?"

"Oh fludajumanutza. Ousha wonna fudamite," Char said, now softly stroking Mina's face with her hand. She got up to leave and she took two steps before turning around.

"You gonna be okay, Lily?"

Mina rubbed her face with her hand. "I think I might be too drunk to be alone. Could you stay a little longer maybe? I mean, Jack's away. I don't know where Esther is. I feel so confused. I feel much too confused to be with Emma by myself. I mean . . . I can't make sense of anything . . ."

Char walked back over to Mina and she put her finger to Mina's lips. "Shhhh," she said. "Don't matter what's in your head, girl. You don't need your head. Your heart gonna get you through," she said.

"That I understood," Mina said.

"Good, Lily. Because schmazzit whosan whainsawhatfor."

"Oh fuck. Oh fuck."

"Gimme that phone, baby."

Mina handed Char-a'tee her phone. Char pressed some buttons and handed the phone back to Mina.

"Look at this phone number. Memorize it and then get rid of it. Because you don't need no one tracing you back to me, believe me. Not with what you're about to face. Just remember the number and get rid of it when you do."

"Okay . . ."

"Look, I gotta get the shit out of here. Baby, try and remember this number. And you call me next time you need me." With that, Char-a'tee Pryce was gone.

Mina collected the glasses and the near-empty bottle off the table. She looked up and saw Esther at her bedroom window, looking out. Mina waved with her free hand, but Esther just closed the curtains. She hoped they hadn't woken her up. Then she remembered her conversation with the mothers. The words "fuck her," took her by complete surprise, even though they jumped out of her own mouth.

# 13

The next morning, after dropping Emma at school, Mina felt terribly guilty about her antics the night before, the mother of all hangovers reminding her with a vengeance that she may have been unfair to Esther. She decided it was the very least she could do to pay Esther a visit and get to the bottom of things.

Esther answered the door on the second ring. Her normally jet-black hair seemed dulled somehow, though it remained wrapped up in her signature beehive. Mina also noticed that she wore a dragonfly pin that looked oddly familiar, though she was sure she would have remembered if Esther had worn it before, considering Mina's new, or maybe not so new, obsession with dragonflies.

"You look terrible, dear," said Esther, words of malice spoken gently, sweetened as if with chocolate.

Mina thought she could say the same of Esther, but decided to stick to her peace-keeping mission. "Yes, I was up late. I hope we didn't keep you up, outside?"

"I don't know what you're talking about?" said Esther.

Mina said, "Me, with my friend. The cement mixer. It must have been late . . ."

Esther chuckled. "No, dear. My waking in the night stopped when my worries did. Just like yours will someday. And besides, with this hearing?" She tapped her earlobe. "You'd be lucky if I could hear you properly even from here. Why don't you come in, dear? I was just making some sandwiches. An early lunch. Have you eaten yet?"

"I haven't, no. Thank you." Mina walked into the house and followed Esther into the kitchen.

"Please, have a seat," Esther said, and she busied herself over the counter. "Turkey good for you?"

"Sure," said Mina. "Thanks."

"Mayo or mustard?"

"Mayo, please."

"Sure thing," said Esther, with a smile. "I only have white bread. I hope that's okay. I know how you young people are with your whole grains, but when you get to be my age, well, you have to compromise on certain things if you don't want to spend your life in the bathroom, you know," Esther said with a laugh.

Now Mina relaxed. Of course everything was going to be fine. Of course she could talk to Esther, woman to woman, friend to friend.

Esther brought two plates to the table, and nodded to Mina to take a bite. The sandwich was delicious and she was grateful to be putting something into the firestorm that was her stomach. Esther pulled a pitcher of lemonade out of the refrigerator and two glasses from the cabinet. She poured them each a large amount and sat down with Mina.

"How did it . . . forget it . . ." Esther trailed off.

"No, it's okay. What do you want to ask me?" Mina took a large bite of her sandwich.

"I just wanted to know if you ended up going to the doctor after all. What he said, you know, about the visions . . . But if it's an intrusion . . ."

Mina wiped her face with her napkin and shook her head as she swallowed her food. "Not so much an intrusion as a big old mystery, I'm afraid."

"Did you uncover anything?"

"Kind of," she said. "But not with Barsheed. On my own." Mina pulled out the article. "Apparently, this is me. Apparently, I used to be someone."

"You're still *someone*, dear," Esther said, and took the clipping from Mina. She picked up her reading glasses and took a look. "Ah yes. Investigative reporter Lexi Randalls. You were quite the little hotshot, you know."

"I'm starting to see . . ."

"Your specialty was righting wrongs. Exposing scandals. A Pollyanna with a poison pen . . ."

"Poison?"

"Well, you may have been a little overzealous sometimes. Maybe not always fair when you could break a story."

"What do you mean?"

She shook her head. "I shouldn't say. Suffice to say, you were good at what you did."

Mina paused a moment. "Can I ask you something?"

"Yes?"

"If I was such a 'hotshot,' as you say, how come Harriet didn't know that I was a reporter. How come . . ."

"Because, like I've told you time and again, Harriet Saunders is a nitwit," said Esther, and she rolled her eyes. "Honestly, I don't know why you insist on keeping company with that woman. She's trash."

Mina felt defensive of Harriet now. "She's not trash. She's my friend—"

"She's a flake and a drunk. And a floozy. Totally unstable."

"Floozy" was new in the mix, but the other words were exactly the accusations made at the playground. Now Mina was angry. "Why did you tell those women I said that? I never said that."

"You're better off without them."

"That's my business, not yours. You know, it's very hard not having any friends. I mean, aside from you. You can't always be around. You won't always be around. And now that Kim's . . . gone . . ." The words got trapped in her throat. "I'm just saying that it's important for me and for Emma to branch out a little bit, you know?"

Esther stared at her coldly, and spoke words equally cold. "Of course, dear. I apologize. Why don't we just drop it then?"

"Okay, then."

"Who is Kim, dear?"

"Kim was my friend. She . . . died. I think she was killed, actually."

Esther took a sip of her lemonade and checked her watch. "That's strange, dear. You never mentioned a Kim before. Are you sure . . . I mean, with things getting a little murky for you. Are you sure she's *real*?"

Mina could feel herself getting annoyed again. "Of course she's real. She's as real as me and you. At least she was."

Esther laughed. "Oh, I'm sorry. I'm not laughing at you," she said. "It's just that . . . it just seems so far-fetched. What makes you think she was killed?"

With every word Esther spoke, Mina began to feel less and less sure that Kim was even real. It's like Char had said . . . Who becomes friend with a bill collector? Mina could feel heat rising in her cheeks and the cognac from last night starting to make its way back up again. "Let's just drop it, okay? It's just not worth getting into any more. She's *real*, I'm sure of it," Mina lied. "She was real."

Esther sighed and paused before she spoke. "Of course she is . . . was . . . dear. So when's Jack due back?

"I think tonight. That's what he said, at least. That he'd try to come home tonight, you know, all things considered."

"Well, good. I'll feel better with him back here, looking after the two of you."

Mina was still angry at Jack. "I suppose it is better for Emma, yes."

"Not for you?"

"I don't know anymore. I'm getting really tired of him not being around, you know? I mean, I know he has to work. Someone has to work. I just wish his job didn't involve so much travel."

Esther paused a moment before she spoke. "Well I suppose it didn't have to," she said.

"What do you mean by that," asked Mina, frustrated that everyone always knew more about her, about her marriage and her husband, than she did.

"Oh it's nothing, dear. It's just that, well, he's kind of a runner, so to speak."

"A runner?"

Esther took a deep breath. "When there's trouble, some people choose to stand and face it, expose it even, turn it around—like you," she said. "Others, like Jack, well, they prefer to flee."

"Jack's job demands travel. He isn't running away."

"Isn't he?" Esther asked.

Mina was quiet. Why was Jack a salesman? Why, of all things, was that the job he had. It hadn't always been his job, that she knew. Had there been other options? Other jobs that would have allowed him more time at home? She started to feel slightly queasy again.

Esther abruptly changed the subject. "Can I take Emma a short while today? I want to take her for a special treat to celebrate her big news."

"Sure. That would be nice," Mina said, happy that she'd have a little more time to explore the basement and maybe even get to the "Clippings - 4" box.

"Will you be okay on your own?" Esther asked.

"I think so," Mina said, but she was starting to feel even more uneasy. Nauseated and a bit dizzy.

"Is everything okay, dear?"

"Sure," Mina lied. "Just a late night."

"Do you need to lie down?"

"It's just that . . ." Mina started talking, but it seemed like she had no control over the words that fell out of her mouth. "It's just that . . ."

"What is it, dear?"

"Ever since going to the dentist. Things have been getting weird. I mean, I know it has nothing to do with the dentist. It's just that strange things have been happening. New discoveries. Talking to people who might not be there . . ."

Mina was starting to get very confused now. "I keep having strange memories. Very vivid. Something isn't right in my head."

Mina watched as Esther stood and made her way to the front window. "Like what?" she said, looking down at her watch. Why did she keep checking her watch?

"Like my uncle. He's dead," she said, her words now getting garbled.

"What's that, dear?" Esther asked.

"My uncle," she said, her mouth starting to feel like it was freezing over. "He's dead."

Esther laughed. "I don't think so, dear. In fact, I think he's very much alive," she said. "Of course, it's not your fault the bullet missed him."

"I don't feel so good," Mina said.

"Is everything alright, dear?" Esther asked.

And then the room went dark.

When Mina awoke, she realized it was impossible she was awake at all because, instead of sitting in Esther's kitchen with Esther, she was somehow standing backstage at a large auditorium. Music blared through the space as a charismatic figure, a man with silver hair and gleaming teeth, pranced and strutted back and forth, a microphone attached to his head with a system of wires that allowed him to move his arms freely, and to effortlessly climb to all the various levels of the set.

"It's all about YOU!" he shouted to the ocean of fans before him. "Your life. Your destiny. Your future. Whatever you want can be yours, just BELIEVE it can be yours. Now go out and get it. Goodnight!"

The stage went dark and all of a sudden Zander Randalls, Mina's creepy-but-not-really Uncle Alex, popped out of the floorboards behind her. Mina was confused for a second before she figured out that he must have come through a trap door that led to the center of the stage.

"What'd you think?" he asked her. He was glistening with sweat. A handler quickly brought him a thick, white towel and a bottle of water, and scurried off just as quickly.

"Great show tonight, Uncle," she told him. "Вы были удивительны."

"*I was amazing?* Really?"

"Really. You were really on fire out there."

He sniffed at his shirt. "Yeah, hence the sulfurous stench," he laughed. "Why don't you come back to my changing room. I'll grab a shower and then maybe we can go get a bite?"

"Okay, but I really can't stay all that long. I have to meet a source."

"That's my busy little peanut," he beamed. "How is the newspaper business treating you?"

She shrugged her shoulders. "It's fine, I guess. I just wish I could be doing more, you know? Something a little more—"

"Zander! Can we get a photo?!" called a paparazzo ten feet from them. Zander put his arm around his niece and they smiled. Then Mina winced.

"What's the matter?" he asked.

"God, you really do reek!" she said, and they both laughed as they headed deeper into the bowels of the auditorium to Zander's changing room.

"How's Jack?" he asked.

"He's fine."

"And our little one?" he nodded at Mina's belly. It was only then that she realized she was pregnant.

"Growing," was all she could say. Why hadn't she realized she was pregnant until he asked her? So strange. Except now she was hyper-aware of it—of the size of her midsection. Of the sensation of movement. Like snakes in a bag, but in a strangely pleasant way. She nearly jumped, feeling a slithering just under her rib cage.

"Moving?" Zander beamed.

Mina nodded, feeling a hot sensation of tears welling up in her eyes, an incredible sense of love welling up in her heart. Her failed memory had robbed her of any recollection of this magical time, of feeling Emma grow and develop within her. She knew this was a dream, but it was all so vivid. She couldn't remember her pregnancy, but now here she was, actually experiencing it. Finally knowing, finally understanding the experience. She hoped she wouldn't wake up too soon.

"May I?" he asked, nodding to her belly.

"Sure," she said. The moment Zander laid his hand on her belly, the baby flipped, and they both laughed.

"Well, looks like she's got some strong opinions already!" he said, and they both laughed again.

"How do you know it's a girl?" she asked.

He shrugged his shoulders. "Don't know. It's your dream."

"Right," she said.

The thought hung between them for a moment before he gestured for her to follow him down a long hallway. At the end, they came to a door with a humongous, cartoonish star painted on it.

"Oh, come on," Mina said.

"Pretty ridiculous, huh," he laughed, nodding to the graphic, and he turned the knob.

The room was over the top, and Mina realized this was probably based on a memory, but not a pure memory. It was completely white, with well-chosen silver accents—a white shag rug, white kidney-shaped leather couches, a giant silver statue of a dog perched on a white lacquered pedestal right in the center of the room.

Zander motioned to Mina to take a seat close to the . . . *fireplace?* . . .and he sat down in front of a mirror dotted with what seemed like a thousand lights. Curiouser and curiouser indeed.

"So what brings you here, peanut?" Zander wiped away at his stage makeup with a towel as he spoke.

"Well . . ." she hesitated. "Honestly, I'm kind of upset about something. I was hoping you could help me out."

"Okay, shoot," he said.

"A man called me. Today at the paper. He told me . . . I guess this is going to sound kind of weird . . . but he told me you kind of . . ."

"Yes?"

"You kind of ruined his life . . ."

"Well, that doesn't sound like me at all, does it? I'm Zander Randalls. I *fix* lives!"

She didn't know why, but his words angered her. Was it what he said? How he had said it? She felt the baby flip a somersault in her tummy, distracting her momentarily. Then she looked back at Zander and the anger returned. She tried to remain composed.

"Well, that's not how he seemed to feel about things. He told me, well, because of what you said. How you are. You made him believe he could believe anything. Do anything . . ."

Zander shrugged his shoulders. "Look, I just spout it. It's not up to me what they do about it."

"He quit his job! He left his wife—no, more like abandoned her and their small children. Thanks to you, he *believed* he *deserved* to embrace the greatness of his destiny, at any cost."

"Mina, come on now. You're not serious. You think this is because of me?"

"You have to admit that he has a point, Uncle. I mean, what you do to these people. The way they take you in. Take in your words like it's scripture. You're like their Jesus—"

"I'm hardly Jesus—"

"Yes. You and I both know that. But they don't. They believe you're somehow the lifeline to their happiness and their success. That you control their lives. They depend on you, you know . . ."

He shook his head. "I think you're drinking the wrong Kool-Aid," he said, dismissively, and she fought back the urge to get up and smack him. She took a deep breath.

"I depend on you."

"Well, that's a little different, don't you think, peanut? You are, after all, my niece. I practically raised you."

"You didn't raise me at all," she said. "You abandoned me."

He stewed quietly for a moment, and then he lost his calm. "How many times must we go through this?" he snapped, and slammed his fist down on the dressing table. He faced her, anger in his eyes. "Honestly, you're a grown woman now. You're practically forty. You have to understand something about life by now," he said, becoming calmer and colder with each word. "But let me spell it out for you again, and hopefully this time it will sink into that small, stubborn brain of yours." He took a deep breath. "I have spent my life building this empire, building this following. I never would have been able to do it fucking around with the PTA and birthday parties and science homework. But the work I did kept you fed and clothed and sent you to that college that apparently taught your heart how to bleed because that, my dear, you did not learn from me!"

"Look—"

"No. You look. No one's happiness or success depends on me. Not even yours, my dear. So if you're feeling empty and neglected and whatever else, again, that's not my problem. That's *yours*."

His words cut through her like a knife. "You know, you're always so kind to others. To *strangers*," she said. "All of your charitable work. Your scholarships . . . Up until you actually have to get closer to anyone than preaching to them across an auditorium or cutting a check. Then you're a fucking bastard."

"What are you talking about?"

"What you do to these people. You take advantage of them. They feel like you know them. That you actually care about them."

"Oh, please. Everyone knows this is a game. That it's all show business. I do my dog-and-pony show, they eat it up. Everyone gets what they want out of it. That's show business. I mean," he chuckled, "you know that I'm not really a messiah. Don't you?"

Mina gulped, considering her next words carefully.

He shook his head. "It's all just common sense, with sequins stapled onto it. Ordinary words laced with fairy dust. Anyone with half a brain knows how sparkly and silly and banal it all is."

Those last words hit her right at the core. "I don't think it's banal . . ."

"Well, then you're naive. Amazing, considering what you've already been through, what you remember of it, at least. Life hasn't exactly been a day at the playground for you, I mean . . ." he stopped, the thought trapped in his throat.

She was finding it hard now to hold back her anger. "What about the people who are supposed to matter to you? What about the lives you're responsible for?"

"I think you're taking all this much too seriously," he said, his tone softer now. "Like I told you. This is a game, peanut. People, those people out there, they're playing it just as much as I am."

"You're an asshole!" she said, and she shot up off the couch.

"Oh come on, peanut. Why are you so angry at me? I never promised you anything. I did the best I could."

"Your best sucked," she spat.

He sat there and stared at her a moment, looking almost wounded. But then, all of a sudden, he started to change. To *physically* change. His eyes lit up red and his body morphed into the form of a fierce and giant dragon. She blinked and shook her head and he was back to normal again.

"What?" he asked her.

"I have to go," she said, standing.

"So you're too mad at your uncle to have dinner."

"I just don't feel so well all of a sudden," she said, and she turned on her heel and left, slamming the door behind her.

As she walked back down the hall toward the stage and the exit of the auditorium, she was filled with rage and confusion. Who the hell did Zander Randalls think he was, that arrogant bastard! Someone definitely needed to shake him right off his pedestal, she thought, concentrating on her anger instead of the hallucination she'd just had.

"So what did he say?" a man's voice spoke to her, as if out of the wall.

Oh, great, she thought. Another hallucination. Well, this was a dream after all. "He said it wasn't his problem."

"What did you say to him?" the voice asked.

"I told him he was an asshole," she said, wishing that was exactly what she had said to him.

"So will you help me, missy?"

Mina felt a small kick under her ribs and knew that she had to get justice—to try and make the world a better place for the child she was about to bring into it.

Just then, the giant dragon she had seen Zander transform into charged down the hall after her and the voice in the wall. As it got closer, it exhaled a giant plume of fire and let out a tremendous cry. The dragon's tail thrashed back and forth, and she felt a pain in her head, as if she had been whacked by its leathery, spiked tail. And then everything went dark again.

# 14

Mina felt a dull pain in her head as she struggled to open her eyes. She could barely see anything as she squinted into the dim room. The longer she stared, the more shapes started to form out of the darkness, edges of objects becoming visible as she grew more conscious, more aware.

A table with a broken leg. A rocking chair. An antique trunk. Storage boxes in various sizes. It was becoming clear that she was in a basement, though not her basement. Definitely not her stuff. She noticed a single bulb suspended from the exposed beams of the unfinished ceiling and decided to see if she could find a switch. It was only then that she realized she was tied to a chair.

Mina tried to wriggle free from her restraints, but it was no use. It seemed the more she pulled on the ropes that tied her, the tighter they got.

"Oh, good. You're awake now," came a familiar voice from the darkness.

"Esther," she managed, groggily. "Are you okay?" Mina felt a twinge of disgust at the fact that whomever had done this to her would do the same to an elderly woman. If she was in pain, she could only imagine how poor Esther felt. "Esther?" Who could have done this to them? Had she really gone too far with the cement in her planting beds? Was her homeowners' association really this insane?

Just then, the exposed light bulb sparked to life and Esther moved under it, smiling kindly. Her smile put Mina at ease. Esther was okay, thank God. Mina was also relieved to see that Esther was free. But how had she managed that?

"Where are we?" she asked Esther. "Are you okay?"

"I'm fine, dear."

"They didn't hurt you? And how did you get free? Can you help me . . ."

Esther cocked her head at Mina. "I don't think so, dear."

Mina was confused; the throbbing pain in her head wasn't helping matters any.

"I don't understand . . . Is this about the planting bed?"

"What?"

"My flower bed. We filled it with cement."

"We? I didn't have anything to do with that."

"No, I meant—"

"This is not about the flower bed."

"Then what? Why are we here? Where are we?"

"Well, dear. I'm here because this is my house. You're here because I drugged you and dragged you down the stairs, and then tied you to the chair."

"Esther, seriously. Have you lost your mind? Does this have to do with the young people? You're mad about the situation between us and you guys in the community? We can talk about it, you know. This all seems a little extreme, don't you think?"

Esther stared at Mina for what felt like ten minutes before letting out a hearty laugh. "Oh, that's a good one, dear. No, I don't really care enough about you and those other twat mothers to do something like this. No," she laughed again. "It has nothing to do with that, I assure you."

Mina was still trying to get over the word "twat" springing so naturally from Esther's mouth, she found it difficult to speak, though finally managed to ask, "Then why?"

Esther pulled a chair close to Mina and sat down. "How do you suppose a little old thing like me can afford to live in this neighborhood? Hmmm?"

"I guess I hadn't thought about it . . ."

"You think Social Security even covers the maintenance? Please!"

"What are you saying?"

"I'm saying that everyone can use a sideline. Some people like to knit and make jewelry and sell it on Etsy for extra cash. Some people moonlight in the food service business or tending bar. You know I can't really do any of those things, not with my arthritis."

"If you got me down here with no help you can't be in such bad shape—"

"Strength is never a problem. How do you think that bag of cement and mixer ended up in front of your house? By magic?" Esther laughed. "I'm still pretty strong, even at my age, dear. The fine motor skills are the first to go. Though you'll never know this firsthand, of course, because you'll never be a day older than you are now. But you'll just have to trust me."

While Mina liked the idea of never getting older than she was, she wasn't so naive that she misunderstood Esther's meaning. Esther planned to kill her. But why?

As if reading her mind, Esther placed a liver-spotted paw on Mina's knee. "I don't get paid until you're dead, dear. You and Jack."

"Paid by who!"

"And Emma . . . That will be a tough one," Esther sighed.

Mina relaxed temporarily, thinking maybe Emma would be spared, until Esther spoke again. "She's such a little hellraiser, that one," she shook her head. "She will not make it easy at all."

All of a sudden everything seemed completely improbable to Mina and she realized her mind might be playing tricks on her again. Rather than entertain imaginings of any harm coming to her daughter, she opted instead to challenge it all. "How do I even know this is *real*?" Mina said. "That this is really happening. Barsheed said . . ."

"Ah, Barsheed. My delightful little pawn. 'Be sure to tell her she'll lose her mind if the memories come back too fast. Be sure to tell her not to search the past—that it needs to come to her . . .' I can't believe any of you fell for that!"

"What are you saying?"

"I'm sorry you fired him when you did, but it looks like he did enough damage to advance things for me, in any case."

"No. This is crazy. This is a dream. This can't be real!"

Esther reached under her chair and pulled up a worn-by-love threadbare little bunny. As a sick and final insult, she grazed Mina's cheek lightly with the bunny's ears; Mina knew the stench was beyond the limits of imagination. Mina knew she wasn't dreaming. Nausea rose up in her. She could physically feel her heart breaking in half. She had failed her child by trusting this woman. This monster. By convincing her child it was okay to trust this monster.

"Where is she?" Mina asked, broken. "Where is Emma?"

"Oh, she isn't home yet," said Esther. "I left a note on your door for that horrible Saunders woman to bring her here after school."

Mina was encouraged, just for a moment. "If Harriet knows where Emma's going to be, how do you think you're going to get away with this?"

Esther smiled. "You must think I'm some kind of amateur or something, don't you?"

"That wasn't exactly the word I had in mind."

"Well, in your bright career as a journalist, you've known very well the stories of mothers who go crazy. They can't take it anymore and they just up and off their kids. Their husbands. Really, it happens all the time. Do you really think all those women murdered their own children? Their families?"

"What are you saying?"

"Yes, it does happen sometimes, but it's rare. Usually it's someone else who comes in, you know, with their own reasons. Like me. Yes, that's generally how it's done."

"What are your reasons?"

"Money, of course. I told you that already. What else is there?" Esther said. "You'll be one of those women now, one of those women who kills her family and then kills herself out of despair. And maybe some journalist will write a nice, forgiving story about you! But, of course, you know it's more likely that they'll paint you as a monster. Like you did for me," she smiled, and the doorbell rang. "Ah, that must be our girl," she said, and she got up to leave.

*Like I did for her?*

Mina struggled to break free as Esther climbed the stairs. "Get back here! Esther!" Esther left the basement and bolted the door behind her. Mina felt hopeless as she struggled to free herself. To save her child. But there was nothing she could do.

Now Mina heard a few muffled voices coming from the upstairs foyer, and then the front door shut. It opened again, and then it slammed shut once more. Mina could kick herself for having given Esther permission to take Emma on a special adventure. And here she was, tied to a chair in the psychopath's basement, unable to do anything at all about it.

Mina struggled with her restraints. She noticed a sharp table edge not far from where she sat. She managed to jump her chair closer to the table, but before she got there, the restraints loosened and fell off.

"Fine motor skills indeed," she said to no one at all.

Mina jumped up and raced up the stairs. Finding the basement door locked, she barreled into it with her shoulder, and behind her were her full weight and the full power of her love for her child and her husband. On the fourth try, she knocked it in.

Mina raced to the hall phone and immediately called Jack. When his cell went right to voice mail, she called his office.

"I'm sorry. There's no way he can be disturbed right now," the receptionist said tersely, "because he never showed up today," and she hung up.

Jack didn't show up at work? Now she panicked. Did they have Jack? She called the police.

"Yep," a man answered.

Mina was confused. "Is this the police station?"

"Yep."

"Well, can I speak with an officer?"

"Depends."

"Depends? What do you mean *depends*? This is an emergency!"

"Who'd you say this was?" the asked.

"My name is Mina Clark. I live on—"

"Mina Clark. Oh yeah, I know your name. We actually just this morning got notified by your shrink someone might be calling about you."

"Barsheed?"

"Sure. Happens more than you think. Shrinks give a heads-up that their patients may be off their meds and may become a threat to themselves or others—"

"I'm not on any meds!"

"Yep. That's our cue to come pick you up and get you hospitalized then. Though usually it's a family member who calls? Well, anyway, you just sit tight little lady and—"

Mina slammed down the phone. She called Harriet but couldn't get her on the phone. She panicked. What was she going to do now? Then she remembered the night before, on her patio. Char gave her a phone number and told her to memorize it. She took a deep breath and leaned against the wall as she tried to remember it.

A flash of numbers came to her and she dialed them, but she hadn't gotten it right. She tried again, and again was wrong. And then wrong again.

"Shit!"

And then one last time.

"Who are you looking for again?" the woman's voice on the other end asked.

"My friend, Char-a'tee. Char-a'tee Pryce."

"Oh. My. God." The woman broke into a fit of giggles. "Who put you up to this?"

"I'm sorry?"

"Was it Frank? Did he tell you to call me? That douchebag," she laughed. "I can't believe this."

"I don't understand. What's so funny."

"Char-a'tee Pryce. From that book."

"Book? What book?"

"What book? It was pretty big a few years back. What, do you live under a rock or something?"

Mina's heart started to race. "Something like that, I guess . . ."

"Like you don't already know this . . . Char-a'tee Pryce is the name of a character in this book called *Random Acts of Char-a'tee*. They were going to make a movie and everything but—"

"*Random Acts of . . .?*"

"Yeah. Very cool revenge story about a woman who got ruined and then set out to ruin everyone. I mean, just about everyone. It was great! She had some unfinished business, what do you call that? Like a cliffhanger ending. Anyway, everyone's been waiting for a sequel, but apparently the author went nuts or something—"

"A character? In a book?"

"Yep. A *great* character. You should check it out—if you don't already know it—ha, ha, wink, wink. Well, say hi to Frank and thanks for the joke. Really made my day," the woman said and hung up the phone.

Mina's head was spinning. Emma was missing and now so was Jack. Esther was a madwoman. Kim was dead. And even if she could get her on the phone, Harriet would never understand what was going on here. And now Char-a'tee was a hallucination . . .

Mina realized there was only one person she could call, and she prayed Jack was wrong about Alex being dead as she dialed. She had no idea where this call would lead, but she was out of options.

She waited three rings before he picked up. "Mina."

"How did you know it was me?"

"No one else calls me."

"Why is that?"

He paused a moment. "Everyone else thinks I'm dead."

"Are you dead, Alex?" she asked.

"What do you think?"

"I don't know what to think anymore. Things are starting to get really crazy right now and I don't know who I can trust . . ." Mina said, now crying.

"Trust *me*," he said. For a second her mind flashed back to her dream. A vision of the man with the red eyes. The dragon. "What choice do you have, Mina?"

She knew, unfortunately, that this pretty much decided everything.

"Where are you?" he asked.

"Next to my house. But I can't stay here." Mina then told Alex everything that had transpired in the past couple of hours . . . everything except her dream about the dragon.

"Listen carefully. Behind your development there's a jogging trail. Do you know it?"

"Yes . . . but . . ."

"Right across from that garden with the giant dahlias is a fence with a sign that reads *State Property, No Trespassing.* Something like that. Climb over the gate and head down the path until you get to a beach. I'll be right there."

Mina hung up the phone. A beach? In the middle of her development? That made no sense at all. But Mina didn't exactly have the luxury of sitting down and trying to figure it out.

As she ran out Esther's back door and toward the jogging trail, she wondered if Alex was really in this to help her. Or if he was going to be the death of them all.

Then Mina tripped over a root and crashed headfirst into a tree and everything went black.

"Can you tell me again, Mr. Paulsen, why *you* think Zander Randalls is responsible for destroying your life? I mean, don't most people consider him a *savior*?" Mina asked the man sitting across the table from her in the Savoy Diner. She was frustrated to be unconscious again but also somewhat delighted, as in this dream she was again pregnant.

The man, probably in his early sixties, with a rugged working man's countenance, a face creased and flecked in salt-and-pepper stubble, took a sip of his coffee. He practically spit it out. "Savior! That's a laugh. That man is a brainwashing devil!"

Mina leaned forward. "And you would be willing to tell him to his face? If I can take you to him, will you tell the world what an evil farce he truly is?"

"Missy, you just get me his ear and I'll give it to him big time, believe me," he said, folding his arms across his chest and sitting back. Then he leaned forward. "But you gotta tell me something. What are you so hot to get him for?"

"He's my uncle," Mina replied, nonchalant.

"And?"

"Let's just say he's been a very shitty uncle and leave it at that."

"Why? He do something fucked up to you?"

Mina didn't respond. She took a sip of her drink while she calculated her response. "He deserted me when I was a kid," she said, her voice cracking. She cleared her throat and started over. "You think you're the only one whose head he crams with crap and nonsense? He fucks everyone and he's got to be stopped."

"Well, you're definitely the one to show him for the fraud he is. Bet you can spot a creep from ten miles. Like that crazy broad no one believed offed her family and you brought down. You know that's why I called you."

"We'll get him," she said, and smiled at the man. "Believe me, we'll put an end to all his nonsense." Just then the baby took a fierce flip inside that nearly knocked Mina out of her chair. She actually grabbed onto the table to brace herself.

"You alright there, missy?"

"Sure," she said, although she couldn't help feeling that this was a lie.

Mina took a deep breath and got back her bearings. She finished her drink. After they'd paid the check and left the diner, Mina rode with the man in his car. They drove in silence as they wound through the various highways that led to the Nassau Coliseum, where Zander Randalls was wrapping a sermon/performance that night.

Using her credentials, Mina escorted Paulsen backstage with her, where they waited for Zander's performance to end.

On the stage, lights flashed and music blared as Zander addressed his flock. "You are your own house of power!" he shouted to the sheep. "Do not let anyone else huff and puff and blow that house down! Good night!"

The auditorium went dark. Mina leaned to whisper in the man's ear. "He'll be here in a minute," she said, and gave him an encouraging light punch in the arm. He only smirked in reply.

"Peanut! You're talking to me again!" came an enthusiastic voice from behind them.

Mina turned to face him. "This is purely business, Uncle."

"Ah, we're back to hating Uncle again. Okay then. What have I done now?"

Mina did not appreciate his patronizing tone. She braced herself and spoke. "I think it's high time you owned what you put out there."

At that moment, Paulsen turned around to face Zander, and Zander's face seemed to lose all color.

"What is it, *Uncle*? You're afraid to face an actual life you've '*saved*,'" she said, using her fingers to accentuate the last word with air quotes.

"Сделайте Вы знаете, кто это?" Zander said coolly, and he shot Mina a disapproving glance. *Do you know who this is?* His expression quickly flashed back to his stage face.

"Сделайте Вас?" *Do you?* she replied, unsure of why he had asked her that question in the first place. *Of course she knew who this man was!* She had brought him here, hadn't she?

Zander extended a hand. "Pleased to meet you . . . what did you say your name was?" he asked, somewhat tentatively.

"Paulsen," the man said, "Arnie Paulsen. And if you don't mind me saying, the pleasure's all yours." He brushed away Zander's hand.

Zander pulled back his hand and a look of worry washed over his face. "So what's the meaning of this, Ali?" he asked Mina. "You're going to grind your personal axe with me in your newspaper then?"

Mina fought to keep from lashing out. "You know it's my job to expose fraud when I see it. I, and Mr. Paulsen, well, we agree that what you're doing here," she said, waving her hand around, "filling all these people's heads with impossible thoughts, well, I think it's fraud. And I think it's high time you manned up and took responsibility for the lives you've, well, changed."

"Ah, yes," said Zander, now cool. "You mean the same fraud who bought you the fancy education and the ability to get into writing for newspapers to begin with? Ironic don't you think?"

"You ruined my life, and now you're going to pay!" said the man reaching into his pocket.

"Look out! He's got a gun!" someone shouted.

And then everything flashed white.

# 15

Mina jerked awake and pulled herself up, wiping dirt and a few crumbled dead leaves from her mouth. The sun was setting now. She wondered what time it was; without her cell phone, she had no idea. She brushed herself off and headed, full speed, to the meeting point where Alex had told her to go.

She found the dahlia garden and the sign, just where he had said it would be, and she scaled the fence. About thirty yards down, she was amazed to find herself at a beach; more amazing than that was that he was there. He had waited for her. He was tapping into an iPad and he wasn't wearing his hat. She now recognized exactly who he was: her uncle, Zander Randalls.

"Uncle?"

"Peanut. I have been so worried about you," he said, and he pulled her into a giant hug. His hat was gone. His beard was gone. "What happened?"

"I guess I hit my head," she said. "I ran into a tree."

He pulled away from her and laughed. "That's typical," he said, and lightly brushed the bruise that had formed on her head with the tip of his thumb. He continued to laugh as he pulled her back into his arms.

The way he smelled, the way he felt . . . Mina started to feel that same uneasiness again in his arms. "I don't see how any of this is funny," she said, squirming slightly to free herself.

Finally he let go. He looked intently into her eyes. "You're afraid of me."

"Can you tell me why?"

"What have you remembered?"

"Not much, really. I just keep having these crazy dreams, you know?"

"The dreams are part of it."

"Part of what?"

"The process."

"I get it. You're not telling me anything. Fine. I don't care."

"Can you just trust me?" he asked. "Just try?"

"Can you at least tell me where we are? And how is there a beach here?"

"I wish I had a better explanation but it's actually not that exciting. Really it's just a catch-basin for water coming off the highway."

"But it's a beach."

"A reservoir really, but yeah, I guess it's also kind of a beach, sure."

"That's just crazy."

"The world's a crazy place. I don't have to tell you that, peanut. So come on. There's no more time to waste."

Mina followed Zander off the beach. The path was dense with foliage, and gnats buzzed in swarms. When she opened her mouth to speak, several flew in. She decided it would probably be better for them to talk later.

Several minutes later, they came to a clearing and then to a road Mina didn't recognize. Parked on the road was a silver Prius, and Zander nodded to Mina to get in.

Zander started the engine and he pulled out his tablet. He passed it to Mina.

"Are you real?" she asked, tentatively.

"You called me, didn't you?"

"I guess I did."

"What do I call you? Uncle? Alex? Zander Randalls?"

"Ah, so you are starting to remember," he said gently, encouragingly.

"A little bit. But if you're Zander Randalls. And everyone seems to believe Zander Randalls is dead, then how are you here? Why does everyone think Zander Randalls is dead?" she asked, point blank.

He looked at her over his eyebrows. "Because he is," he said, and he peeled off into the road.

She buried her face in her hands. "So you're saying I'm riding in a car with a hallucination."

"No, I told you. I'm real."

She looked up at him. "Char-at'ee isn't real."

"I know."

"But it just doesn't make any sense, you know? You *spoke* with her, just as I did. You interacted with her. You took her coat . . ."

"Remember that I met Char after you did. She wasn't your first imagined friend."

"Great. Who else are you going to tell me isn't real now. Esther?"

He seemed to ignore her. "Do you remember Lucy? You also used to let me speak to Lucy."

"You know, I didn't before. But I guess I've been seeing her now, yes. Only in dreams though. Barsheed asked me about her too. I know she isn't real."

"She used to be quite real to you, once."

"But you won't tell me why."

"I can't. But I will tell you this. Believe it or not, with Char-a'tee in your life, and now that you've been having these dreams, you are on your way to remembering things again. It's really amazing how similar it is this time . . . The same as when you were a child. First the dreams. Then the friend. Truly crazy. Sorry. But you know what I mean."

Of course she didn't. "Sure," she said, resigned, looking out the window. "Where are we going?" she asked.

"If we can build this bridge for you, between your dreams and your memories, you're going to be able to find Jack and Emma. So you'll stop asking questions now and just trust me?"

"What choice do I have?"

"Good," he said. "Now, while you're sitting there, I want you to open the screen on that tablet and take a look at what I found while I was waiting for you."

Mina complied. She tapped the tablet and a website came up. "What is this?"

"I know. Try and ignore that it's kind of a kooky conspiracy website."

"It looks like a dentistry site."

"Keep reading and you'll see."

Mina scrolled through the article on the screen but couldn't find anything relevant. "I don't get it," she said.

Zander pulled over and took back the tablet. He tapped at it a couple of times; the look on his face indicated that he'd found what he was looking for. "Here we go," he said. "So things may be a whole lot worse than they seem." He tapped some more. "Tell me about that thing in your mouth."

"What? You mean the gold crown?"

"This website has a theory..."

"Oh, good. Now another person thinking that the Internet—"

"Just bear with me. The place you got that put in? Pearls of Wisdom?"

"Yes?"

"And your bank, the one that owns your house. First Federal?"

"So?"

He looked up at her. "Did you know that First Federal also owns Pearls of Wisdom?"

"I imagine banks own a lot of things."

"Yes. Securities. Souls. But dental spas? Doesn't it seem a little peculiar to you?"

"I don't know. Maybe?"

"Yeah, it's odd. So open your mouth. Let me get a better look."

"Are you kidding me?"

"Mina, come on. Open." Once again Mina complied.

Zander held her by the chin and titled her head back and forth. "Okay, let's check it out," he said, and he tapped more into his tablet. "Fuck."

"What?"

He sighed. "This website has a theory . . ."

"Okay . . .?"

"This sounds totally fucking nuts, I know. But it does all start to add up . . ."

Mina was losing patience. "What's the theory?"

He hesitated a moment before he spoke. "Well, the website claims that Pearls of Wisdom exists to help the bank get more control of its customers."

"In what way?"

"The gold crowns, it seems. There are two types. One is a mind-control device."

Mina pulled her hand to her face.

He shook his head. "I'm sure you don't have the mind control one. I think yours is a little more dangerous."

"Something more dangerous than mind control?" Mina said, once again pulling her hand to her face. She gasped. "It's not some kind of detonator or something!"

"No, not at all. No. Let me think for a second... They must not know you're free yet. That you got away. There's still time."

At that moment, Zander shockingly sprang out of the driver's seat and straddled Mina, holding her down. "I'm sorry, peanut," he said, and when she opened her mouth to scream, he forced her mouth to stay open. She could swear his eyes flashed that demon, dragon red for a moment before he pulled a pair of pliers from the center console, reached into Mina's mouth, and tore out her crown.

"What the fuck!" she screamed. "Get the fuck off of me! You sick bastard! Get the fuck off of me," Mina spat blood with her words.

Zander held up the pliers with the extracted tooth; and then he passed out.

Mina struggled to get him off her but she couldn't budge him. "Wake up, you sick fuck! Wake up and get the fuck off of me!" He still didn't budge.

What was Mina going to do now? As she sat there underneath him, crying, all she could think about was how stupid she had been to trust this man. It really would be over now for all of them.

She tried to heave Zander off her again as her thoughts turned to her husband. Her daughter. She'd fucked up, trusting all the wrong people, and now they were doomed.

But then the thought of "trusting all the wrong people" began to simmer while she sat there, caged by her crackpot uncle. *Trusting all the wrong people*. Her mind flashed to Esther. To Alex. And then to the dream she had had after she'd hit her head . . .

*Your dreams are the bridge to your memories . . .*

The man . . . Paulsen . . . The interview . . . The confrontation . . . The look of *knowing* on Zander's face when he saw Paulsen . . . How did Zander know Paulsen? Speaking to her in Russian . . . Asking her if she knew . . . And the gun . . . Zander Randalls was shot . . . And it was Mina's fault . . .

Now Zander jerked awake. He jumped off of Mina and returned to the driver's seat. He chucked the pliers and the gold tooth-GPS out the window, into the brush, and pulled a box of Wet Ones out of the console. He handed it to Mina, started the car, and pulled back onto the road.

"I'm sorry, Mina. I know that was gross. Devastating and gross. And I know you don't believe it, but I would *never, never* do anything to hurt you. I really didn't have a choice. If they know where you are, you're all going down."

"Just forget it," she said, and they drove in silence, Mina poking the tip of her tongue into the hole left by the extracted device.

"We're going to get them back, okay? And then you can tell me to fuck off and get out of your life. But first we're going to get them back."

"Zander Randalls was murdered."

"That's what the world believes, yes."

"It was my fault."

"Don't think like that, Mina. You didn't pull the trigger."

"But I led him to you. I thought he killed you, and that it was my fault. That's the terrible thing that happened to me. But why would I do that? Why was I so angry at you? That's what I can't remember . . ."

He pulled over once again and threw the car into park. He grabbed Mina's hand in his and he squeezed it tight. He looked intently into her yes. "Zander Randalls is dead, and believe me, that's a good thing. He had to go. Showy, self-absorbed prick that he was. Now it's just me, okay? Now it's just Alex."

"Uncle Alex."

He smiled warmly. "Your one and only."

They drove on again. "So why did the bank put a tracking device in my mouth?"

"Because they wanted to keep tabs on you, naturally."

"That's ridiculous, though. They know where I am. They all know where I am. They call me forty freaking times a day!"

"Well, I'm no detective, but I'm going to say it has to do with what just happened with Esther. I have some ideas."

"Like what?"

"Do you and Jack have life insurance?"

"We have a child."

"Okay, so, Emma's the beneficiary?"

"Of course. I mean, I think so. Why wouldn't she be?"

He shook his head. "Don't be so sure," he said.

"What are you talking about?"

"Did you read the fine print?"

"Honestly, Jack usually takes care of these things. I don't even think we have the policy at home. I'm pretty sure he keeps all that stuff in his office."

"Well, if you read the fine print in your agreement, you'll see that if your loan defaults more than a certain number of days, First Federal will become the beneficiary of your life insurance policy."

"Jack never told me that," she said, shaking her head. "That can't be true."

"The website says . . ."

"Doesn't that seem a little insane to you?"

"I've seen it before."

"On the Internet," she scoffed.

"Uh, no. I always read the fine print. You should always read the fine print."

"Thanks," she said.

"Are you behind on your payments?"

Mina felt the familiar shame rising up in her. "A couple of months maybe."

"I bet that's what it is then. They want their money and they're willing to kill you all for it. We have to get our hands on that policy."

"That's ridiculous!"

"That's corporate America."

"But why not just foreclose on us? Take the house away and sell it?"

"That neighborhood you live in? You know your house isn't worth anywhere near what you paid for it. The bank doesn't want to lose that kind of money. Now, say you and Jack are each insured for one mil—or one and a half?"

"Sounds about right."

"Voila. So the bank loses nothing, and in the event of your death, it actually makes a whopping profit."

"So how does Esther profit in all of this? Do you think she works for the bank? That they hired her?"

His eyes lit up. "Bingo! You see, that's why we need to get your head on this because this is just the sort of reporting you used to do."

"Vindicating the victims. Bringing down the bad guys. Like you."

"Maybe, but I think it's best we drop that for now."

"Well, I'm sorry but I can't. Why am I so angry at you? Why did I do that to you? What did you do to me that was so awful? I keep thinking . . . Forget it."

He took a deep breath. "You resented me. As Zander, I traveled constantly and you never believed I was there for you. I was always there for you when I could be. But you wanted more. And you deserved more. You were right. And Jack blames me for . . ."

"For what?"

"Never mind. Just forget it for now."

"Well what about my parents? My mother? Was that why I stopped remembering before? And come to think of it, how could you leave me after that?"

"Ultimately, you ended up in a good place, but . . . no. It wasn't always good. While they were placing you, you jumped around from one foster home to the next."

"And you *let* that happen to me."

"I realize now that I had a choice, but back then I didn't see it that way. I could have done things differently but I chose wrongly. I can admit that. Though I will add that the experience did make you *strong*. I know you'll never believe me about that. But the way you grew up, it taught you to never take any bullshit from anyone. I think that's what helped you write Char-a'tee so well."

"*Wrote* Char-a'tee? What does that mean?"

"Your friend, your hallucination. She's your character," he laughed. "You created her. *Random Acts Of Char-a'tee*—that's your book."

"I thought I was a reporter? You're telling me I wrote this book too? How come there's no record of me writing that. Wouldn't someone have said something? If it was such a big book. . . My name . . ."

"You wrote it under a pen name. 'Blonde Satin.'"

"Great. Another identity."

"We all wear many hats."

"Why am I Mina?"

"Alessandra Philomina Randalls. You were always Ali, but when you got past what happened with your mother, and you lived with Stan and Tanya, you decided you wanted to be called Mina instead. It was easier for them to say anyway."

"And Lexi?"

"You picked that up as a reporter. Because of the kinds of stories you did, you wanted to keep your professional life separate from your personal life."

"You mean stories that ruined people. Like the one that ruined you . . ."

"You never got around to writing that story, actually. You know, because of your illness. But yes, that was the general idea."

"Okay, but what I don't understand is that if I destroyed you, *why* are you helping me? Why have you been giving me money and why did you get my car back? And why are you here now? Are you also working with Esther and the bank? How do I know I can trust you?"

Alex scratched his chin. "You know, I was angry at you for a long time. Deeply disappointed and deeply hurt. If we're to be honest about things, I was mad as hell. I wanted you to suffer for what you did. For ruining me. *Me!* Of all people! For a long time, I could only see how I was affected by all of it. How hard I worked to get you into the best schools. How you of all people could betray me so deeply and horribly."

"I saw it differently, I guess."

"Yes. Well, if you can see it, you can believe it . . ."

"That's not really helping."

"Sorry. Anyway, after a while, being 'dead,' I started to see that maybe you *were* right. That I was making a lot of money at the expense of people. Vulnerable people."

"Oh. Like the man . . ."

His eyes flashed angrily. "No. Not like him."

"Sorry. I—"

He shook his head. "You couldn't have known. He tricked you. He knew you were vulnerable, at least in one way." He shook his head. "I always told you that you were strong. That the only strength you can ever count on is the strength you have within. Do you remember that day? Your mother's funeral? The dragonfly?"

"I had a dream, I guess. I think I do now, yes."

"Well, I'm not like you. Jack's not like you. He's soft, sensitive. Maybe a little cowardly."

"Hey!"

Alex shook his head and kept talking. "Jack is a sweet soul. An artist. He counts on you for strength, or at least he did. He softens you."

She thought about Esther's words, that Jack didn't have to travel. That he chose to travel. To get away from her... "He runs away from me. I'm afraid he may be having an affair. With his boss. Her name is Amber..."

"He's not running from you, Mina. He's just running. That's just the way he is. He's not much for confrontation, for facing things. That's more your thing. He runs away because he doesn't know what else to do. And I'm certain he's not having an affair. He loves you, Mina. I'm sure he does. But, like I said, he's kind of a coward."

Mina felt annoyed at his assessment of her husband but decided to let it go.

"And you? What about you, Uncle?"

"Me? I'm shallow, flashy. A con artist. In any case, we're the kind of people who *need* people like you to keep us strong. Well, Jack strong. Me, honest."

"But Jack's the one who . . . And you . . ."

"You don't see it so clearly, maybe because of your condition, but you're the one who keeps him strong. You always have been. At least you were."

Mina considered this for a moment but for as long as she could remember, there was no proof of this at all in their marriage. Except the night that she took the phone from him. What had he said to her . . . *You seemed a little more like you* . . .

"Most people need something they believe is strong to cling to, which is why I got to be so famous. Pretending to be that kind of person. A fucking messiah! A gleaming dragonfly with a shiny, colorful exoskeleton and shimmering wings. All flashy and distracting on the outside and totally weak within . . . Jesus. What an ass I was. Sure, I was helping some people, maybe. But I was neglecting the one person I should have been helping all along. I really didn't believe you needed me. But I was wrong. I was so fucking wrong . . ."

"But then you found me?"

"I never lost you. I always knew *where* you were. If you ask Jack, I'm the one who quote-end-quote *imprisoned* you there. It was only in the past several weeks that I realized what a hollow prick I had been. That it was time to, well, face up to my part in it all. And I felt like maybe, just maybe, I could forgive you."

"So you do forgive me then? You're not angry with me anymore?"

"Do you want the honest answer?"

"I guess maybe now's not the best time."

"Time heals all wounds, or so they say. Look, I'm sure things will be right between us, between me and you and me and Jack someday," he said, staring off into the distance.

"So now what?"

"Now we save your family."

"And you and me?"

"I'm sure we'll work it out. First things first: Let's go get that policy."

# 16

Balabaster Design Fittings was located in the most soulless of places, a suburban industrial park buried behind a landfill in the dead middle of Long Island. There was nothing inviting about the drive to the squat little building that housed Jack's office. Mina had been there once, maybe twice, but she'd never before felt such guilt that someone like Jack, someone with such a deep appreciation of art and beauty, had to report almost every day of his life to a place like this. Mina's eyes filled with tears. She decided that if they got out of this current terrible mess, the first thing she would work to change would be Jack's job. She almost didn't care if he still traveled, just so long as he never had to come back here.

Alex pulled into a spot in front of the building and hopped out of the car. "You coming?"

"Yeah," said Mina. She wiped her face with the back of her hand and followed him to the front door.

"So who's the lead here?" he asked.

She stared blankly at him. He shook his head. "Who's doing the talking? Part of me thinks you're better because you're the wife and the badass . . . though partly I think maybe me, you know, because of the whole Zander magic thing."

She stared blankly at him.

"Let's just say I can be persuasive. You'll see."

"You lead," she said, and she pushed open the door and walked ahead of him.

Once inside, Mina approached the reception desk. Now she could see the face of the snotty little tormenter who controlled whether or not she could speak to her husband on the phone. It gave her great pleasure to feel her special feeling rise within her, that tingly empowering sense of awesome. Just as Alex opened his mouth to speak, Mina jumped in front of him and pounded her fist on the girl's desk. "I want to see my husband. Now, bitch!"

The girl was startled, and looked to Alex for an explanation. He shrugged his shoulders in reply. "This is her show," he said, a chuckle in his voice, and he stepped back.

"I said I want to speak to my *fucking* husband now. You better make it happen. Go get me Jack Clark. Now!"

Recognition washed over the girl's face. "Oh, yes," she said, less startled, more smug. "Jack's crazy stalker wife."

Mina felt the urge to throttle the girl, which Alex must have sensed, as he gently placed his hands on Mina's shoulders to hold her back.

"Jack's not here," she said, smug and bored, as she looked away from Mina and casually flipped through some papers on her desk.

"Well, then I guess I'm going to have to go see for myself then, aren't I?" said Mina. She turned to Alex. "It's this way. Come on." He obediently followed.

"You can't go back there!" the girl screeched. "I'll call security!"

Mina turned to face the girl. "Bitch, I'm his wife. I can go wherever I want." And she and Alex darted through a commune of cubicles to get to Jack's office, another deeply soulless space.

Alex and Mina rummaged around, pulling open credenza doors and filing cabinet drawers, producing nothing worthwhile. When Mina headed to Jack's desk, her eyes stopped for a moment. The surface was covered in scrap papers, filled with random doodles. The one photo he had was a framed picture of her and Emma, smiling in the sun. Aside from the doodles, it was the only remnant in the space that belied a human being sometimes occupied it. Mina thought back to the day that Jack took it, the three of them spending a summer afternoon together, playing in the park. Alex now joined Mina behind the desk and started pulling open drawers.

"Bingo!" he called out when he got to the bottom drawer, shaking Mina out of her reverie.

"You found it?"

"I think so. Who's your life insurance with?"

"Uh, let me think. Is it HighLife maybe?"

"Got it," he said, holding it up.

"Can I help you?" came a woman's voice from the door. "What is your business here?"

Mina looked up to see a stout woman in her late fifties, nearly as round as she was tall. Her well-creased face was made up as if she'd gotten ready in the dark; her gray suit, creased like her face, seemed starched stiff, as if made of cardboard. "Who the hell are you?" Mina asked.

Aside from a slight twitching in her left eye and her lips, the woman remained cool and collected. "I'm Amber Fox. Regional manager."

"You're Amber Fox? *You*? You're Amber?" Mina replied.

"More like something encased in amber," Alex quipped under his breath.

Mina shot him a disapproving glance.

"You know what they say, 'Face your fears . . .'" he whispered softly, a chuckle in his voice.

"What is your business here?" Amber asked.

"I'm Jack's wife," Mina said.

Amber's face seemed to soften slightly. "Well, maybe you could tell us where is Jack then? No one here's heard from him since he left Omaha last night."

"Neither have we," said Mina.

"Really? I thought for sure he was with you. I know there have been . . . issues. He said he needed to cut his trip short . . . that you . . ." she looked away, clearly embarrassed.

Alex piped up. "There are problems alright, but not with Mina. We have to find Jack—and Emma, now. We have reason to believe they're in danger. I think you have the power to help us out," he began, starting to spin some of the old Zander Randalls mind-washing magic. *"Do you believe you have the power to make a difference?"* he challenged.

Amber's eyes suddenly began to glimmer with life and promise. It was as if she had become possessed."Of course!" she said. "I have the power to make a difference!"

"How do you do that?" Mina whispered.

"Jedi mind trick?" he whispered back. She rolled her eyes. "Well, my version of it anyway."

Mina faced Amber. "Is there anything more you can tell me about the last time you spoke to Jack? Any clue he may have given about where he was headed?"

Amber shook her head and pursed her lips. Suddenly her face lit up. "Wait a minute!" she said. "I can't believe I didn't think about this before. Let me get in there," she continued, trying to squeeze herself between them and the desk.

Mina and Alex stepped aside, and Amber sat down and flipped on Jack's computer, logging on with her code. "Stupid. Of course!"

"What is it?" Mina asked, peering over Amber's shoulder, breathing in a hint of mold coming off Amber's starchy suit.

"All of our employees have cell phones with GPS chips. It's so we can track them in the field—so we know they're actually making their sales calls instead of ducking into the movies or something."

"That seems a little insidious, don't you think?" Mina challenged.

Amber looked up. "I do. That's why I forgot all about it. I never use it." Amber pecked away at the keyboard and suddenly a map filled the screen.

"Aha!" she said, and kept typing. "The technology isn't quite perfected yet to pinpoint exactly where someone is, but . . . let's see." Amber tapped the screen with a squat sausage finger. "I can't make out where this is. All I see is golf courses and . . . looks like maybe some houses . . . Wait, what is this? A beach?"

Mina shot Alex a knowing glance. "Looks like he's home?" said Alex. "Or close to it?"

"Odd, but it looks like he's closer to the playground or something," Mina said. "Let's go." She darted for the door but then turned back into the office and rushed to the desk. She grabbed the framed picture from Jack's desk and looked at Amber. "Thank you," she said.

"*You've accomplished a great greatness here today*," said Alex, and Amber's eyes got that glimmer again.

"Jack's very important to us. I'm happy I could help," she said, and Mina and Alex ran out of the building and headed to the car.

"Why don't you drive," he said, tossing her the keys. "I'll read."

They jumped into the car and Mina peeled out of the parking lot.

A minute or so later, Alex said, "This may be worse than I thought. At least it's more insidious."

"Why?" she asked.

"Who do you suppose owns HighLife?"

"Not First Federal?"

"You got it!"

"Son of a bitch," she said, and floored the engine.

Mina raced to Easton Estates, but once through security, she slowed to about fifteen miles an hour.

"Don't you want to step it up a bit?" asked Alex.

"They're very particular about speeding here," she said. "Lots of kids and dog walkers."

As if on cue, a couple of dog walkers materialized, each holding a leash in one hand, a bag of droppings in the other. When Mina and Alex drove past, they each waved the hand with the droppings at them.

"Your neighbors just waved dogshit at you," Alex said.

"Yes, that's kind of what they do here," she said, and she sped up slightly to get to the playground. "I don't think it means anything except that they're clueless."

"Still . . ."

When they arrived at the playground, they noticed a fence had been erected around the perimeter. "What the—" Mina said out loud as she turned off the car and headed to the entrance. Alex followed.

"I guess this is meant to keep creeps like me away?" he said.

"I don't think this is keeping anyone away," Mina said, nodding to the gate. The fence was only about three and a half feet high. Mothers and nannies simply lifted the children over the gate; once inside, they tripped the lock and let the adults in.

"Another one of Witmore's bright ideas," said Harriet when Mina and Alex approached.

Also outside the gate was a small group of scowling older residents. "You shouldn't be doing that!" one of the fossils screeched.

"You should be using your key!" yelled another one dressed all in beige.

"The rule says '*Use your key*'," a man in plaid shorts piped up.

Ellen stepped over to the throng of old people and said, "You think we don't know that we need a key?"

Alex entered the fray. "It appears that none of these women were given keys," he said to the older crowd, and their eyes took on that familiar glimmer as he spoke to them. "*You can make this situation right again. You have the power,*" he said.

The older residents couldn't take their eyes off Alex and the woman dressed in beige spoke again. "Charlie gave us all keys. He came to our houses. He dropped them off last week when he told us about the fence."

Now Marie spoke. "Well, we never heard about any fence, and we weren't given keys."

"That's preposterous," said the man with the plaid shorts. "Why, you're the ones that use the park!"

"That's Witmore," said Harriet.

"*How can you make this situation right again?*" Alex addressed the older group and the woman in beige stepped forward. She handed Harriet her key. "You take this, dear, and make copies," she said sweetly. "We'll make some copies of ours too."

"Thanks," said Ellen, who looked at Claire. "I told you they weren't all obnoxious windbags." Claire turned bright red and stepped away.

"I still don't know how you do that," Mina said, and Alex shrugged his shoulders.

"Who's this guy?" Harriet asked.

"Not important right now," Mina said, the urgency returning. "Have you seen Esther?"

"Not since I dropped Emma off at her house. Honestly, I still don't see—"

"What about Jack?" Alex asked.

"I don't think I would know Jack if he ran me over in the street," Harriet said.

The woman in beige spoke, looking at her watch. "If I know Esther, she's at the community center now," she said. "Today's Thursday, and every Thursday she plays mahjong. Four to six-thirty. I saw her going in there at four on the dot. You can probably still catch her if—"

"Thanks!" Mina called over her shoulder as she and Alex darted for the car.

"Now what?" said Alex as they slipped into the car.

"First we check to make sure Esther is otherwise occupied. Then we break into her house and steal back my family."

# 17

The community center at Easton Estates was a building erected to give all members of the community a place to gather and relax—one of Easton's designs for his vision of Harmonious Living. And much like his other misguided visions, the space featured sprawling areas for playing cards and other table games, and not a single area of recreation for children, despite a recent renovation. For Mina and Alex's purposes, at least this day, that fact served them well. The main room was taken over by the mahjong players, whom they could see clearly from the structure's side windows. From this vantage point, they'd be able to tell without much struggle whether Esther was here or not.

"I see her!" Alex said.

"How would you know? You've never met her," said Mina, approaching the window.

"Because she's wearing something of yours," he said, nodding to the window.

Mina peered in. There was Esther, playing her game as if nothing weird was going on in the world. Mina could see she was wearing a dragonfly pendant around her neck. Mina's dragonfly pendant.

"I knew I recognized that piece. She's worn it as a pin."

"Well, apparently now she thinks she's wearing it as a trophy. She looks pretty busy, and she clearly doesn't know you're out. Come on, let's go!"

Alex and Mina headed to Esther's house. The front door was locked, but Mina knew where Esther hid her spare key. She flipped over a lawn gnome on Esther's patio and produced it, and they pushed their way into the house.

"Jack!" she called. "Emma!"

"You look around down here. I'll check the upstairs," Alex said, and he raced in that direction.

"Emma, sweetie? Mama's here!" she called. "Jack?"

It unnerved Mina how nothing in Esther's house seemed disturbed in any way. It seemed just as she had left it. What other horrors was Esther hiding here? "Emma?"

Alex ran up behind her. "Nothing upstairs," he said.

They both headed to the basement, Mina racing ahead. She turned on the light and her heart dropped.

"Stupid! Of course they're not here! She would know I wasn't and then she wouldn't be at the community center thinking everything was okay with the world. Fuck!"

"You don't suppose they're at your house?" said Alex, and they ran out of Esther's unit through the back way without closing the door.

They raced across the lawn. "Wait," she said. "Alex, you should go first. You know, in case the police are here . . ."

"Right," he said, and crashed through the French doors in the back of the house.

"You could have just opened . . ."

"Coast is clear. Come on," he said.

"Jack? Emma?" Mina called, and she waved Alex to follow her to the basement. "Jack?"

"Mina!" she heard her husband's muffled voice coming from the basement. Her heart raced as she pulled on the doorknob. It was locked.

"Oh shit!" she cried. "He fixed the doorknob!"

"What?"

"It's locked! I can't get it open!"

Alex pulled on the knob as well. "I think we can break it. Looks like a cheap piece of crap. Do you have a hammer?"

Mina nodded. She ran to the kitchen drawer and pulled one out. She raced back and handed it to Alex. He tried to pull off the knob using the claw; the door around the knob collapsed like rice paper.

Mina tore open the door and ran down the stairs. Her husband was alive.

"Jack!" she called. "Is Emma with you?"

Just as she asked, her own question was answered, for there was Emma, sitting on the floor, scribbling all over one of Mina's old clippings with a giant red Sharpie.

"Hi Monny."

"Somehow she managed to untie herself," he said, nodding to a chair next to him, "but I haven't been able to convince her to untie me."

Mina raced over to Jack and kissed him. Now Alex joined them as Mina struggled to get Jack untied.

"Holy mother of god," Jack said. "So you weren't hallucinating," he said to Mina.

"I can't get these untied!" she snapped, frustrated.

"I can help," said Alex.

"Oh, I don't think we need any more help from you," said Jack.

"If it wasn't for him . . ." Mina began.

"I have a lot of sentences that begin that way. 'If it wasn't for your uncle . . .'"

"Jack, just shut up already and tell us what happened," said Alex, as he loosened Jack's restraints. Mina glared at Alex and he changed his tone. "*You have the power to get us* . . ."

"You know that bullshit never worked on me," Jack snapped.

"That's a fine way to address the guy who just helped save your life."

"I would call you lots of things, *Zander*, but savior isn't one of them."

"Fair enough," said Alex.

"Please, guys, there isn't time," said Mina, pulling Emma into her arms. "Just tell us what happened. How you got here?" Mina asked.

"You tell me," Jack said. "I flew in last night, to be with you, and a car met me at the airport. Which never happens, by the way. But the driver was holding a sign with my name and told me I'd won some sales quota competition. He had a gold tooth right in the middle of his mouth now that I think of it," he said, and Mina and Alex exchanged a knowing glance. Another mind control device at work. "So I followed him. I got into his car, he offered me a scotch, and the next thing I know, I'm tied up in the basement here. With a freaking headache like you would not believe."

"Oh, Jack. I'm sorry, sweetie," Mina said, and she planted a soft kiss on his forehead. "Look, there's no time to explain everything now, but I have reason to believe we're in deep shit right now."

"Monny say sheet! Monny say—"

As Mina headed toward Emma, she spotted what Emma had been scribbling all over. It was the piece she'd written about the Ski Lodge Murderess, who poisoned her family and nearly escaped. The face was younger but undeniably recognizable: Esther Erasmus. The article was more than ten years old but the crime had happened long before that. And the woman was identified as Regina Hammer. Mina knew now it was Esther, and she was amazed at how much she suddenly remembered.

Feeling overwhelmed now, Mina collected herself. "Look, mahjong is almost over and so will we be if we're still here when Esther gets back."

"Esther?"

"She's trying to kill us," she said. "She was waiting for us all to be together—"

"Esther? But she's, like, ninety!"

"Eighty, but she's also a vicious bitch," Mina said, grabbing the clipping and holding it up. "Look."

"Holy frack," Jack said, "I remember that!"

"Well now so do I!"

And just then they heard the sound of the front door opening.

The sound of an explosion came from upstairs. Mina scooped Emma into her arms and followed Jack and Alex up the stairs.

As they raced to the front door, Esther appeared, cutting them off. "Where do you think you're going?!" Esther raged, and, improbably, pulled a sledgehammer from behind her slender back, bringing it down on Mina's leg, shattering her knee.

"Ouch!" Mina wailed, and dropped Emma, who ran to Jack.

"I have a plan here, dearie. I told you. I have a lifestyle to maintain. And I'll be damned if you're going to ruin that for me! I promised three bodies," she said, now looking at Alex, "but four's not going to be a problem," she said.

Esther raised the sledgehammer, but before she could bring it down on Mina again, Mina felt the familiar molecules beginning to percolate again. The sense of fearlessness. The sense of power. She grabbed the sledgehammer away from Esther and managed to swing it into her back.

Esther fell to the floor, and her black beehive popped right off her head. Now she looked up at Emma, who was watching with great interest and a small amount of confusion. "You're not going to let Mama hurt Gramma Esther like this, are you, child?"

Emma buried her face in her father's chest and Esther got back up again. Mina still held the sledgehammer but the pain in her crushed leg was almost too much to bear. Esther lunged at Mina again just as another explosion sounded. Now a river of fire poured down the stairs, not unnoticed by all present.

"*You are the light of the world*, Esther. Do you know that?" Alex said out of nowhere.

Confused, Esther looked at Alex quizzically. And in just that split second, Mina managed to tear her pendant from Esther's neck, and then swung the sledgehammer at Esther, knocking her down the basement stairs.

"How does he *do* that?" Jack asked, more to himself than to anyone else, but getting incredulous looks from both Mina and Alex that this would be what he noticed.

The house was becoming engulfed in flames. "We have to run. Now!" said Alex. "We have to get out of the house!"

A flash of light crackled in Mina's mind as she took in those words. *We have to get out of the house!*

She started to take off after them but collapsed. "I can't walk!"

And just in that moment, Emma cried out. "PP! I need my PP!"

"We have to get out of here, and now," said Alex. It took just a fleeting second, in all the confusion, for Emma to untangle herself from the adults and run up the stairs, a flaming beam falling after her, blocking them all from her.

"Emma!" Mina screamed, the terror in her voice raw. She struggled to go after her, but she could barely move at all. Now Alex held her down.

"Peanut. You can't."

"Get off of me! That's my kid! Get the fuck off of me!" Mina shouted as she tried to wriggle out of his too-strong grasp.

Alex looked up at Jack and the men shared a knowing look. One of them had to go after the child; Alex surmised it wouldn't be Jack. "You take care of Mina," Alex said. "I'll get Emma."

Jack nodded his head. He kneeled next to Mina and cupped her face in his hands. "Everything will be alright," he said. He kissed her lightly on the lips. And then he darted into the flames.

"No! Jack!" Mina cried. "No!"

"Come on," said Alex. "Come on."

"I won't. I won't leave them. Get the fuck off of me!" she screamed, and beat him with her fists. Alex picked up Mina as if she were made of air. He lifted her over his back and she punched him furiously with every step he took away from the burning house.

The cement "garden" she had "planted" had created a kind of barrier; without foliage to burn, the fire had no place to be but the house. Exhausted, Alex placed Mina gently on the grass.

"You have to stay here," he said. "There's nothing you can do in there but get yourself killed."

Mina exploded into a torrent of frustrated tears, tears that burned her eyes and face as they fell. Then she looked up to see Alex moving back toward the burning house. She struggled to pull herself closer but the pain in her broken leg was too much. She couldn't move, and there was no will power in the world strong enough to make her.

But just as Alex got close to the house, another image appeared. A silhouette of man, a child in his arms. At the sight, more images crackled to life in Mina's mind.

A flash of a woman she knew was her mother. A blonde, petite woman with shining eyes and soft skin that smelled like strawberries and sweet cream. The woman and the little girl planting seeds together in a planter by the fireplace.

A flash of her with her mother and her uncle playing in the sun at the park. Uncle pushing her on a swing. Mother laughing, shielding the sun from her eyes with her hand.

A flash of her mother opening a letter. Her mother sitting on the stairs, looking sadder than she had ever seen her. Sitting next to her mother and, with her tiny hands, pulling her mother's tear-drenched hair away from her beautiful blue eyes.

A flash of a man standing in her house. A face she doesn't recognize yet, but a face she would know later. Arnie Paulsen. Younger and more fierce, but Paulsen all the same. A horrible screaming fight between the man and her mother. Him shoving her mother and then knocking her to the ground. Her mother's head hitting the jagged stone fireplace and seeming to explode all over their now-bloomed pot of chrysanthemums. "Mama!" the child cries out.

A flash of the man turning to the child, who's been watching and has seen everything. She runs and he chases her. She races into her room and hides under her bed as the man comes for her.

A flash of the small girl shaking under her bed as a shadow passes through her room, a shadow with heavy steps, a shadow that smells rancid and pickled. The smell of stale gin and anger.

"Where the fuck did you go?" he yells. "Ali! You spoiled little bitch! Where did you go?!" He gives up quickly. He leaves the room.

A flash of the small girl, too terrified to leave, too terrified to cry out, and now another smell fills the room. Burning smoke chokes her. And then intense light and heat.

A flash of a man's arms reaching under her bed. Grabbing her. Pulling her. "We have to get out of here!" he screams. And it's Uncle, and she knows him and now she feels safe.

"Mama!" she cries, as the house burns around them.

"I'm sorry, peanut. I was too late. She was gone when I found her. When I got here. We have to get out of the house."

"Mama! We can't leave Mama!"

"We have to go. We have to get out! Now!" The man pulls the child to him, guards her face with his hand, buries her into his chest. She can smell his Old Spice cologne and she can feel the tickle of his chest hair through his shirt. She can hear the beating of his heart. She knows he's right, that they have to get out of the house, and quickly. And only now, pressed into his arms, only now does she feel safe.

A flash of a man carrying a child away from a house disintegrating in flames. A scene just like this. A scene that feels like it happened a hundred years ago . . .

A flash, a flash in real time now. A man emerging from the flames, clutching a small child, the child clutching a frayed and singed toy bunny.

"Jack!" Mina cried, and struggled to pull her broken body to him. Jack ran to Mina and placed Emma in her arms. He wrapped his arms, his body, around them both as they watched the house burn to the ground.

"That was very brave and very stupid," said Alex, bending down to them.

"Well sometimes you have to believe it to make it so, or whatever," Jack said. He shook Alex's hand.

Emma squirmed away from her mother and jumped right into Alex's arms. "Grandpa Alex!" she squealed, and he held her tight as the sound of sirens in the distance got louder and louder. Alex kissed Emma on the top of her head.

Somehow, the head of the homeowners' association, Charlie Witmore, materialized out of the chaos. "You're going to pay for this!" he shouted at them. "Oh, are you ever going to pay!"

Jack and Mina did not acknowledge him; they just stared off into the distance, watching their "prison" implode. A minute later, Jack, never taking his eyes off the burning spectacle before them flatly asked: "The homeowner's insurance?"

A new surge of panic welled up in Mina, as she knew that expense was definitely on the "pay later" pile.

Then Alex piped up. "I paid it," he said. Jack and Mina collapsed into each other's arms.

A crowd had now amassed from all around the neighborhood, neighbors curious about the events disturbing their peace, a reminder that here no secrets were ever safe, especially as a throng of reporters was now part of the mix.

Mina reached out and grabbed Alex's hand. "You saved me. Now and then. It was *you* who saved *me*."

"You remember?"

"I remember."

Suddenly, Mina began to realize what all of this would mean for her uncle, that Zander Randalls could no longer pretend to be dead, especially as she knew her people, these reporters, were going to smell blood and they were going to attack. "What are you going to do?" Mina asked him.

"Don't worry, peanut," he said, his soft warm eyes emanating a calming peace. "Things will work out as they're meant to. *If you believe it to be true . . .*"

"Alright already," Jack said. "We get it!"

# 18

Mina's coffee, black, cooled on the table in front of her as she thumbed through her new notebook, pages of idea fragments, all fictional, waiting to be sewn together and brought to life in a new story of her devising.

She was writing again and it felt good. Once Mina Clark had let journalist Lexi Randalls come back to life, she published a huge and scathing exposé on what had occurred with First Federal, and her impeccable facts and powerful storytelling launched an intensive investigation into the bank's seedy practices, which went well beyond bogus fees and improper foreclosures. Though an exhausting eighteen months had passed since the incredible chain of events that destroyed Mina's house and nearly got her and her family killed, the bank was still in business as the investigation ensued.

At least Mina was able to makes some headway. Her suggestion that bank employees who forced foreclosures would have to be in charge of personally dismantling the homes they foreclosed on was a big hit with socially-conscious legislatures. Unfortunately, because she and Alex has discarded her crown, and Pearls of Wisdom was, ironically, destroyed in a fire around the same time the Clarks' home went up in smoke, the criminal investigation into the case, and Esther's involvement in it, was slogging along. It didn't matter much to Mina anymore, except that she was determined to prove the bank had killed Kim. One day she'd piece it together and get justice for her friend. She was sure of it.

The cause of the fire was attributed to a blockage in the dryer, something Esther had arranged for long before that fateful day. Bob, the water heater repair guy, had planted it when he "fixed" the dryer, she was sure, but Bob and his "Best In the Business" white van had mysteriously disappeared after the fire.

One other person who had also disappeared, unfortunately, was Arnie Paulsen. Once Mina made the connection between the man who had begged her help to bring down Zander Randalls and the man who had been in her mother's house . . . the man who had killed her mother . . . and once Alex had admitted that this man had indeed been her father, who hated Alex desperately and had vowed to ruin him for as long as Mina had been alive, Mina had nearly had another psychotic collapse. With the help of her family, however, and the gentle skill of a new therapist, one recommended to them by Amber of all people, Mina began to heal. She had some anxiety that Paulsen might show up in their lives again, but she hoped that the spectacle that arose from the last person who'd tried to mess with them would keep him at bay.

*The last person . . .*

Mina was still finding it difficult to believe that Esther Erasmus had been that vile murderess she'd brought down so early in her career. Her first targeted exposé. Regina Hammer. She had been free for years when Mina found her out; Mina's story brought her to justice. Unfortunately, though, Mina's mental collapse thinned the evidence implicating Regina, and she was released. Mina still had yet to figure out how she and the bank connected in all of this. Another mystery she was sure one day she would solve.

Esther's betrayal still burned deeply within her, and Emma still sometimes asked for her. Mina hoped that, over time, over the normal course of things, Emma would start to forget Esther and the old house. That building new memories would knock out the poisonous old ones. As for Mina, however, this memory of Esther was something she knew she would have for the rest of her life.

Mina closed her notebook and sat back in her cozy leather chair, taking a long sip of her coffee and letting herself think. The doctor allowed her this one eight-ounce decaffeinated indulgence a day, and she savored every drop. A fluttering much like the feeling of popcorn popping inside her tummy made her wonder if this new kid was enjoying the coffee as much as she was.

She absently thumbed her prized dragonfly pendant. If all was not yet right in the world, things were at least moving in that direction.

"Mama!" came a little voice that broke her reverie. Emma bounced into the room, her sweet face framed by pigtails tied by red ribbons on either side.

"How was school, baby?"

Emma's face twisted into the scowl that used to be common in her baby and toddler years, but had all but disappeared this year from her repertoire of facial expressions. The scowl now only came out when Emma felt particularly wronged. Like now. "I'm not a baby."

"Of course you're not," said Mina, placing her coffee on a nearby table and scooping Emma into her lap. "How was school, my big girl?"

Emma's face lit up as she regaled Mina with stories of quiet play and snack time, of spending time with the letter C and story time.

The Treefont School was no Acela Academy, but Acela, and the whole suburban existence that surrounded it, was now but a bittersweet memory for them all. Though Mina kept in touch with Harriet, and even with Claire and Marie and Ellen, via Facebook. She'd learned that Harriet was pregnant again, and had also learned from Harriet that Charlie Witmore had suffered a freak accident and died. Apparently, he had caught wind that one of the Easton Estates residents had planted a small organic garden on their roof, which Witmore surmised would be against the rules if someone had thought to make and enforce a rule for that. During his inspection, Witmore unwittingly slipped on a pile of compost and took a fatal face-plant into the resident's yard. (Speaking of flowers, none had been used at Witmore's funeral, out of respect for the fact that he'd died in a flower bed.)

Emma had left Mina's office door open, and Mina could hear voices in the foyer shared between the downstairs, a four-bedroom unit where she and Jack and Emma, and soon the new baby, lived, and the upstairs. "Who picked you up today?" asked Mina.

"Daddy!" she squealed. "And Grandpa Alex!"

"Both of them?"

"Uh-huh!"

After the night that Alex had helped Mina rescue Jack and Emma, Jack and Alex had been cordial with one another, but it took several months for them to truly make amends. Mina had never realized just how deeply Jack could hold a grudge, but Alex had been able to wear him down eventually, no doubt calling on some of his dusty old new age philosophies and a little "snake oil."

Because Alex hadn't committed any kind of financial fraud by pretending to be dead, because there was no life insurance illegally paid out and no other ramifications of Zander Randalls's death beyond the dementedly devout losing their lord and savior, he was not even fined for faking his death. In fact, most of the people who questioned him could easily see why he'd want out of that particular existence, and even applauded his escape method. A little more of the Zander Randalls brainwashing magic at work.

And when the tabloids got a hold of the story, well, he got a whole new flock of followers. Though he was through with touring and recording, there was an incredible surge in sales for his existing body of work, one that ensured he'd be comfortable, and keep his family comfortable, for the rest of their days. Though even with all his newfound wealth, he couldn't imagine living anywhere else but right here, with his family.

"Alex?" Mina called, and both Jack and Alex showed up at her office door. Seeing the two of them there, the two most important men in her life, warmed her as another flutter took hold in her tummy, this one a distinctive kick.

"Ouch!" Mina cried.

"Ouch!" parroted Emma.

"You felt that?" Mina asked. Even though Emma was sprawled out over her bump, she found it hard to believe such a little baby could have so much impact.

"He kicked me!" Emma scowled. "You are a very bad boy!" she said to the bump.

Jack, dressed comfortably in a pair of form-fitting jeans and a white, paint-flecked T-shirt, came over and kneeled down beside them. "Young lady, what makes you so sure it's a brother?" he asked, as he affectionately stroked Mina's tummy with a hand that was also flecked in paint.

The baby gave another giant kick. "I see he takes after his mother," Alex joked, and they all laughed.

"*As maçãs respondem-se com maçãs*," said Jack.

"What was that?" Mina asked.

"Just something my mother used to say. The apple doesn't fall far from the tree."

"But what language is that?" she asked.

"Mina, it's Portuguese. You haven't remembered yet that's where your husband's family's from? You mean to tell me you don't remember I still kind of had an accent when we met?"

Mina felt the old familiar heat rising in her cheeks. Her thing for Portuguese accents, of course. Another mystery solved.

"You used to mess with me all the time about it," Jack laughed.

She looked blankly at him. He shook his head. "Every time I said something stupid in front of people, you'd joke that 'English wasn't my first language'?"

Now Alex laughed. "Oh yes, that's true. What a little pain in the ass you were," he said.

"See!" Jack said, waving at Alex. "So I guess over time I just learned to speak without it."

"I shouldn't have done that," Mina said.

"I could bring it back . . ." he said, his accent now evident.

"Maybe only sometimes," she said, smiling a devilish grin, which he returned.

Not having the giant house hanging over their heads would have been enough for Jack to quit Balabaster Design Fittings and find something new to do, but the cushion created by the insurance payout and buying their new home in cash meant Jack didn't have to be a slave to a job he hated anymore, and he too could spend his time doing what he loved, with the people he loved most. Mina was happy to have her husband around at last.

How would the sequel to *Random Acts of Char'a-tee* unfold? Would there only be one sequel? What would the fate of her beloved street diva heroine Char be? None of that really mattered right now. For now, she was just enjoying the process and living in every wonderful, memorable moment.

The phone rang, and Mina felt the old panic rising up in her, as it still kind of did every time the phone rang. Emma sprang up to answer it.

"Hello? She is. Hang on."

Emma brought the phone over to her mother.

"Who is it?" Mina asked.

"It's Frank," she said, and when her mother didn't grab the phone right away, she impatiently added, "Your agent?"

Everyone breathed a collective sigh of relief as Mina took the phone from Emma.

"This is Mina."

# ACKNOWLEDGMENTS

No matter how many of these babies I put to bed, it's never something I can do on my own. And for that, people deserve to be thanked! Lots of awesome people! So first . . .

Thank you to the folks at Diversion Books, especially Mary Cummings, for believing in me and for making it happen!

Susan Lauzau, I always suspected you were a better editor than I. In fact, you are extraordinary. Wow! Thank you for your careful eye and catching those things I never would. I am forever indebted to you for your mad skills and your wonderful friendship.

A huge thank you to Diana Gliedman, Fred Pineiro, and my parents, Paul and Francine Hornberger, for your invaluable insights in bringing together such a complicated narrative. Your suggestions definitely improved things! (May I suggest, dear reader, that if you ever endeavor to write a novel of your own, avoid having an insane amnesiac as your protagonist. It kinda complicates things.) Oh and Fred, your tag lines? *C'est magnifique!*

Tricia McGoey. Oh Trish... Not only did you dazzle with the cover for my last book, *Rita Hayworth's Shoes*, you so amazingly and beautifully made the cover of this book shine. You know it goes without saying, but I just can't help saying it: I care for this! Thank you! (And also for your insightful and significant manuscript critiques!)

A very special thank you goes to a handful of dear friends who agreed to read the layout and check for errors before it was finalized: Ruthie Brown, Carolyne LaSala, April Banaitis, Ian Chow-Miller, Douglas Slagowitz, and especially Carolyn Dembeck Mosciatti. The divine Ms. Mosciatti was amazingly thorough in finding errors I had read over and never seen a thousand times. Carolyn, I can't tell you enough how incredibly grateful I am for the painstaking effort you put in to your read.

When you're a little author fish in an ocean of well-known and well-established authors, you definitely come to rely on your "school" or community of other writers who help you navigate the unknown seas of what you do after you write the book. There are many to thank, but most especially Meredith Schorr and Tracie Banister, who introduced me to the world of blog hops and Facebook writers' groups and Twitter re-tweets, and who each graciously accepted being interviewed for my own blog, "Clippings In The Shed." Thank you both for your guidance and mentorship. A big wet sloppy thank you also goes to blogger-extraordinaire Elizabeth Cassidy for always doing such kickass interviews with me!

A big hug of thanks to Steve Maraboli, the "anti-Zander," whose pure and beautiful insights and simple, soulful messages always inspire me to believe in me.

To my dear friend and mentor, Roger Cooper, thank you for your tireless and amazing efforts in championing me and my work.

Thank you to Marie Aikman, my eighth grade English teacher. It was you who first introduced me to "Jabberwocky" and led me down the rabbit hole of imagination where I do most like to dwell. (You should also know that I can still recite that poem, word for word, whenever prompted.)

To my children, Madeleine and Juliana . . . When you are old enough to read this you may be alarmed to know that some of your "finer moments" have been exploited to make Emma the little demon she is. But I am deeply and sincerely thankful to you both for who you usually are—precious bundles of sweetness that make me laugh and inspire my heart and soul. You are my special angels and I treasure you both so much.

And speaking of treasures . . . It is not an exaggeration to say I would be nowhere without my husband, Christopher. I will never forget that moment on our front patio when we made the decision to stand together and hold on tightly to each other while our "ship" splintered apart and sank around us. Thank you for your support. Your patience. Your humor. You, my love, are my finest treasure. (Oh and I think I owe you a doormat.)